THE
JIGSAW
MAN

DEANIE FRANCIS MILLS

J

JOVE BOOKS, NEW YORK

THE JIGSAW MAN

A Jove Book / published by arrangement with
the author

PRINTING HISTORY
Jove edition / February 1997

The Putnam Berkley World Wide Web site address is
http://www.berkley.com/berkley

ISBN: 0-515-12019-7

A JOVE BOOK®
Jove Books are published by The Berkley Publishing Group,
200 Madison Avenue, New York, New York 10016.
JOVE and the "J" design are trademarks
belonging to Jove Publications, Inc.

PRINTED IN THE UNITED STATES OF AMERICA

10 9 8 7 6 5 4 3 2 1

For my dad, Ken Henderson,
who was born in my twenty-sixth year
and
for my daddy, Bill Francis,
who died too soon

You have always been my heroes.

A fixed idea ends in madness or heroism.

—Victor Hugo

THE
JIGSAW
MAN

I

Woe to them! For they have gone the way of Cain . . . caring for themselves . . . doubly dead . . . wandering stars for whom the blackness of darkness has been reserved forever.

—JUDE, V.11-12
NEW AMERICAN STANDARD VERSION

The way of Cain

—ANCIENT HEBREW EXPRESSION FOR MURDER

ONE

FROM CHILDHOOD ON, SHE HAS *always referred to him as the "Jigsaw Man." This is because, in her dreams, she only sees certain portions of his face at once—never the whole thing. There seem to be crooked lines separating each part, so that one piece might be his left eye and forehead; another might be his mouth and chin and, say, his right cheek. Once, when she happened to see a promotional spot on TV for a traveling production of Broadway's The Phantom of the Opera, she broke into a cold sweat and became ridiculously frightened.*

Like the fictional Phantom, the Jigsaw Man always seems to be shrouded in mist. He towers over her, dressed all in black, wisps of moisture clinging to his dark hair, his puzzle-piece face glaring down, mouthing words at her she cannot hear.

He always chases her through the fog. They dart in and out and between these creepy Wizard of Oz–like trees that reach out for her as she runs with black, gnarled talons, snatching at her hair and muffling her screams with their twisted boughs.

She always screams, of course. Which finally, bless-edly, wakes her.

But when she awakens, the darkness never really both-ers her quite as much as the silence.

It was the stillness to the house which struck Gypsy when she first walked in, a silent watchfulness. It crept down her spine as she reached up to punch in the code which would disarm the security system of their suburban Dallas home. A quiet of sorts, separate from her usual silence.

Annie scampered on ahead and toward the darkened bedroom, still bouncing like Winnie-the-Pooh's Tigger even after a busy second-grade day. It was all Gypsy could do not to call her back.

Silly, Gypsy told herself. *Ridiculous.* Still, she snapped on lights all over the den. Within split seconds, Annie had returned, bewilderment scrunching up her little face as she signed to her mother that Daddy was not at home. Gypsy could have told her that much. There was always a cessation of energy when John was absent, as if his very presence charged the atmosphere with a crackling of elec-tricity that could only be settled and still when he was gone, leaving behind a lonely void.

But this time, there was something not right about the emptiness of the house. Gypsy could *feel* it.

John was not scheduled to leave for the deep-night watch at the Dallas PD, where he worked as an officer in the intelligence division, for a couple more hours. That short stretch of time was precious to their little family; the only time of day when they could all be together.

Gypsy worked days as a crime lab tech for the South-west Institute of Forensic Sciences. She spent her working hours hunched over a microscope, comparing pubic hairs or blood stains or searching for glass fragments in a pair

of jeans that had been washed repeatedly, or simply identifying odd stains. Sorting methodically through the detri-
tus of violent death with a tweezer—that was Gypsy's
job, and she viewed it with the detachment of any professional who is trained to pick out just the right piece of
truth to complete the puzzle.

Though some of her friends regarded it as a gruesome
way to make a living, Gypsy gained a great deal of personal satisfaction from it, especially when her careful
work revealed just the crucial piece of forensic evidence
needed to convict and put away the bad guys.

Gypsy was good at her job; so good, in fact, that she
was a favorite among the city's prosecutors. It had been
Gypsy's job performance which had helped crack one
sensational serial murder case nine years before. A handsome, charming officer named John Halden (who was
working homicide in the Crimes Against Persons division
at the time), was the primary investigator on that case.
Their combined testimony had put the defense to rest, sent
a multiple child killer to death row, and changed Gypsy's
life forever.

And yet, to this day, she still had trouble understanding
why—of all the glamorous professional women John had
dated—he still chose her. Even after all this time, his love
for her was as simple and clean as ever; it had never fal-
tered. Each day, she still got a little thrill at the thought of
seeing him after work.

This brief time span with John and Annie was Gypsy's
unmasking time, her letdown time, her time to relax with
someone who could sign as well as she, someone who accepted her just as she was, someone who expected no
more or no less of her than she was able to give.

When a quick search of the house revealed no note or
any evidence as to why John had left or where he was or

when she could expect him back, the uneasiness which had cobwebbed Gypsy's mind the minute she walked in the door tightened.

She told herself not to worry. Told herself he had undoubtedly been called away by his lieutenant on a moment's notice and would get in touch with her as soon as he could. After all, it's not like it hadn't happened before, particularly when he was working undercover.

It had been a long day and she was tired, that's all it was. Gypsy reminded herself of this as she heated a can of SpaghettiOs for Annie. On this day, she'd been in court.

Testifying was always a bitch, and since both of her usual courtroom interpreters had been home sick, Gypsy had to rely on lip-reading. And the damn prosecutor had mumbled behind a moustache while the defense attorney chattered like a nervous Uzi.

Most people had a romanticized idea of lip-reading, based on the proficiency shown by actors in movies and on TV. The truth was that lip-reading was an inexact skill. Many words in the English language looked the same when being pronounced, such as *stick* and *click*, or *who* and *shoe*. Sometimes Gypsy had to ask that people write out what they were trying to say, which meant that on this day, the court was forced to endure the laborious process in order to ensure an accurate testimony.

"Annie! Supper's ready!" she called.

At least her speech was clear and understandable, a fact which helped her a great deal in the continual struggle to communicate. Gypsy had been fully hearing until she was Annie's age, a moment in time which neatly split her life into before and after.

Before was the wind soughing through the trees, and Daddy bellowing out *I am the Walrus* along with the Beatles on the hi-fi, and Mama's good-night whisper, and

Archie Bunker hollering at the Meathead on TV, and the squawk of chalk on the blackboard at school.

Before was the call of Daddy's good-bye as he donned his crisp blue uniform with the shining silver badge and drove off into the sunny day, and the anxious murmurings over her head when he still had not come back three days later, and the cries of her mother when they found him, and the *crack*-report of the Honor Guard's revolvers at the funeral—twenty-one times, (she had counted)—and the uneasy quiet around the house as her mother packed their things without even so much as KLIF on the radio to keep her company, and the gentle lap of water against the pier when they moved so far away down to the coast.

Before was the sound of her mother's screams yanking her from sleep, the night the Jigsaw Man came.

And after that . . . only silence and death.

"Su Lee? This is Gypsy Martin Halden—John's wife." Gypsy took a deep breath. She was thirty-two years old; she should be able to call her husband's office without feeling apologetic.

"HEY GIRL," read the digital message across her special telephone. *"LONG TIME NO HEAR. WHAT CAN I DO YOU FOR?"*

Picturing the tiny chain-smoking, foul-mouthed, black-eyed Vietnamese dynamo at the other end of the line was a comfort in itself. Gypsy smiled. "I just wondered if you had any idea where John might be. He wasn't here when we got home and he didn't leave a note or anything. Did he get called in or something?"

"NOW GYPSY, YOU KNOW WE DO ALL KINDS OF TOP-SECRET SHIT AROUND HERE. YOU WANT ME TO BREAK THE CODE OR SOMETHING?"

"Only if you know where my husband is."

"OH WELL, IN THAT CASE. LET ME CHECK AROUND AND I'LL GET BACK TO YOU, OK?"

"Okay. Thanks, Su Lee."

"CAN DO EASY GI, FIE MINUTES." Referring to the promise made by wartime Vietnamese whores to the American soldiers who hired them was Su Lee's favorite sign-off. Once, after too many Mai Tais at a party, she had confessed to Gypsy that she never knew her father, an American GI.

Annie went streaking through the den at that moment buck-naked, her black curls stuck damply to the back of her neck where they had come loose from the pins, cheeks rosy from the shower-warm bathroom, her nightie wadded in her arms against her chest as her little butt dimpled with each bounding stride.

"I forgot my panties!" she motioned to her mother, dropping the gown as she did so, scooping it up and dashing out of the room, her shoulders shaking with giggles.

Gypsy supposed she must teach the child modesty someday but so far, she hadn't the heart. Annie was just too cherubic at this stage. Gypsy didn't want it to end.

She wanted Annie to always be a child; at least, for as long as she possibly could.

She never wanted her to know terror and abandonment and grief. Never wanted Annie to have an after.

The years after the Jigsaw Man came loomed giant in Gypsy's mind, years of silence and terrible loneliness, confusion and loss as her mother was put into the ground and she was shunted from one foster family to another. Some were cruel, some were kind, but none of them noticed the deafness.

Time and again she was slapped or otherwise punished for not coming when she was called, or for not doing things she'd been told to, or for ignoring her elders when spoken to. Dismal grades provided further evidence to them that she was slow and stupid and gave more ammunition to classmates and foster siblings to use in tormenting and teasing the solitary, awkward child who inched daily more and more out of reach, a small boat who'd slipped its moorings and drifted ever further from shore.

If it hadn't been for an observant high school English teacher, Gypsy might have been lost forever. At long last, her hearing impairment was diagnosed. Training followed, and a hearing aid which helped somewhat.

She'd come such a long way since then, but even with the successes Gypsy had been able to achieve in the years since those bleak days, she had never quite been able to shake the idea that she was still that stupid, clumsy kid who could never do anything right.

John and Annie now kept Gypsy tied firmly to the dock. As much as she loved her work, the truth of the matter was that lab techs came and went, but here, in this house, she *mattered.*

Once she was dressed in her crumpled nightie, Annie came over to the couch where Gypsy sat and crawled into her lap, holding her Pooh-Bear in the crook of her arm and handing Gypsy a copy of the latest *Sesame Street* magazine. They both knew that Annie had long since outgrown the simple publication and should be moving on to the more sophisticated *3–2–1 Contact,* but neither of them were in any particular rush to give up this special time.

As Gypsy read aloud the happy little stories and played the easy games with Annie, she glanced at the clock from time to time and tried to ignore the growing panic which was beginning to take root deep inside her.

It's not the same, she reassured herself as Annie traced an uncomplicated maze with her chubby finger. *Daddy was a beat cop in a bad neighborhood. Anybody could have jumped him for any reason.*

Of course, John worked intelligence and often took dangerous undercover assignments. Who knew what kind of peril he might be in.

"Mommy?" Annie placed the palms of her hands on Gypsy's cheeks and forced her to look into wide, blue, black-lashed eyes. John's eyes. "Aren't you going to read the last story?"

"Why don't we save it for tomorrow night?" Gypsy said. "It's time for you to go to bed."

"But I'm not sleepy," Annie signed, her small hands stubborn and emphatic. She was a natural ham, the expressions on her face exaggerated just right so that her meaning could not be mistaken.

"Well, you'll be sleepy in the morning when Mr. Alarm Clock goes off if you don't go on to bed now."

"No I won't. Tiffany's mom lets her stay up until David Letterman comes on."

"Yes. And Tiffany falls asleep in class, too."

"But I won't fall asleep. Can't I just watch TV a little while?"

"No."

"How 'bout if I read a book?" Annie asked slyly.

"No books, no TV, no toys. Just you and Pooh-Bear, snuggled under the covers." Gypsy glanced at the clock.

"I'm hungry." Annie crossed her arms over her chest.

Gypsy sighed. "You can't be hungry. You just had cookies and milk and now you've brushed your teeth."

"Then I'm thiirs-ty," Annie said without signing, drawing out each word as if speaking to a moron.

Gypsy frowned. "I'll bring you a drink of water. Now go to bed!"

Annie's forehead crinkled. "I wanna see Daddy."

Gypsy shook her head. "He's at work."

"Can I call him on the telephone?" Signing again, she rushed a bit.

"No. Annie . . ."

"I'll just talk a little while—"

"I said go to bed, Annie!" Gypsy shouted, fatigue and worry tugging loose her self-control.

Eyes like accusing thunderclouds, Annie jumped off of Gypsy's lap and stomped into her room. Just before crossing the threshold of the door, she glanced back at her mother. Tears clotted fanlike lashes, piercing Gypsy to the core.

Annie was Gypsy's soul mate. She learned to sign the same time she learned to speak, and the bond between Gypsy and her child had become so strong as to be almost spiritual. Over the years, they'd invented their own private little forms of communication, and Annie often took over the grown-up role of helping Gypsy relate to people outside the family when she could see her mother having difficulty understanding that, say, they were all sold out of sandalfoot pantyhose but were expecting a shipment in next week, or that the doctor was called away unexpectedly and they would have to reschedule their appointment.

This role was not one which Gypsy thoughtlessly thrust upon the child, but one which she happily embraced at a very young age and never seemed to mind. With her mother's glossy, thick, black, unruly curls and her father's strong jaw and supple lips, most people found the bubbly little girl who matter-of-factly signed for her mother when necessary enchanting. Especially when Annie pronounced all sorts of frank judgments upon a world which seemed to cause most children a great, nameless anxiety.

Once, when Gypsy had been unable to shield the child

from a news report of a man who had shot up a crowd of people in a restaurant before turning the gun on himself, Annie had turned to her mother and said, in their odd mixture of words and signs, "Why didn't he just do that in the first place, and save everybody a lot of trouble?"

Her precociousness was caused, in part, by her status as the only child of a hearing-impaired parent and partly by her keen intelligence which Gypsy had always assumed she inherited from her dad.

But the bond between them was so strong and supple that Gypsy sometimes worried that she did not know where she ended and the child began. When Annie hurt, Gypsy felt the pain.

What she did not want—ever—was for Annie to feel her mother's pain.

Gypsy almost never shouted at Annie; there was seldom any need. She got to her feet and went into the child's room, where an Eeyore night-light glowed dimly, outlining the cockeyed jumble of books, the careless scattering of clothing, the overstuffed box of Barbies. Kneeling beside the bed, Gypsy lay her face on the pillow beside her daughter's, cheek-to-cheek, their breaths mingling, until one small hand finally reached up and softly patted Gypsy's hair.

Inhaling the subtle scent of baby shampoo, Gypsy closed her eyes and for one brief moment, felt at peace.

When she left Annie's room, the lights were blinking, signifying the ringing of the phone. She dove for it.

It was Su Lee.

"I'M CALLING YOU BECAUSE EVERYONE ELSE WILL JUST HAND YOU A PILE OF SHIT," read Su Lee's customary blunt commentary across the top of Gypsy's telephone. *"NOBODY KNOWS WHERE THE FUCK*

JOHN IS, BUT THE CHIEF,"—referring to the deputy chief in charge of Intelligence, Abe Strickland—*"CAME DOWN HERE ABOUT AN HOUR AGO, AND WHEN I ASKED HIM, HE GOT THIS WEIRD LOOK ON HIS FACE."*

For one painful instant, Gypsy's heart seemed to stand still. "What do you mean, *weird*?"

"I DON'T KNOW. SHOCKED, I GUESS. KIND OF SCARED."

"Why would he be scared?"

"THAT'S THE THING. MAYBE I'M READING TOO MUCH INTO IT. YOU KNOW HOW PARANOID I AM. IT WAS JUST A STRANGE REACTION TO A SIMPLE QUESTION, I THOUGHT."

"Did he say if John was on assignment?"

"NO."

Gypsy had to fight the overwhelming sense of frustration that the wives and husbands or lovers of undercover officers face all the time, when their beloveds seem to vanish into some sinister, shadowy world where they become, quite literally, someone else. Some prolonged investigations could take months—even years—and spouses were expected not only to keep the household running smoothly during those long absences, but not to ask any questions until it was all over. If they were still around. There was a very high divorce rate in both the vice and intelligence divisions.

But for Chief Strickland to act shocked and even worse, *scared* when asked about John's absence carved an echoing hole deep inside Gypsy.

Su Lee promised to dig up what she could. She offered a few words of encouragement, then left Gypsy alone with her awful anxiety.

She couldn't help thinking of her father. She tried not to, but it was inevitable.

She could remember so little about him. His big hands, his broad shoulders, his laugh as he swung her high in the air, her mother's giggle when he bundled her up in his sheltering strong arms.

Her mother's laugh. Gypsy could hear it then, clear and ringing, and her daddy's pretend-gruff voice as he nuzzled her neck.

His voice, she could remember. It was his face Gypsy had so much trouble calling to mind anymore.

But she could remember that day, that long and awful day when Daddy didn't come home from work, the fevered bustle of adults trying to act unworried, her mother's uncommon quietness.

She wasn't supposed to know how badly beaten the body had been when they finally found it, a carcass dumped in a landfill. The details were whispered in her presence, but her hearing was keen in those "before" days and her interest fierce and she heard, she heard.

Gypsy couldn't remember much about the funeral anymore except the sea of blue uniforms, so many they spilled over the other graves as far as she could see. The line of men in uniform firing off their revolvers in the air, and her mother jumping each and every time.

The house grew dark then, and too quiet, and her mother's laughter stopped. For reasons Gypsy's child-mind could not grasp, there was a tight sort of wariness in her mother's eyes all the time after that, and in only a few short weeks they had packed up everything they could possibly fit into their old Plymouth and left Dallas far behind.

The last clear sound Gypsy would ever hear came some

six months later. It was the sound of her mother's screams, the night the Jigsaw Man came.

Now, these many years later, as Gypsy paced the floor and fretted while she awaited word on her missing husband, it was not her mother's last screams that seared into her memories, so much as it was the awful truth that she could never, ever forget.

Because deep, deep down inside, Gypsy harbored a secret, a terrible secret of what happened that night when she lost her hearing, the night her mother died in front of her eyes, the night the Jigsaw Man came.

TWO

THE DALLAS FIELD OFFICE FOR the FBI looked like anything but what it was, mused Special Agent in Charge Parker Jefferson as he headed into the handsome tan-painted brick building known as Landmark Center, located on Ross and Lamar in the trendy West End marketplace area of Dallas, just a few blocks away from the spot where President Kennedy was murdered.

The streets were paved with restored bricks, and the walkways leading to the building had green canvas awnings over them. A courtyard was lit by attractive gas lamps and dotted with neat shrubs.

Most of the buildings in this area were renovated warehouses that now held pricey shops and funky restaurants. The hunter-green lobby of the building housing the FBI was lavished with plants; the high ceiling was antique punctured tin.

The offices themselves had clean, cream-colored walls and maroon carpeting. More potted plants. *Hell, the only thing the room lacks is a piano bar,* Jefferson thought as he walked through it. The only hint that it was actually an FBI office was the thick bullet-proof glass which sheltered the receptionists.

Parker Jefferson overlooked the twelfth largest field office in the Bureau, with some 240 agents. This office had been responsible for some of the most important investigations in American history.

At his office door, Jefferson punched in a code and stood to peer into a scanner, where the pattern for the blood vessels in his eyeball was retained on memory. The door clicked open, registering his name and time of entry on record.

Compared to the front office, Jefferson's was strictly utilitarian. A large framed portrait of J. Edgar Hoover dominated the wall behind his desk. Surrounding the portrait, like satellites around Mother Earth, were photographs of Jefferson with various presidents, public service plaques, and framed awards.

But every other surface was a study in controlled chaos, from the stacks of files and documents on his desk to boxes of marked videotapes on his floor in front of a small TV to book-crammed shelves in the corners. Doris had taped several messages to the telephone, a last-ditch attempt to make sure he saw them before they were forever lost in the maelstrom. Known as a "Betty Bureau"— a support employee who'd devoted a lifetime to the FBI—and serving a total of eight different SACs (Special Agents in Charge) in the Dallas field office, Jefferson's secretary sported an iron-gray skullcap of curls and warm brown eyes. She kept him—and most everybody else in the office—in line, and Jefferson didn't know what he'd do without her.

Ignoring the phone messages for the time being, he retrieved the latest *Dallas Morning News* from beneath a tottering stack of files and scanned through it, a morning ritual he never missed. After almost thirty years in the FBI, including a stint at what Hoover used to call the

Seat of Government—at headquarters in Washington, D.C. as assistant director in charge of the criminal investigative division, Jefferson had learned the importance of image over content.

FBI agents could do a crackerjack investigation—as they had done with the Kennedy assassination—but if the public *perceived* them as having botched the job, then none of their hard work mattered where it counted: in Congress, where the budget was appropriated.

It was his job, among others, to make sure that only the most visible successes got hyped and the failures hidden or spin-doctored. The way Jefferson saw it, that had been the problem with the Branch Davidian fiasco. The ATF fucked up the whole thing from the beginning, even inviting the *media* to come along, and who was sent in to clean up the mess? The FBI, of course, who never would have gotten them into such a state in the first place. It was impossible from the word go.

Fortunately for him, the San Antonio office had been in charge on the ground, with close supervision from Washington, naturally. Still, he hadn't gotten as far as he had in the Bureau by being associated with spectacular failures.

Quite simply, Parker Jefferson was married to the Bureau. It was all he had ever wanted to be, growing up in a small dusty Texas town, watching the G-men beat out the bad guys time after time down at the cinema on Saturday afternoons. Back then, everybody respected the FBI, who stood for truth, justice, and the American way. He couldn't wait to get out of Nowheresville and go join the action.

To this day, he loved the job, the diversity, the prestige, the travel, the occasional excitement. Several framed incentive awards on the wall behind him and the

Meritorious Achievement Medal attested to the fact that, though his ambition showed itself from time to time, Parker Jefferson was still very, very good at what he did.

Through the years, Jefferson had developed an uncanny ability to be in the right place at the right time when the heat was coming down or when the brass came for a visit. During his days on the bricks, he always knew how to word his reports, called 302s, in just the right way, and how to handle his superiors during file review and the biannual case file inspections from on high.

He even knew which divisions got the most PR and which squads in which field offices to request in those divisions. He knew when to leave the bricks for management, when to do his stint at headquarters.

And he never let himself be encumbered with a spouse and kids the way so many of them did, either. Since every promotion for management meant a corresponding transfer, those agents who had families were sometimes slowed down or even stunted in their career aspirations when the family balked at yet one more move. Especially in the Hoover days, when you could be moved from one coast to another and back every six months for the most arbitrary reasons.

Jefferson had requested the Dallas office because it was close to his Texas roots and because there was no better job in the Bureau than SAC, where he could work in virtual independence and answered to no one on a daily basis; he answered to no one, in fact, other than the director himself.

Besides, he had started his career here more than thirty years ago, a nervous trainee terrified of doing anything that might "embarrass the Bureau" (translation:

Hoover), and it felt good to come back now in a position of power.

Glancing over the headlines, Jefferson was pleased to see that indictments were due to be handed down on several bank fraud cases his team had been working for the past two years, since even before he had arrived, and nodded with approval at the way his media rep had fended off questions about a Vietnamese drug cartel which his people had heavily infiltrated through superb undercover work in tandem with the Dallas PD.

Street gang activity was on the rise—soulless kids preying on the weak, murdering for the fun of it. Dallas, once a brave and beautiful city, had fallen victim to the same cancerous crime growth as other big cities. Now she was growing bald and thin and he wondered if she— if any of them— would be able to survive the disease.

One small news item caught his attention and brought him full upright in his chair: a Dallas PD intelligence officer, John Halden, was missing.

A PD spokesperson stated that Halden had not been seen at home or at work for two days and was not on assignment. His wife, Gypsy, had told reporters that her husband had given her no warning that he planned to leave; none of his clothes were missing and he had given her no indication of emotional depression or trouble of any kind. She sent out a plea for any information that anybody who knew John could provide. A Dallas PD phone number was provided.

Jefferson picked up the phone, his palm covering the taped-on messages, and put a call through to special agent Doug Nicks, known to most of the guys in the office as "Nicky." A former all-American linebacker, Nicky was big and black and no-nonsense. He had a reputation for bulldogging cases so relentlessly that other agents were sometimes reluctant to work with him. That was why Jefferson liked him.

"Nicks."

"Nicky? Jefferson here. I just got in this morning from out of town and read about this Dallas cop—John Halden."

"The guy who's missing."

"Right. We've worked with him on task force before, haven't we?"

"Couple times."

"You guys hear anything about this?"

"Not yet. DPD hasn't asked us to help, either."

"Well that's fine. I didn't figure they had. I just remember him as a good cop. It seems peculiar, him disappearing like that. I just wondered if there was any scuttlebutt on it."

"None that I know of. But hell, any cop who's done cover work for very long makes enemies; you know that, Mr. Jefferson. There's no telling what happened to the poor slob."

"Still. Let's run a discreet check or two. See if he's been using his credit cards or anything."

"You think he skipped?"

"I don't know. And I'm not saying he has, understand? I'd just like you to check around a little bit."

"Should we tell the PD?"

"No. Hell no. It'll just piss 'em off. No—wait 'til they come to us, then show 'em if they ask. In the meantime, let's see what we can find out."

"Got it."

"After all, we've done task force work with the guy. If he's in any kind of trouble, I don't want it to reflect badly on us."

"Who knows?" said Nicky. "Maybe they'll turn up a body and we can all breathe a sigh of relief."

Jefferson waited just long enough in simmering silence to let Nicky know he had really screwed up, then he gently replaced the receiver in the cradle.

THREE

ON SATURDAY AFTERNOON—THE THIRD day since John had disappeared, a DPD unit pulled up outside Gypsy's house. Two uniformed officers and Su Lee got out and headed up the walkway to the front door.

Gypsy knew this because she was standing to the side of the front window, watching through the curtains. Her heart was caught in an icy grip so suffocating she couldn't breathe. She wondered for a fleeting moment if she might faint and tried to take a deep breath to prevent such a thing from happening.

Her mind became a mixed jumble of thoughts, impressions, and emotions: *Thank God Annie is at a Saturday afternoon matinee with two other cops' wives and their kids; this is exactly how it was when they found Daddy; I've met one of those officers before but I don't think I know the other one; please, please God don't let him be dead; maybe if I don't answer the door they'll go away and I'll never have to know; oh Mama, how did you bear it?*

The lights began to blink twice in quick succession, signaling the doorbell.

Gypsy closed her eyes and sank to the floor, her knees tight against her chest, her heart pounding so hard it shook her whole body.

Hammering on the door vibrated the wall against which Gypsy huddled. Part of her detached itself and stood back, saying, *Get up, you idiot. Let them in and find out what happened to John. You've got to, old girl, that's all there is to it.*

But all strength seemed to have drained from her body and she knew that if she tried to stand, she'd just plop right down like the Scarecrow on *The Wizard of Oz*. A great pressure expanded within her chest, and she considered the fact that she may be having a heart attack.

Don't be such a weenie. Get the hell up and let those guys in.

A strength outside and apart from herself seemed to nudge her to her hands and knees. It was only a couple of steps to the door, so she just reached up and unlocked it, letting her arm fall like so much dead weight.

Su Lee sprang through the door, glanced around, then whirled and stared at Gypsy. "Oh God, you poor kid!" she cried, her face stricken. "I should have called first. Hell, I didn't mean to scare the shit out of you."

Dropping to her knees, she took Gypsy into her arms and whispered, "He's not dead, he's not dead, he's not dead—at least, we don't think so. We don't know."

Gypsy pulled back and studied her friend's black eyes. "You've got to say it to my face, Su Lee."

"Oh shit. Forgive me." Su Lee repeated what she had said.

Gypsy stared at her. "What do you mean, you don't know?"

"I'll tell it to you straight. They found his car. There's

no sign of foul play, no indication of a struggle—no blood or anything."

"But no John."

Pursing her lips, Su Lee shook her head.

"So he could still be dead!"

"And he could just as well still be alive!" Su Lee took Gypsy's arms in her hands and shook her slightly. "Gypsy. He could still be alive."

Gypsy started to cry, nervous, tension-releasing sobs. Su Lee got her to her feet and the officers who had accompanied her helped to half-carry Gypsy to the sofa. Su Lee brought her a glass of water; Gypsy's hand shook so hard that some of it slopped out onto her lap.

He could still be alive. On the other hand, they could find his body in a city dump somewhere, too.

Su Lee started making phone calls, and in what seemed like a very short period of time, the house began to fill with people, the so-called brethren: that family of cops and their loved ones who are connected by a bond thicker, sometimes, than blood, who stand together in solidarity against a world gone mad.

You didn't have to be a cop to be a part of it; you could be born into it or marry into it, but you could never be one with it otherwise. It was that shared understanding that spouses especially intuited, that their dear ones provided the only shield the general public had, the only thing which stood between the everyday citizen and anarchy.

Lately, especially, wives and husbands left home every day to cross into a war zone, to wage endless battle with an enemy which had no regard for human life, no respect for home and family, no appreciation of the difference between right and wrong. Half the time, even the victims of violent crime turned on the assisting officers as if they were to blame for the pain.

And more often than not, the officers themselves became casualties of that very war.

John was well-liked and respected by everybody who knew him. As word spread, most everyone who worked with him made it a point to go by the house and check on Gypsy, to see if there was anything they could do.

Such overwhelming support and encouragement was heartwarming to Gypsy, but the sad truth was that the presence of so many people around her talking at once rendered her hearing aid virtually useless and confused what little bit of hearing she did possess. Vast chunks of conversation were lost to her. The strain of trying to keep up drained what few reserves of strength she had left and sent vicious headaches to torment her.

The result was a sense of isolation more acute than any she had ever felt when sitting alone in an empty room.

Ironically, she had come to depend on John through the years to help run interference for her in such busy social situations. With his fluid signing and her ability to speak clearly, she normally had no trouble following the thread of the most complicated three-way conversations.

It made her miss him even more.

It was as if someone had come along with a hatchet and chopped in two the solidly tied rope that moored her little boat to the dock. She could see herself drifting out to sea once again, lost, lost.

Still, she was keenly aware of Annie and tried very hard not to overlook the child or even to depend on her to fill the gap left in her father's absence. It was impossible to keep from her the news about the discovery of her daddy's car, but it was hard to know what the child was thinking as she grew more and more quiet and withdrawn—in her own solitary boat, bobbing along just out of reach.

Alone in bed at night after everyone had finally left, Gypsy wept and prayed for her husband in the velvet darkness. She could sense him out there calling to her, but no matter how hard she strained to hear him, there was only nothingness.

Only the dead stillness. Only the terrible silence.

SAC Parker Jefferson had just been briefed by Agent Spencer of the SOG (Special Operations Group) about an ongoing surveillance operation when Agent Nicks caught up with him. The dim, blue-carpeted SOG room located behind thick glass windows on the third floor of the field office contained a jumble of tape recorders and monitoring positions for various wiretapping and bugging devices.

A computer-lettered sign on one wall read, THE FLOGGINGS WILL CONTINUE UNTIL MORALE IMPROVES!

Nicks tapped on the window to get Jefferson's attention, then waited politely for his boss to step out into the narrow hallway.

"Whatcha got?" Jefferson did not smile at the agent. He was still punishing him for that crack about finding a body.

"Well, he's not using any of his credit cards, but there's something else I'm looking into."

"What's that?"

"John Halden has an undercover alias that he hasn't used in quite some time: Hal Johnson."

"Okay. And?"

"Well, from what I can tell, there have been a number of credit cards issued to a Halden Johnson in recent weeks."

"Credit limit?"

"Substantial."

"Hmmm. Have you cross-referenced the name? Checked to make sure it's not some guy with the same name?"

"I'm doing that now. I'd have had it done already if I didn't have to share computer time," he grumbled. "I'll stay late if I have to."

"Good." Jefferson sympathized with Nicky about the FBI's antiquated computer system, which was only recently coming up to the standards set by the CIA twenty years ago. Still, it seemed natural to him that Nicky would stay late to finish the job. "Anything else?"

"Yeah. Well, couple things. First, if I'm going to do very much more on this case, sir, you kind of need to say something to my supervisor about it. He's beginning to wonder."

"Oh, of course. No problem. I'll have a word with him as soon as we're finished. And the other thing?"

"Well, I had lunch with an old buddy of mine, a cop who's working Halden's division now."

"And?"

"Well, we were just shooting the breeze, you know. Shoptalk. I didn't make it sound like an official inquiry or anything, but I more or less quizzed him about whether John Halden might be deep undercover right now."

"What did he say?"

"He said, 'If John Halden's deep undercover, it's so damn deep *none* of us knows about it, including his wife.' "

Jefferson said, "Keep digging. Let me know what you turn up." He turned to go, but Nicky hesitated. *"What?"*

Nicky said, "They found the guy's car you know."

"I know."

"I've just got this feeling that he did what most of us wish we could every now and then. Just walked the hell away from it all and made a new life for himself somewhere."

Jefferson gave him a small smile. "You gettin' ideas, Nicky?"

Nicky shook his head. "Nah. I tried that, my wife'd track me down and kill me." He chuckled.

"Speaking of . . ."

"Yeah?"

"Why don't you see if any large sums of money have been withdrawn recently from any of their bank accounts."

"Okay."

"And while you're at it, see if you can find any new accounts in any local banks under the name Halden Johnson."

"All right."

"Hell, we may have to check out the whole state."

Nicky looked as if he were suppressing the desire to say, *Oh shit.*

"And Nicky, keep me apprised. Call me at home if necessary. Worse comes to worst, we may have to take what we know to the PD, whether they want to hear it or not. I'd rather begin work on this case now and worry about jurisdiction later. Oh, and we may even have to have a little talk with Halden's wife."

"You think she knows something?"

Jefferson shrugged. "Case like this, you never can tell. Just find out all you can on this Halden Johnson guy and keep me posted."

"Right." Nicky turned to go.

"And Nicky—"

The agent turned back with a long-suffering look on his face. Jefferson suppressed a grin. "Good work."

Nicky nodded and took off down the hall, whistling.

Management, Jefferson reflected, was a whole lot like parenting, especially in the FBI, which regarded itself as one big family. He didn't have any kids of his own, of course, but like most childless people, figured he knew more than those friends of his who were parents. The trick was to maintain discipline with the agents in his charge, but not be so harsh that it broke their spirits; offer praise for a job well done, but not so much that they took it for granted.

And never let them forget just who was boss.

As he headed back to his office, he wished he didn't have to deal with the Dallas PD at all. The FBI was a thousand times better at handling these sorts of investigations than police departments, especially when it involved one of their own.

But there was such a thing as jurisdiction, and professional courtesy, which dictated that the FBI not get involved unless specifically requested to do so by the police department in question, unless the investigation clearly crossed into federal jurisdiction and, so far, they had no evidence of that.

In the meantime, he would have Nicky make his discreet inquiries. He would keep an eye on what the PD was doing, and he would wait for further developments.

Because there was one thing of which he was certain: Halden Johnson was going to give them further developments.

"GYPSY. THIS IS CHIEF STRICKLAND."

Gypsy felt a rush of relief at the phone call from John's deputy chief. She could picture the portly, warm veteran cop with the road-map face as if he were standing in front of her. The Chief was immensely popular with his officers, who dreaded his upcoming retirement. They knew nobody could fill the shoes of the man whose thirty years of experience had made him a "cop's cop."

"I'M SORRY I'VE WAITED SO LONG TO GET IN TOUCH WITH YOU. IT'S BEEN NEARLY FOUR DAYS NOW SINCE JOHN DISAPPEARED AND I NEVER SHOULD HAVE LET THIS MUCH TIME GET BY BEFORE I SPOKE TO YOU."

"Chief Strickland—I have to know—is John undercover? If you'll just tell me that, I'll be able to sleep nights."

"I DON'T WANT TO TALK TO YOU OVER THE PHONE. THERE'S JUST TOO MUCH—"

"What? What are you talking about?" The Chief's disjointed message was frightening Gypsy. Was John undercover or not? Couldn't he just say yes or no and tell her more later?

"PLEASE FORGIVE ME. I REALLY CANNOT DISCUSS THIS WITH YOU OVER THE PHONE. JUST HANG IN THERE, AND I WILL BE OVER THIS EVENING TO TALK TO YOU. I'LL EXPLAIN WHAT I KNOW THEN. I WILL TELL YOU THIS . . ."

There was a long hesitation. So long that Gypsy wondered if he was even still there. She waited, her heart racketing against her ribcage.

"IT'S ABOUT YOUR DAD'S MURDER, GYPSY. YOU KNOW THAT CASE WAS NEVER CLOSED, AND THERE'S SOMETHING ABOUT IT THAT I SHOULD HAVE TOLD YOU YEARS AGO . . . I JUST WASN'T SURE UNTIL RECENTLY."

For the Chief to mention her murdered dad during a phone call about her missing husband chilled Gypsy to the roots of her hair. The truth was that, in all Gypsy's years of working with and around Dallas cops, she had never told anyone that her father was once a Dallas cop himself—not even John.

Silly though it might sound—even to her—Gypsy had always had a secret fear that if she ever did anything to delve into that old mystery, the Jigsaw Man would come back. And this time he would get her.

Or if not her . . . then maybe Annie.

Gypsy remembered being horrified once by watching twelve-year-old murder victim Polly Klaas's father tell a television interviewer that the child's greatest fear had always been that the bogey man would somehow come into the house and snatch her away. As parents, they had always tried to reassure the child that such a thing could never happen.

But it had.

Gypsy had always harbored that same fear.

Because even though Gypsy's mother had fled with her and hidden them far away, it was not far enough away, apparently. For the Jigsaw Man had found them after all, and strangled her mother as seven-year-old Gypsy stood paralyzed on the stair landing and watched.

But skeletons had a way of rattling out of closets when you least expected them. With one word from the chief, that childhood specter reached out and grabbed her in one bony fist.

"I KNOW THIS IS A LOT FOR YOU TO HANDLE RIGHT NOW, GYPSY. IF I DIDN'T THINK IT WAS IM-PORTANT, I WOULDN'T EVEN BRING IT UP."

She tried to unglue her thoughts, tried to say something, anything, but the flood of mental images and emotions was rushing through her mind too fast, dragging along debris she'd long since hidden away.

"I'LL TALK TO YOU TONIGHT, HON. WE'LL WORK EVERYTHING OUT THEN. NOW, YOU TRY AND GET

SOME REST UNTIL THEN, OKAY? GOOD-BYE FOR NOW."

And before she could get out a word, they were disconnected.

A sick feeling of dread settled into her gut like a bad, heavy meal.

She was so confused, so weary of just thinking all the time, of trying to put on a brave face in front of a too-bright and perceptive little girl, of trying to smile for the people who visited bearing food and encouraging words she couldn't even understand half the time.

Now this.

She found herself wondering if she were somehow doomed to live her mother's life.

And if that were the case, then what was to happen to Annie?

Later that day, overcome by mental and physical exhaustion, Gypsy fell asleep on the couch in front of the TV.

But she was not to rest. Instead, she ran through the mist and the grasping wicked trees, panting and screaming. Something grabbed her shirt, but when she tried to squirm out of it, she looked up to see, not another tree, but the Jigsaw Man. Laughing.

The Chief didn't come. Gypsy waited all evening long, pacing the floor and willing herself not to call. Finally, when she couldn't stand it any longer, she checked in with his office and found out that he'd left hours ago.

It seemed she'd walked to the front window and parted the drapes a hundred times, watching for car headlights, starting if she saw any, standing forlorn in disappointment as she watched them fade into the distance.

She read a book to Annie, but just a few minutes later,

couldn't remember which one. Tried to watch TV, but was too jumpy and drained to follow along with all the closed-captions. Flipped through magazines, but hardly noticed even the pictures.

Watched the clock.

Pacing the floor, she considered listening to music, but she would have had to turn it up so loud that Annie would never be able to sleep.

Silence, to Gypsy, usually meant only solitude and peace, but on this night, it meant loneliness.

And that stillness. That awful stillness in the house.

Like death.

Most homes made all sorts of little housey sounds: the hum of the refrigerator, the tick of the clock, the click-on of the air-conditioning or heating unit, the creak of a settling beam. Even neighborhoods had their homey noises: the bark of the dog next door, the chatter of birds in the trees, the rush of a passing car, the thrum of an airplane.

But for Gypsy, there was only silence, and that emptiness shouted John's absence to her louder and louder every day.

She couldn't stand it.

By ten P.M. she flipped on the TV to catch the evening news in a futile attempt to distract herself. She hadn't even been bothering to read the captions when a sudden photograph of Chief Strickland flashed across the screen.

Clutching the arms of a wingback chair, she perched birdlike on the edge of the seat, her whole body stiff, her breath coming out in short little gasps.

Video appeared of a car ditched on the side of the road, the driver's side door open.

A body, tangled in the shoulder harness of the seatbelt, slumped forward over the steering wheel.

The captions read: " . . . *BODY WAS FOUND SHOT*

*TO DEATH IN THE FACE AT CLOSE RANGE WITH
SOME SORT OF LARGE CALIBER GUN. DEPUTY
CHIEF STRICKLAND APPEARS TO HAVE BEEN TRY-
ING TO GET OUT OF THE CAR AT THE TIME OF THE
SHOOTING."*

Su Lee appeared on-screen, looking tiny and stunned
next to the brawny reporter. *"IT LOOKS LIKE SOME-
BODY MIGHT HAVE RUN DEPUTY CHIEF STRICK-
LAND'S CAR OFF THE ROAD. WE DON'T KNOW IF
THAT SAME PERSON OR PERSONS WAS THEN RE-
SPONSIBLE FOR THE SHOOTING OR NOT."* Her nor-
mally inscrutable face trembling in a losing battle against
tears, she shook her head. *"HE WAS ONLY THREE DAYS
AWAY FROM RETIREMENT. THIS IS A TERRIBLE,
TERRIBLE THING, AND OUR HEARTS GO OUT TO
HIS FAMILY."* With that, she turned abruptly and walked
away from the camera.

Gypsy didn't hear or see anything after that. The next
commercial break found her huddled in a tight ball on the
floor in front of the wingback chair, her face pressed into
her knees, trying with all her might to keep from screaming.

FOUR

"IT'S A TRAIN WRECK OVER there at the PD," confided Nicky to Jefferson on Monday morning. They were in the SAC's office with the door closed. "You know they found the weapon used in the deputy chief's murder. Or what they think is the murder weapon. Their ballistics is checking it out now."

"A thirty-eight, right?"

"Right. Charter and Arms snub-nosed Chief's special. Loaded with hollow-points. But there's more." It was all he could do to keep from rubbing his hands together.

Jefferson waited. Nicky'd been working hard. He deserved a little triumph.

"They ran a make on the gun. Seems it's registered to one John Halden. Used to be his service revolver before they switched to nine-millimeters."

Jefferson let out a low whistle. "No shit."

Nicky grinned. "Yes shit. And I think I found a legit way we can get involved."

"Tell me."

"I found a P.O. box. In the name of Halden Johnson."

"What's in it?"

"Letters from different states. Looks like they may contain checks."

"You don't know for sure?"

Nicky shrugged. "Without a search warrant, I didn't have a right to open the envelopes once the post office let me check out the contents of the box."

"Right." Jefferson pursed his lips. "You thinking what I'm thinking?"

"Got to be some kind of mail fraud. It would explain the dough he's been pulling in lately."

"If you're right, that would make it a federal crime."

"You want me to put the box under surveillance?"

"Well, that goes without saying. Get Angelino and Sanderson to help you. And let's get that warrant. We've got enough to go on now, I think."

Nicky headed for the door, then stopped. "You gonna tell the PD?"

"Let's check out those letters first. After all, they just lost a beloved officer, and it looks like one of their own may have killed him. Emotions'll be running high. I don't want to go blundering in and cause bad feelings. We'll give it a day or two."

"Right." Still, Nicky hesitated. "Hell of a thing," he said.

Jefferson nodded.

"You know Halden?"

"Met him a time or two."

"Just as nice a guy as you'd ever want to meet. A good cop, too. Never had a problem with turf, you know?" he said, referring to disputes which often took place between the FBI and local law enforcement when investigating the same crime. Some task force jobs went smoothly; others got tangled up in egos and turf wars between the branches.

Jefferson sighed. "Just goes to show that people are never what they seem." As he leaned back in his chair and watched Nicky close the door behind him, it occurred to Jefferson that he had never in his life felt wearier.

He had a bad feeling about this one.

Even worse, he wondered where it was all going to end.

Gypsy Halden knew just what awaited the Chief.

In order to determine exactly what had happened to cause the death of Deputy Chief Abe Strickland, his body and clothing would be divided into fragments and sent to various labs and rooms and offices at the Southwest Institute of Forensic Sciences, a five-story white building (not counting the basement), located adjacent to Parkland Memorial Hospital.

Prior to autopsy, the body would be brought into the basement on a gurney and brought by elevator up to the fourth floor, where it would receive an identifying toe tag before being lined up alongside all the other bodies in a large refrigerated storage room, where it would patiently wait its turn.

Contrary to depictions on TV and in the movies, the Institute did not store bodies in drawers, the theory being that the less a body was handled, the less likely valuable evidence might be lost. Consequently, no sheet would be placed atop the body, and relatives would not be taken to view the body itself. Instead, they would be merely shown photographs of the face by a field agent, which was usually sufficient for identification.

The Chief's blood-soaked clothing would be carefully cut off and placed in marked brown paper bags, where it would be sent to the criminal investigations lab on the third floor for microscopic evaluation by Gypsy's coworkers.

Without removing the Chief's body from the gurney, it would then be wheeled down the hall into the autopsy room, where it would be x-rayed and photographed. After autopsy, samples of his blood and other body fluids would be sent to the histology lab on the first floor and toxicology on the second floor.

During the autopsy, an investigating homicide detective would be standing at the ready. The medical examiner would place the squashed hollow-point bullet which was removed from the Chief's head—bits of his brain still clinging—directly into the detective's hand, who would then make a tiny identifying mark on the base end of the bullet to help preserve the chain of evidence before wrapping it in a soft cotton tissue and stuffing it into a small tube similar to a film cartridge, which he would then hand-label with case identifying data.

The detective would have the thirty-eight caliber Charter and Arms snub-nosed Chief's special found near the scene dusted for fingerprints in the criminal investigation lab, although Gypsy knew as well as anyone that fingerprints were rarely successfully lifted from guns; and then he would carry it in a sealed, marked manila envelope upstairs to the weapons test range on the fourth floor.

Gypsy knew all this, and so she was waiting right outside the elevator door on the day John's gun was brought to the weapons test range.

The homicide detective, a veteran tired-eyed bloodhound-faced man named Walter Bixby was startled when the doors opened and revealed Gypsy standing there like a palace guard. To Gypsy's surprise and Bixby's obvious irritation, Su Lee also stood at his side in the elevator.

"What the hell are you doing here?" Bixby asked

Gypsy. "Just your presence alone could taint the evidence."

"For God's sake, Bixby, cut her some slack," said Su Lee. "You're not going to let that gun or anything else out of your sight, and neither am I. Just let her watch."

He narrowed his eyes at Gypsy. "Stay out of the way," he said grumpily.

She nodded.

"I'll be there in just a minute," Su Lee told Bixby, and waited for him to disappear through the test range door before looking Gypsy full in the face and mouthing, *"I didn't want CAPers to fuck this one up."*

She was referring to the Crimes Against Persons division, of which homicide was a part. Like Gypsy, she was deeply worried about the make on John's gun. They both wanted to be absolutely certain that a mistake had not been made somewhere, and most especially certain that nothing went wrong in the crucial evidence chain.

In the test range, a squat-bodied, bespectacled technician with Brillo-pad hair was filling out a form and examining the tagged gun with a surgically gloved hand. "Got some blow-back here on the barrel," he commented, referring to blood and brain matter which would have exploded from the Chief's head on impact. "Must have been pretty close range."

"There was powder tattooing on the victim's face," said Bixby. He glanced over at Gypsy. "What was left of it, anyway."

She regarded him with a cool eye. This was her turf. Here, she could divorce her emotions from everything that was happening. It was a practice developed early on by anyone involved in law enforcement; a necessary protection from constant exposure to daily miseries of the human condition. In the lab, she never gave much thought to the bloody garments and semen samples and nicked knives that crossed her microscopic path.

Only once had she nearly lost it at work: when she'd been called upon to examine a blood-drenched flannel nightie just like one owned by Annie at the time. Sized *eighteen months*. There had been thirty-six stab holes in the nightie, and Gypsy had not slept worth a damn for six months after that.

But she could handle this. She was sure of it. And although she couldn't hear verbatim every word said by the tech, she could figure it out easily enough from long experience.

The tech squinted at the firearm. "There is a small cross scratched into the frame, just in front of the cylinder," he commented.

"That's my identifying mark," said Bixby. "Signifying that this is the gun we found near the scene of the shooting."

"Read me the serial number from your notes taken at the scene."

Bixby obeyed. Following along by examining the revolver, the tech nodded, compared the serial number which was written on the tag attached to the trigger guard, and made another note on his form.

The snub-nosed Chief's special contained five rounds. One had been fired. The tech examined each of the remaining four bullets in the chambers and numbered them, and made notes on the exact placement of each cartridge.

"Got any brass from the scene?" asked the tech.

Bixby shook his head. "The revolver was apparently the only weapon used, so the empty shell's still in the cylinder."

The tech nodded. "Right. We'll wait until we test-fire it to remove and mark the shell casings."

When everything that could be examined, checked, and double-checked had been, the tech took the thirty-eight and affixed it to a wooden viselike frame and adjusted it to the distance estimated by the homicide detective as having been the range fired when the Chief was killed.

Even though Gypsy was watching, and even though the concussion was muffled to her, she still jumped when he pulled the trigger.

The ballistics microscope was somewhat different from microscopes used in other analysis. This one allowed what was called a photomicrograph, which placed both slugs—the one taken from the Chief's brain, and the one just fired—side-by-side for comparison.

She knew the tech was talking to Bixby while he was looking, but she couldn't make out what he was saying. After a moment, he slid to the side in his castered chair and Bixby crouched over the eyepieces and squinted into them.

A glance at Su Lee's face told Gypsy everything she needed to know, but it wasn't enough. She had to see for herself.

"May I take a look?" she asked, and everybody stepped back, Bixby watching her every move.

Because they were hollow-points, much of the bullets were flattened, but enough remained of them to mirror the spiral grooves and raised lands of the revolver's barrel: the grooves in the soft lead of the slugs showed up under the photomicrograph as shallow raised areas: the lands like tiny grooves.

The patterns were an exact match.

The evidence was perfectly clear: the service revolver once carried by her beloved husband had been used to murder Deputy Chief Abe Strickland.

There was no doubt. She could see it with her own eyes.

And John was nowhere around to answer the charges against him.

FIVE

IT WAS THE KIND OF autumn day Dallas does best: warm, buttery sunshine and cool, sweet breezes; and everything was so photogenic for the cameras, from the soft emerald expanse of cemetery underfoot to the azure canopy of sky overhead to the hundreds of crisp, dark uniforms that filled the scene as far as the eye could see.

One hundred sixteen squad cars and the entire motorcycle division had led the funeral procession for Deputy Chief Abe Strickland for miles through blocked city streets. Everywhere they passed, idling automobiles turned on their headlights. There had even been too many uniformed people to fit in the church, and they spilled out into the parking area, black tape over their badges, murmuring softly to each other and looking around with sharp, hardened eyes.

Two of the Chief's sons and a daughter were Dallas cops. They came to the funeral in uniform. There were dignitaries in attendance, including the governor, who was trying to push a strong anti-crime bill through the Texas House, and the director of the Texas Department of Corrections. A black civic leader who had once been a troubled youth but had been taken in hand and turned around by the Chief, spoke during the service. Sound bites from the speech were picked up and aired by all three evening network news broadcasts, and the man was interviewed by CNN.

Word was out that the gun which had killed the Chief was registered to missing Dallas police officer John Halden. It was just the kind of information the media thrived on, and they swarmed the funeral like bats looking for blood to suck.

There they found Gypsy.

Friends had advised her not to go, but she had ignored the advice because she felt so strongly that John would have wanted her to be there, and because she couldn't imagine not paying her respects. It had never been her intention to intrude on the family's privacy; she only meant to blend into the fringes of the crowd.

Emotionally, she was holding together fairly well, until the Honor Guard began firing their revolvers in the air. She felt trapped in time then, in a weird double exposure of memory and reality, remembered grief and raw fresh wounds.

Oh Mama, she thought, eyes blurring with tears both old and new, *I never realized before how young you were when you lost Daddy.*

On the other hand, she pondered, *What's worse? Putting your husband in the ground to a hero's burial and a twenty-one gun salute . . . or hanging suspended in this horrible limbo of doubt and worry and wondering if the man you love with all your soul could actually be a stranger?*

She couldn't take it anymore. She had to get out of there before the revolvers were through echoing their final accusations over the heads of men and women who once thought they knew John and now wondered if they ever really did.

It was a good time to leave, anyway. Her plan was to slip out surreptitiously through the crowd and get away before drawing any attention from the Strickland family. She touched the arm of her friend Natalie Abrams. Natalie was middle-aged, pear-shaped, short, practical—and skilled at sign language. She had volunteered to accompany Gypsy to the funeral and sign for her, instinctively understanding that Gypsy would want to sit unobtrusively in the back.

They began to edge their way through the throngs of people standing in clots, necks craned to watch the Honor Guard tri-fold the flag and present it to Strickland's widow. Finally Gypsy and Natalie broke through the last little group and strode rapidly across the cemetery grounds toward Gypsy's car, which was parked some distance away, well beyond the endless line of squad cars.

Gypsy's thoughtful attempt at discretion proved to be her undoing. The various TV news reporters and their accompanying camera crews, as well as writers and photographers from *Texas Monthly*, the *Dallas Morning News*, and *Dallas Life* were all lurking about, waiting for the service to end so that they could descend en masse on the family as they headed for the limousine.

Gypsy caught the full brunt of the onslaught when, to her overwhelming horror and embarrassment, she found herself confronted by a shoving horde of eager bodies, each thrusting either a microphone or a tape recorder in her face and mouthing so many questions at once as to make the Tower of Babel seem comprehensible. Desperately, she looked for a way out, but she and Natalie were surrounded. There was simply no graceful way to make an exit.

One aggressive young man from the Dallas ABC news affiliate managed to push himself so close to Gypsy's face that she was able to read his lips fairly easily. "How do you feel about the fact that your missing husband is a suspect in the murder of Deputy Chief Strickland?" he asked, and a relative hush fell over the crowd as they awaited an answer.

She stared at the faces before her. As camera people and sound engineers jockeyed closer for better positions, she wondered how on earth she was supposed to answer a question like that. *How do I feel?* she wanted to ask. *I feel like I want to die. I feel trapped in a terrible lie with no way to find the truth. I feel so sad and frightened that I can hardly get up in the morning. That's how I feel.*

Finally, she said, "I don't know who killed the Chief, but I do know it was not my John. He loved Chief Strickland—we all did—and I just hope they find whoever did this terrible thing."

Chaos erupted. Gypsy glanced helplessly at Natalie, who shrugged and signed, *"This turd over here wants to know if you know where John is."* She rolled her eyes heavenward.

Gypsy said, "I have no idea where my husband is, but I do know in my heart that he did not go willingly."

Someone elbowed his way to the front of the crowd and shouted something at her. Natalie stared at him, her face horror-struck. Then, slowly, she turned to Gypsy and signed, *"This man claims they've found secret bank accounts belonging to John, along with a post office box and new credit card accounts . . . Gypsy . . . he wants to know if you knew about that."*

Gypsy felt all the blood drain from her face. Hot and cold needles tingled throughout her body. Her mouth so dry she had trouble speaking, Gypsy finally signed for

Natalie to interpret: *"That's a vicious lie. Where did you hear such a thing?"*

The man said something Gypsy didn't understand. Grim-faced, Natalie signed *"Son of a bitch won't reveal his sources."*

The crowd suddenly grew dead still, watching her with predatory eyes, waiting to swoop down and snatch up her words in bloody talons.

Swallowing hard, fighting for control, Gypsy said, "I don't know what you're talking about. My husband doesn't have any secret accounts. Whoever told you that must be crazy. I'm not going to answer any more questions. Please excuse me."

They didn't, of course. She had to fight her way through the mob.

And of the hundreds of uniformed officers standing around nearby, none stepped forward to help her.

The Dallas SAC was watching the evening news in his office when the phone rang even before coverage of Strickland's funeral was over. It was Strickland's successor, acting Deputy Chief in charge of intelligence James Fitzgerald. Jefferson had only met him once, and found him to be the most physically unattractive man he'd ever seen. His homeliness must have put a chip on his shoulder, because his disposition was just as bad.

"What the fuck is this about secret bank accounts, Agent Jefferson? I know a goddamned FBI leak when I see one."

Even the guy's voice was ugly. Jefferson adopted his calmest tone. "I can certainly understand your anger, Chief Fitzgerald," he said, "and I guarantee you that if it came from any of my people, heads will roll."

There was a brief silence. Then, in a slightly mollified

voice, Fitzgerald said, "What are you guys doing investigating the Chief's death, anyway? You got no jurisdiction in this matter, and we didn't ask for your help."

"I assure you it was not our intention to offend the police department in any way, Chief Fitzgerald, but one of our agents uncovered a possible mail fraud scheme on the part of John Halden. We were already investigating that when your ballistics ID'ed his gun as the murder weapon."

"Well then, why didn't you get your ass over here and talk to us about it?"

"We were going to. First thing in the morning, after the Chief's funeral. I thought it could wait until then."

Another silence. "You're probably right. We didn't do much on the case today. Everybody wanted to go to the funeral."

"I understand. I met Abe Strickland a time or two, you know, through mutual task force work. I didn't know the man real well, but he was an exemplary officer and a credit to your department."

"The best there ever was."

"How's his family holding up?" Jefferson asked politely.

"They're all pretty shook up. Man puts in thirty years on the streets, never gets shot, then three days before retirement he gets his head blown off. Next thing you know one of his own men is a suspect."

"Have you made any more progress on the investigation?"

"Well I'll tell you this much: if you guys could help us track down John Halden I'd personally kiss your feet."

"Are you formally requesting that we get involved?"

"Shi-it, Jefferson, you already *are* involved. Like I say, I know an FBI leak when I see one."

"Then if you like, we'll get together first thing in the morning and swap leads."

"Now you're talkin'. I'm ready to get this show on the road. You can't imagine what this whole thing has done to morale."

"Pretty low, huh?"

"Half the guys are ready to hang Halden. The other half swear he's being framed. And everybody feels so damn shitty about the Chief they can't hardly function."

"Maybe some fresh blood will help jump-start you."

"You'll have to get in line," Fitzgerald said gloomily.

"What do you mean?"

"So far we got CAPers, intelligence, missing persons, and internal affairs working on this case. Everybody's got bunions from stepping on each other's toes. I'm afraid the FBI's just going to have to join the crowd."

No way, thought Jefferson. *We'll be above the crowd, not part of it.* Already he didn't trust a police department to adequately investigate one of its own, even if the victim was also one of the fold.

One thing for sure, he was going to have to keep an eye on Fitzgerald. Jefferson didn't trust the guy. It was obvious he had some kind of hidden agenda. Not only that, but if anything went wrong, there was no question whom Fitzgerald would blame—loudly and publicly.

Fitzgerald must be covering something up. Otherwise he wouldn't be so worried that all the different divisions plus the feds were in on the investigation. He especially seemed to have it in for Jefferson, something he was going to have to handle very delicately.

A major part of Jefferson's job would be simple finesse—working through a tangled mess of egos, making sure tasks weren't being duplicated, organizing and unifying efforts, recognizing and acknowledging successful leads (no matter who found them), and seeing to it that the media was managed as smoothly as possible.

He didn't want any leaks getting out that he hadn't personally approved.

If it wasn't for my work, Gypsy thought to herself Tuesday morning after the Chief's funeral, *I know I'd go batty.*

She was still reeling from the latest accusations against John. Though the rumors had made all the local news broadcasts—twice—and were plastered all over the *Dallas Morning News* this morning, she still had no idea who was responsible for them.

And did it really matter? Once a theory such as that hit the media, you were already tried and fried. They didn't have to be true, or even come from a reliable source for people to believe it once they saw it on TV.

Friends Gypsy had once considered family had distanced themselves from her in recent days. Others, like Su Lee, were still fiercely loyal and yet . . . there was that doubt. That awful, terrible doubt that Gypsy could see now in everyone's eyes. *Could he? Did he?*

There had been a case in the news, she remembered, about a mild-mannered CIA agent who—to the endless shock of everyone who'd known him—turned out to be spying for the Russians. And another case she could recall, in which New York city police officers were found to have been dealing drugs.

Gypsy was living in an increasingly cynical society where presidents were expected to lie and cops were not always considered the good guys. Why should anybody believe that her husband was innocent, when his continued absence from the scene almost shouted his guilt?

Just that morning, a coworker had insinuated that

Gypsy was incredibly naive to continue to believe that her husband was himself a victim.

God, she was tired.

She couldn't remember when she'd last slept through the night, or even a time when her head didn't ache. Propping her elbows on the lab table, Gypsy rested her face on her cold hands, an oddly soothing gesture for her burning head.

"Gypsy?" She felt a hand on her shoulder. Startled, Gypsy's elbow slipped off the table, cracking her forearm painfully against the edge. It was the deputy chief medical examiner, Charles Sedgewick, M.D. Her boss.

"Excuse me, dear, but I need to see you in my office." As his tall back receded down the rows of lab tables, several lab techs watched with open curiosity as she followed meekly behind.

Sedgewick was lanky, balding, and hawk-eyed. His aquiline nose gave him even more the air of a bird of prey, and when he stared down his wire-rimmed half-glasses at her, she felt like a little kid in front of the principal. As soon as he began a sentence with "It has come to my attention—" she knew she was in as much trouble as she'd ever been in school.

"—that you might be better off taking a leave of absence for a while, at least until this, er, matter . . . is cleared up."

Her heart clenched. *No. Please, God, don't take my work away from me.* "I don't understand," she said.

"I said, 'It has come to my attention—'"

"No, no—I understood what you said, Dr. Sedgewick, but I don't understand *why*. I mean, I know I've been a little distracted lately, but I don't think my work has suffered—

"Oh no, it's not the quality of your work," he assured

her. "It's just, well, some of us feel that your being here at the crime lab represents a certain conflict of interest."

She was flabbergasted. "*What?* What do you mean? I haven't come into contact with any of the evidence related to my husband's case."

He tilted back his head and looked down his nose at her. "That's not entirely true, my dear, is it? I understand you were present at the firing range when the murder weapon in the Strickland case was test-fired."

Stymied, she hesitated.

"Your pay will continue . . . at least for the time being."

You mean, until my husband has been completely pilloried in the press. Gypsy began trembling, a deep inner quaking that took root in the center of her being and spread out in concentric ripples over her entire body.

She wanted so desperately to be outraged and forceful, but when she spoke, she could barely get the words out. "But, c-couldn't I work in one of the other labs? I could work toxicology—"

He was shaking his head, as if she were already being dismissed. "I'm sorry, Gypsy. You have to understand what a political hot potato it is for you to be here at the Institute when your husband is under suspicion for the murder of a high-ranking police officer."

She felt her knees knocking together and leaned against Dr. Sedgewick's desk, clasping her hands so that he wouldn't see them shaking.

"I could do clerical," she said, despising her own pitifulness.

"I'm sorry. If you need any help with your things—"

Lifting her chin in a pathetic show of defiance, she said, "No need. I assume you'll mail my paychecks?"

"Certainly. No problem. I'll take care of it personally."

You don't have to be so goddamn eager to get rid of

me, she thought, fighting back tears as she left his office, more deeply humiliated than at any other time of her life.

Gypsy had friends at work, but she didn't think this was the time or place to speak to them about this, and it was all she could do not to break down anyway as she quickly gathered up her things and fairly ran out of the building.

The drive home was a blur. Those miserable, lonely days of her childhood came rushing back, those days when she had no one to turn to and nowhere to go.

And then she got home.

Parked in front of the house were two plain cars she knew had to belong to the feds. Standing on her front porch were four men: two FBI agents and two plain-clothes detectives from internal affairs. She recognized the detectives: Art Sakowsky and Barry Angleton. But when she spoke to them, they seemed unable to make eye contact.

One of the agents was a big black man, handsome in an intense sort of way, who identified himself as Agent Nicks and presented her with a search warrant.

Gypsy was still shaking from her encounter with Dr. Sedgewick, and this was a double hammer-blow that rendered her speechless. She unlocked the front door with her key and they all followed her inside.

The first thing they asked to see was the family's home computer, which they carried out lock, stock, and barrel—along with all their computer disks, including the ones which contained some of Gypsy's lab reports and Annie's *Where in the World is Carmen Sandiego?* game.

All the financial records that Gypsy used to figure their taxes each year, along with bank statements and other receipts, were loaded into cardboard boxes and hauled out.

Shock set in. The whole thing took on the soft-focus

aura of unreality, as if it weren't really happening in real life but was merely a movie that she—a casual observer only—was watching. She answered their questions in a disconnected monotone, a voice not really a part of her.

They asked for a key to the family's safety deposit box and she gave it to them. They rooted through the closets and drawers and Annie's room and crawled up into the attic. Gypsy knew that under the terms of a search warrant, only those items which held a direct bearing on the crime being investigated could be removed from the house, but it didn't keep her from feeling violated—simultaneously embarrassed by the messy state of the closets and outraged that her privacy had been laid open so completely and so quickly.

It was just too much like a nightmare. *Soon*, she thought, *I will wake up and this will all end.*

Then Agent Nicks, somber but respectful, politely asked if Gypsy would mind accompanying the men back to the police department to answer a few questions.

That's when—with jarring finality—the real world came crashing down upon her.

SIX

"WE QUESTIONED HER FOR twelve hours," reported Agent Nicks to Jefferson the next morning. "Rodriguez assisted. Both her parents are deaf and she's fluent in sign language. Anyway, I don't think Mrs. Halden knows anything."

"Polygraph?"

"She volunteered to take one."

"So you don't think she's harboring him somewhere."

"We've had her under surveillance for several days now, and I don't see anything out of order. Yet."

"How about a court order for a wiretap?"

"That could take some time. We really don't have any evidence that she has had any prior knowledge of her husband's activities or that she has been in contact with him."

"Still. We've got to explore that avenue. Get the paperwork underway."

"Will do."

"What about the computer disks?"

Nicky rubbed his hands together. "Now that's been a lot more productive. I'll send Agent Johnson in to brief you. He knows more about it than me."

"In a nutshell, Nicky."

Nicky grinned. "In a nutshell? Mail fraud through selling phony items via computer bulletin boards."

Jefferson clapped his hands together. "Got him!"

"Yeah—If not for murder, then for this."

"We'll get him for murder," said Jefferson. "I assume he's already listed with NCIC, the National Crime Information Center?"

"Oh yeah. First thing."

Jefferson leaned back in his chair, hands clasped behind his head. "Any flak from the cops?"

"Not from the rank and file. But that Fitzgerald is an asshole. We can't take a step without tripping over him."

"Don't worry about him. I've seen his type before. He gives you much grief, let me know."

"We can probably handle it. It's just a pain, is all. They say his wife left him. For another cop. He's so whacked-out about it they may find somebody else to take Strickland's job."

"What about the wife? I mean Halden's wife."

"What about her?"

"How's she holding up?"

Nicky frowned. "That's the worst part. You can't help feeling sorry for her."

"Why? Because she's deaf?"

"Well, partly, but mainly because she seems so lost. That son of a bitch apparently pulled this off without giving her so much as a clue. They've been married, what, eight—nine years? One day she wakes up and her old man's not only gone, but turns out to be a crook, to boot."

Jefferson said "It's hard for me to imagine that she didn't notice *a thing*. I mean, really. How can you live with somebody and not know?"

Nicky shrugged. "Happens all the time."

"I guess."

"Anyway. I think she's about to crack up. I really do. And I couldn't blame her if she did."

The demons were always worse at night.

They crowded round her bed, plucking at her with skeletal fingers, whispering in her ear with foul breath, yammering in her head so loudly she thought she might go insane.

"Do you have any reason to believe your husband might be having an affair?" Agent Nicks had asked.

Like, maybe he got tired of dragging his disabled wife around on a chain, signing for her at parties, protecting her from insensitive strangers, dealing with everyday mix-ups or even big blowups that had occurred when she misunderstood something crucial?

A reason like that, you mean?

Like, maybe he had finally seen for himself just how boring and dumb she really was? Like, maybe he finally went out and found someone bright and beautiful and full of grace . . . someone who could actually *hear* his terms of endearment in bed?

Something like that, you mean?

"Your husband made withdrawals of substantial amounts of money from his secret bank accounts," Agent Nicks had said. "Where do you suppose he got the money?"

Where do I suppose? Where do I suppose?

I have no idea what I suppose! she wanted to scream. *I don't suppose anything! I just want my husband back.*

"We have reason to believe your husband was using your home computer and modem to conduct an illegal mail fraud operation from your home. What do you know about that?"

Nothing. I know absolutely nothing.

"C'mon, Mrs. Halden. You both use the same computer. Are you telling me you had no idea what he was doing?"

We respect each other's privacy, she tried to say. He doesn't snoop into my computer files and I don't snoop into his.

"But didn't you suspect something from the amount of time he was spending at the computer?"

How could I? she wondered. *I worked days, John worked nights. We hardly saw each other.*

That was it, then. They didn't even have a marriage. Not a real one anyway. How could they, when he seemed to be living this secret double life?

Then the demons always crowded around her bed and screamed in her head: *You stupid, stupid bitch! Only somebody as stupid as you could have lived a lie with a man and not even* realized *it!*

And the Chief. Dear God, the Chief.

Could the man she loved and cherished and shared a child with . . . could he have faced that old man down and calmly blown his head practically off his shoulders?

Only an idiot like you could have married a monster and not even known it.

But every time the demons threatened to dominate Gypsy and send her screaming over the edge . . . John would come to her. In the half-life between dreams and waking, she would feel his gentle caresses, and see his clownish signing, and watch him with Annie . . . Annie, their precious Annie . . . Could he have ever, *ever* done anything to deliberately hurt that child?

No, she would scream back at the demons. *NO!*

All Gypsy's career life, she had analyzed cold, hard evidence with the unemotional eye of a scientist. Now the tables had turned. A virtual tidal wave of evidence was staring at *her*—God knows, the demons reminded her of this every waking moment—and all she had to counter it was her stubborn, persistent love for her husband.

But sometimes, as she finally slipped off into restless sleep, her dreams would be shadowed by a dread, a sense of something dark poised just out of her line of sight. She would be frightened and she would call for John, and though she would search for him everywhere and call and call, when she looked up, it would not be John standing over her.

It would be the Jigsaw Man.

"Mr. Jefferson, hold for the White House."

"Special Agent Jefferson? This is Ellen Blackman. I've been asked by the president to let you know that your name appears on our short list of candidates to be considered for appointment as director of the FBI."

Powerful emotion caught Jefferson by surprise and completely closed his throat. For a long moment, he was speechless.

"Agent Jefferson? Are you there?"

"Yes—yes, certainly. I just—I'm very flattered."

"You came very highly recommended by Director Kellerman himself. The last several appointees have been federal judges, and Director Kellerman felt it was time we chose someone from the ranks. The president has seen your resume and is very impressed by it."

"Well . . . thank you. I knew Director Kellerman was ill, but I wasn't aware his illness had progressed this fast."

"I think he wanted to make a contribution to the selection process now, while he is still feeling reasonably well."

Jefferson's heart began a slow, steady thrumming in his ears. *This is it,* he thought. *Dear Jesus, this is it.*

"The president would like to meet with you next week, if that's possible, to discuss this further."

"Of course."

"All right then. If you'll put your secretary with my secretary, we'll get the arrangements made."

With shaking fingers, Jefferson transferred the line to his secretary. He was still sitting there ten minutes later, still shaking, when, with a wild whoop of congratulations, Doris came running into his office and threw her arms around his neck.

Two days after the Chief's funeral, the phone rang at Gypsy's house.

As usual, she flew to answer it. The message was digit-clear across her special phone:

"GYPSY, HONEY, YOU'VE GOT TO FIND THE LET-TERS. I'M A DEAD MAN IF YOU DON'T. YOU MUST NOT TELL ANYBODY. DO YOU UNDERSTAND? NO-BODY. JUST FIND THOSE LETTERS, AND WAIT TO HEAR FROM ME AGAIN. I LO—"

And though she cried and screamed and banged the receiver of the telephone hard against the desk, the line had long since been disconnected, and there was no other word from her missing husband.

"You crazy bastard!" cried John Halden, straining mightily against the chains which bound him to the wall next to the cot upon which he sat. "When I get out of this, I swear to God, I'll kill you with my bare hands!"

The man, standing just inches out of John's reach, telephone receiver in hand, grinned at John and shook his head. "Better men than you have tried," he said. Replacing the phone on the cheap desk, he sat down in the chair, swiveled, and leaned back, arms crossed over his chest, pale blue eyes studying John in much the same way an exterminator might study a bug.

John, panting, wiped spittle off his stubbled chin with the back of his hand and regarded the man who was regarding him.

John had met this man before through his work, but it didn't make him any less creepy-looking. Strange scars criss-crossed his face, leaving odd patches of skin either ruddy in complexion or alarmingly white. Those patches stood out, almost in bas relief. There were similar scars on his hands.

Yet in spite of the scarring, he had a ramrod-dignified carriage that emphasized his height (somewhere over six feet), and brought a certain grace to bear on his dark silver-streaked hair, cut military short. Though possibly in his fifties, he looked ten years younger.

John still couldn't believe that after fifteen years' experience, his cop's gut had given him no warning about this man, that he had followed him willingly into his car, that he had never stopped to think just how dangerous he could be.

The sense of powerlessness that now raked against John's skin like fingernails was not just caused by his imprisonment. He broke eye contact and glanced behind his guard at the sophisticated surveillance equipment that was set up and ready to go.

The man registered John's glance and nodded approvingly. "State-of-the-art," he said, patting the device like a pet. "ICOM R9000. It receives 100kc to 2gc. Got a built-in computer with a data/video display screen." He smiled with pride. "It's a repeater system. The RF transmitter is easy to hide. Puts out 30 watts and travels as many miles." He added, "Lets me keep a close eye on Annie while she looks for those letters."

John kept a steady gaze. The man's use of the name "Annie" to refer to Gypsy was unnerving. He stifled a shudder. *Never show fear.* It was the first rule of undercover work, John knew. *A con can sniff it out like a dog, and you'll be dead before you can blink.*

"You should see the keen fiber-optic probes I've got threaded through the house," continued the man, clearly proud of his work. "All it takes is a little-bitty hole, maybe an eighth of an inch, for me to see all I need. But then, you probably know all about that, you being a big-shot *intelligence* officer and all. Some intelligence. Just look at you now." He chuckled, and it came out sounding like a deep-throated growl.

Struggling to keep his face impassive, John stared at the man and wondered if he was psychotic or just plain evil. His whole family was at the mercy of this nutcase, and it was all his fault.

He should have known better than to go poking around.

SEVEN

PANIC ALMOST GOT HER.

With Annie away at school, Gypsy didn't have to keep up a brave front. Pacing the house from one end to the other, she allowed herself to weep and tear her hair, cursing and screaming.

Letters? What letters? She had no idea what John was talking about.

Where was he? What was happening to him?

Half a dozen times she reached for the phone. She could call Su Lee, maybe. Somebody, anybody who could help her.

Once she fetched the business card Agent Nicks had given her. Maybe she should call him. After all, this was a clear case of kidnapping, wasn't it?

But each time, something always held her back. Again and again she slammed down the receiver or just stopped dialing halfway.

Think about it, she told herself. Hadn't she already endured hours of suspicious questioning? And all the evidence seemed to point to the fact that John had left of his own free will; had, indeed, been planning it for some time. Even had a great deal of money to finance it. Illegal money, apparently.

And worse, it appeared to be John's gun which killed the Chief. She had seen that for herself.

Even those who didn't want to believe it couldn't help but admit that it looked bad, real bad, for John. And there was a growing number of them who accepted everything at face value and condemned her husband.

Some of them even suspected *her* of being involved.

If she were to go to them now and tell them about the phone message, would they believe her? She had no printed readout of it or anything. All they would have was her word.

A word many of them already suspected.

She wanted to hope that the FBI might be somehow different, sort of *above* the interdepartmental rivalries and jealousies and loyalties that inevitably tainted a police department investigation of one of their own.

But Gypsy, of all people, knew just how incriminating hard evidence could really be.

Granted, secret bank accounts and credit cards—or even evidence of fraud—did not make John a murderer. Nor did the fact that his gun was the weapon which murdered the Chief mean that he had pulled the trigger.

But law enforcement officers, just like anyone else, had their prejudices, Gypsy knew. She'd taken part in enough criminal investigations to know that cops often formulated opinions fairly early on, and then searched for evidence to back them up. Sometimes they even ignored evidence that could prove otherwise.

They all denied it, of course. They all said that they were simply searching for the truth. And many of them did. Unfortunately, just as many did not. And no matter how many defense lawyers called such things as hidden bank accounts "circumstantial," the truth was that many jurors shared those same prejudices.

Hell, it was just plain human nature.

Gradually, Gypsy's own rational mind began to pierce through the rush of emotion which had possessed her when John first called. She splashed cold water on her face and sat down in a comfortable chair in the living room, forcing herself to take deep breaths and calm herself.

Then, she faced some cold, hard truths of her own.

She was not going to be able to ask for help through the traditional channels; of that she was certain. She was going to have to handle this thing herself.

Because, the bottom line was that *John needed her.*

With haunting sadness, she realized that, for most of the past decade, anyway, her husband had been her valiant protector.

During all those "after" years, Gypsy had never had one before John came into her life, and it was now stunning to realize how very much she had come to depend on him in the years since.

And now . . . he was depending on *her.* Now *she* would have to be the valiant protector.

Was she up to the task? She didn't feel like it, but she was going to have to be.

Resting her head back on the chair's cushion, she let her mind free-fall through the years, trying to think what letters John could mean . . .

The jolt of memory, when it came, seared her insides with a cold fire.

"I don't have the letters! I don't know what you're talking about!" Her mother's cries . . . echoing through the years.

"You lying bitch! I'm sick of your lies, do you hear me?

Sick of them! Tell me where the letters are! Tell me! Tell me!" Gypsy's stomach rolled. She could see the man again, as clearly as if he was in the room with her, crouching over her mother's body. His hands were around her throat, and he punctuated each *"Tell me!"* with a tightening of his fingers. Her mother's choking sounds began to be gurgles.

Roused from bed by her mother's screams, she had stood frozen on the stair landing in her bare feet and white cotton nightie, watching this hulking dark figure stoop over Anna, striking her in the face when she did not say what he wanted her to say.

And now he was trying to kill her.

Flinging her body down the stairs, she flew across the room, where she leapt onto the man's back and began pummeling him with her tiny fists, screaming, *"Leave my mama alone!"*

Shaking her off like a great shaggy dog after a bath, he stood up, drew back a hand, and slapped her so hard on the left side of her face that she was literally picked up off her feet and tossed backward, where she landed in a crumpled heap next to her mother's prone and too, too still body.

Ignoring the high-pitched ringing that suddenly drowned out all sound, Gypsy crab-walked over to her mother and picked up her limp hand. Sensing the big man behind her, she whirled around and looked up. He was tall, so tall his head almost bumped into the ceiling fixture and the bright white light sent little black dots swirling around her eyes until he stepped in front of it and leaned over her.

The Jigsaw Man.

His face was marked like a puzzle, and the black dots in her eyes blanked out parts of it, like little missing pieces. She wanted to scream and she opened her mouth but nothing came out.

He reached for her.

She ran . . .

The lights started to blink, signifying someone at the door, crashing Gypsy back into the present. She leapt to her feet as though the Jigsaw Man was really after her. She wanted to run—just as she did that night—

She was trembling so violently now—just at the memory of it—that she clutched her arms to her chest, gulping air to keep from hyperventilating.

The lights continued to blink. Slowly shaking her head, she moved to the door and peered out the side window. Two middle-aged women and a man were standing patiently on the porch, holding leather carryalls and clutching thick Bibles to their chests.

Backing away from the door, Gypsy sank back into the chair.

She knew what she must do.

She was going to have to go back. Back to the old house by the sea where her mother died. Back to the past.

Back to the horror.

Everything inside of her was screaming *"NO!"* But her love for her husband was a strong and steady presence that overshadowed all doubt, all fear.

From a drawer in a small table by the chair she removed a yellow pad and pen and started to make a list. The lights stopped blinking. She wrote:

—*Call the Rockport realtor and ask him to restore electricity and water to the old house. Also have phone installed.*
—*Go by school and talk with Annie's teacher. Get books and lesson plans for indefinite absence.*
—*Have newspaper and mail stopped here/give plants to neighbors to take care of.*

—*Have car completely serviced for long trip.*
—*Get down Smith & Wesson .38 from top of closet/clean it/stock up on ammo.*
—*Ditto the .410 shotgun.*

By the end of the list, her hand had stopped shaking.

John Halden spent his days lying or sitting on a standard Army cot, a loaf of bread and package of bologna on the floor beside him next to a two-gallon jug of water. A plastic five-gallon bucket set at the other end of the bed sent noxious odors into the room that disappeared only when his captor showed up to haul it away, which tended to be once every two or three days.

Prison leg-irons had been adjusted to fit around his wrists, and the accompanying chains reached to a steel pipe which ran from the floor through a hole in the ceiling. The chains extended about six feet in length—just far enough to enable him to do push-ups and sit-ups on the hardwood floor beside the cot or to use the bucket.

The room was small, about eight-by-ten, and windowless. It was a false room. John knew this because three of the walls appeared, judging from the thick wooden baseboards, high ceiling, and faded wallpaper, to be the standard walls of a room in an old house. But the wall across from him and facing the bed was only cheap wallboard, with a door-sized rectangle cut out and held in place by wooden backing blocks screwed into a wall frame constructed of two-by-fours. Whenever his captor entered the room, he pulled the "door"—from which long screws protruded—shut behind him. The backing blocks fit the screws. When he tightened the blocks, the door became flush with the wall.

Ingenious. John wondered what the wall looked like on

the other side, whether it was covered with fresh wallpaper that could possibly alert someone to the presence of the false room. Provided anybody was there who was of a mind to hunt for such a thing, which he doubted. He suspected the false wall was probably also well insulated, so as to allow no sound to escape.

The only light to his little cell came from a single bulb in the ceiling that glared mercilessly day and night. Along one wall crowded a cumbersome gray metal Army surplus desk, upon which rested the surveillance equipment receivers and computer equipment, along with a telephone, tantalizingly close and yet so very far. A floor fan ran constantly—not for John's comfort, but to protect the electronic equipment from getting too hot in the close room.

He had tried everything to escape.

His wrists were swollen and raw from yanking fruitlessly against the chains, his feet sore from kicking against the floor and walls, hoping against hope that somebody somewhere might hear the noise and come to investigate. He had a bump on his head from the time he stood up on the iron railing of his bed in his sock feet (he never knew what happened to his shoes), straining to see if he could figure a way to dislodge the pipe, and fell off—his chains yanking his head into the bedstead.

Naturally, he had tried screaming for help—tried until his voice turned to sawdust, but to no avail.

Though he couldn't tell for sure where he was, the heavy atmosphere and the unseasonal warmth told him it was probably not Dallas, which was already beginning to bundle up for winter.

Down south somewhere, then, but he had no way of knowing even if he was still in the state of Texas, since he was drugged for the entire trip. Thank God he was still wearing the sturdy sports watch he always wore on duty, which let him know the date and told him he'd been away from his family for more than two weeks.

His breath and clothes stank from bologna and sweat and fear, and he knew the landscape of the ceiling by heart as he lay awake for hours on end, wracked with worry about his family.

When he thought about how much he loved his wife, it made his chest ache. John knew she felt inferior to the high-class attorneys and sinewy smart police officers he saw every day on the job, even worried, sometimes, that he might be tempted to leave her someday for one of them.

If she only knew.

When John found Gypsy, it was as if he had come home to a place of soothing quiet and comfort, a place where he was never expected to be something he was not, a place where shy humor and soft pleasures in bed made him homesick even when he was at work. And, corny though it may seem in the self-sufficient nineties, home was a place where John was needed.

It wasn't as if Gypsy hadn't been taking perfectly capable care of herself for years before she met John, but underneath that competent exterior beat a vulnerable heart, a bruised and battered soul, a little girl who never got over missing her mama and daddy. When he took her in his arms, he felt more a man than at any time when swapping machismo with dangerous felons on the mean streets of the city.

And the beautiful child they had created together, his sweet Annie, why, he loved her more than life itself.

And now—through his own almost phenomenal stupidity—he had left them abandoned, alone, afraid, and in very real peril.

II

The voice of your brother's blood is crying to me from the ground.

—Genesis 4:10
New American Standard version

EIGHT

GYPSY DISCOVERED THE BUMPER BEEPER later
that afternoon.

While out in the garage, rummaging around for luggage, she dislodged an old soccer ball which rolled underneath the car. When Gypsy dropped to her stomach and
crawled beneath the car, arm outstretched to fetch the
ball, a thin rubber-coated wire traced across her cheek.
Looking up, she spotted the magnet which attached the
signal transmitter to the underside of the Blazer. The wire
served as the device's antenna.

If she hadn't been married to an intelligence cop, she'd
never have been alerted to the presence of the wire in the
first place. But there it was, plain as day: proof that she
was under surveillance. This "bumper beeper" would
allow those following her to have a clear signal of her
whereabouts even if they had lost sight of the car itself.

Heart pounding, Gypsy lay flat on her back on the cold
concrete floor of her garage, eyes squeezed shut, trying to
think what to do next.

Shit. Shitshitshit.

How was she ever going to get to Rockport without the

entire United States government knowing about it? John had warned her not to tell anyone.

Of course, that's what kidnappers and their victims always said when they established contact.

Maybe she should call Agent Nicks after all and explain what was going on.

And maybe she should tell him she'd seen pink polka-dotted elephants in her backyard too. He'd believe that just about as much.

Forgetting all about the ball, Gypsy heaved herself out from under the car, opened the car door, and plunked down in the passenger seat, her head back on the seat rest, thinking.

From what John had told her about doing task force work with the FBI, the one thing that always drove cops crazy about the feds was the overkill factor. "Why bring three agents to make an arrest when thirty will do?" he'd joked one time. The FBI theory was that the more agents they had involved in any given situation, the less the chances one of them might get hurt. The less chance, too, of failure.

Where cops might put one or two cars tailing a suspect, the FBI would put five or ten. With a surveillance plane—capable of conducting surveillance from four thousand feet—to boot.

Shit!

Okay. Calm down. Think. Twenty undercover vehicles had been used to tail convicted spy John Walker. But she was no spy. How bad were John's suspected crimes in comparison, anyway? Using that as a gauge, then how many cars were likely to be tailing *her?* Five? Two?

Think. If they were planning a big operation, especially one in tandem with John's old colleagues, then they wouldn't necessarily *need* a bumper beeper, would they?

If they were using numerous cars and a plane, they would have her in clear sight wherever she went.

So. If they were using a bumper beeper, she surmised, then they must not have that many agents and/or cops on the case. At least, not yet.

Now. If the cops were watching her, wouldn't at least Su Lee give her some warning?

Hard to tell these days.

She shook her head. No. Something told her John's old friends in intelligence weren't in on this—not yet, anyway.

A new thought brought her upright. Was her phone tapped and, if so, had they heard John's call? And if they had, then wouldn't they help her? Wouldn't they *know* that John was an innocent victim?

Slow down. Think.

It had only been four days since the Chief's death—about two weeks since John disappeared. Getting court approval for a wiretap was no easy thing. A pretty conclusive case had to be made before a judge would approve such an invasion of privacy, and Gypsy doubted they'd had time to make that case. Yet. She had no doubt they were trying, though.

In the meantime, they were watching every move Gypsy made.

Thank goodness she'd been evasive to Annie's teacher that afternoon when she collected her daughter's books and assignments. Now she was certain that the feds would be questioning the woman as soon as she got away.

If she got away.

For the time being, Gypsy removed the bumper beeper and tossed it into the front seat. She had plans for it.

Then she lugged some bags into the house and packed as best she could for both herself and Annie. The little girl seemed disinterested in the procedure, choosing to sit in front of the TV and watch a *Beauty and the Beast* video. Gypsy was worried about her child. She needed to cuddle the little girl and explain everything to her, but there wasn't time and now she couldn't be sure their conversation wasn't being monitored.

Keeping the garage door closed, she made trips back and forth through the kitchen door, stuffing the car full of everything she could imagine they might need and then some. For Annie, she constructed a little nest in the back seat of pillows and her favorite toys and books and crayons, along with a portable tape recorder and some of her favorite tapes and books on tape. Next to Gypsy on the front seat was a small bag with "trip treats" she'd bought that afternoon at a discount store to alleviate boredom. Maps went on the dash.

Sandwiches, snacks, and a loaded cooler went into the Blazer next to last. Then, Gypsy carefully placed the unloaded shotgun on the floorboards at her feet and the loaded thirty-eight on the seat beside her, covered with a towel.

Done.

By then it was dark. Gypsy and Annie ate a quick, light supper and Gypsy made a run through the house, setting light timers and checking things as if she were leaving on a pleasant vacation and not a desperate attempt to save her husband's life.

There wasn't anything left to do then, but leave.

Heart in her throat, Gypsy backed the Blazer out of the garage and pushed the button on the garage door opener to close it as she pulled slowly down the street, one eye glued to the Blazer's side mirrors, but it was impossible to tell anything after dark. After driving about a mile in apparent oblivion to her pursuers, Gypsy slowed to a crawl as if looking for an address, knowing that as she did so, her followers would slow as well. Then, without speeding up at all, she suddenly whipped to the right around a corner and then accelerated, dousing the lights as she did so. At the next corner, still driving without her lights, she took another quick turn into an alley and drove to the next block, watching behind her for pursuing lights.

There were none.

Now she exited the alley onto the center lane of a major thoroughfare in heavy traffic, put on her headlights, and followed it to the nearest traffic signal, slowing slightly until it turned red and unfastening her seatbelt as the Blazer came to a stop. Slamming the car into "park", she leapt out, stooped, and stuck the bumper beeper on the underside of the car next to hers, which happened to be a Ford Bronco—not exactly a Chevrolet Blazer, but close enough in the dark.

When the light turned green, Gypsy hesitated until the Bronco had passed, then she careened the Blazer into a lefthand turn in front of oncoming traffic and accelerated down that street, more or less backtracking the path she'd taken in the alley. From that point, she hit the overcrowded Loop 12, circling with the gigantic Texas Stadium looming behind, and headed west on I–20.

It took her two hours before she felt safe enough to turn the Blazer south toward the Gulf.

As far as Gypsy could tell, nobody followed.

"You *what?*" screamed Jefferson.

"We lost her, sir." A contrite Nicky stood slump-shouldered in front of him. A slight tick in his left eyelid betrayed his nervousness.

"I can't believe this. How many cars did you have tailing her?"

"Two. I was in one with Wilkenson. Angelino and Sanderson were in another."

"I thought you had a beeper on her."

"We did . . . er . . . it turned up on a Ford Bronco."

"A Bronco. *You dumb fuck!* How many times do I have to tell you, huh? *Never underestimate the enemy!*"

"Well, she's hardly an *enemy,* Mr. Jefferson. She's a woman with a little kid whose husband's missing."

Jefferson smiled. It was the sweet smile that he only reserved for children and imbeciles. "You, of all people, should know a little something about stereotypes, Nicks."

Nicky looked as though he were about to speak but thought better of it.

"You stereotyped her. Put her in the slot marked, 'housewife.' Figured she was good for, what, the latest sale on cabbage at the supermarket?"

The eyelid jumped.

"You thought this little gal would never outsmart a couple of big bad FBI agents like you and Wilkenson, right?"

"Angelino and Sanderson were there too, sir."

"I don't give a shit if the entire United States Army was there! You still lost her! You fucked up, Nicks!"

In a futile effort to stop the tick, Nicks blinked.

Jefferson bored into the agent with eyes he knew reflected light like cold steel. "Now. Tell me the part again about how she didn't come home last night, and how you haven't seen her this morning."

Nicky blinked again.

"In other words, the only real connection we may have to a cop-killer and a federal fraud has now skipped town—does that about cover it, Nicky?"

"Yes. Sir."

Jefferson glared at the agent, whose forehead had now broken into a thin film of sweat.

Nicky said, "We've got several leads on where she may have gone, Mr. Jefferson. I'll get right on it—"

"No. You won't get right on it. I'm taking you off this case, and I'm taking you off the violent crimes squad."

The agent's lips parted, and his whole face sagged. It had taken him two years to work his way onto the violent crimes squad, and he loved being there.

"But my cases—"

"I'll brief the others on the squad. They'll divvy them up. And I'll speak to Caldwell," he added, referring to Nicks's supervisor.

Nicky was no longer making any attempt to hide his crestfallen expression.

Jefferson paid no attention. "Meanwhile, Nicky, we've got a warehouse full of bank records that need to be gone through. Those savings and loan scandals are a bitch to investigate. Takes months, you know, just going over all those numbers. They'll be glad for the help over in the bank fraud squad."

He sat down behind his desk and began sorting through the confusion of papers, ignoring the big agent until he realized that he had been dismissed.

Nicks left, yanking the door firmly shut behind him, just short of a slam.

Jefferson gave the door a thoughtful stare. Whenever his daddy had given him a spanking, he used to say, "This hurts me, son, more than it hurts you."

He'd never really understood that until he was in a position himself to discipline others. And it was true. It did hurt him worse than it did Nicky.

But then, he doubted ol' Nicks would ever lose a tail again.

John's worst enemy, each and every day, was himself.

In spite of his watch, the light bulb in the windowless room confused his sense of day and night. His sleep was sporadic and restless, leaving him fatigued and confused. Before long, doubts began to assail him.

Had he been left to die?

There was just so far the bread and bologna—now growing rancid—would go. And what about his family? Anyone who had gone to so much trouble to install such high-spy surveillance equipment would monitor it, wouldn't they? Not leave it to gather dust. Unless they didn't need it anymore. Unless Gypsy and Annie were no longer . . .

John tried not to think about that.

He wondered if there were even anybody near enough to eventually be able to smell his decomposing body. If not, he could be here for years. He—or his body, anyway—might never be found.

He worried endlessly about Gypsy. She *needed* him! What was she going to do without him? How would she manage?

He didn't even get to tell her how much he loved her.

Just the thought of his wife and child filled him with anguish, and he had to fight despair each and every day.

If he'd just minded his own business, kept *out* of it, for God's sake. Let sleeping dogs lie.

He wondered if Gypsy would ever be able to forgive him.

And then sometimes he would sob, too weary with thinking even to do his exercises, too sad to mark the day off on the wall.

As if pursued by the devil himself, Gypsy drove all night.

It was hard to tell, from reading a map or even from tracing the distance with her finger, how huge the state of Texas really was. A thousand miles stretched from east to west and another thousand from north to south, and Gypsy felt every last one of them as she—at last!—drove through the sleepy little community of Rockport on the Gulf Coast and made her way past the harbor and along Fulton Beach Road toward the old house.

The closer she got to it, the more she was rendered virtually speechless with dread. The morning air was thick with autumn mist and a briny, salty scent as she climbed stiffly out of the car, heart thudding heavily against her lungs.

The spooky, twisted oak trees were just as she remembered them, slanting crazily all to one side, the tangled boughs stretching toward the house as if the sea winds were too harsh to take and they were imploring to be let inside.

The house was set high back from the road at the top of a steep incline, shrouded with the gnarled trees like the veiled eyes of an old woman peeking between arthritic fingers. Surrounding acreage set the house apart from any neighbors, and the encroaching trees acted as a wall, ensuring privacy. A rickety, timeworn wooden boardwalk led down to Fulton Beach Road, which curved around the base of the hill, and just across the road was the endless expanse of water, smudged slate beneath matching clouds and seamless haze. A battered and sun-bleached wooden pier—missing many boards—extended out into the mirror-calm water, protected by a shrimp-rich bay, for about fifty yards.

For many years Gypsy had wondered why her mother stipulated in her will that the rambling old house not be sold. When she came of age, the house became hers, but

Gypsy would have no part in it. For years a local realtor had rented it out to summer vacationers and winter snow-birds, but the upkeep became too much of a burden. And so in recent years it had simply sat unoccupied, a visible symbol of Gypsy's own indecision. John had wanted her to either use it for a second home or contest the will and sell it. She had been unable to do either.

Now it stood filthy, creepy, and hot. Annie, unaware of her mother's anguish and finally set free of the back seat, was enchanted by the place with its climbable trees and explorable nooks and crannies. Scampering from one awesome discovery to another, she chattered nonstop as she hadn't done since her father's disappearance. Finally, Gypsy took Annie's hand in her own, to quell the rapid fluttering signs.

How ironic that it would be this place, *this* place . . . that would set the child's spirit free.

But the minute Gypsy set foot in the house, keys clutched in a sweaty palm, the memory of her mother's death slapped the breath out of her, forcing her to sit down on a sheeted chair. To Gypsy, the house seemed like some sort of living, menacing presence, thrusting un-wanted memories upon her and haunting her with sounds she would never hear again.

Vividly as if it only happened yesterday, she saw her-self, *felt* herself standing horror-struck on the stair land-ing, tongue-tied and useless as the Jigsaw Man choked her mother to death.

Why didn't you call for help? insinuated the wormy lit-tle thought she'd kept so carefully tucked away for so long. *There was a telephone right on the landing. You could have saved your mother's life, and you didn't.*

A sob escaped her and she struggled to maintain a mea-sure of control for Annie's sake.

Because the accusation was there—had been all along—serving notice to all her other secret tortured thoughts: *You could have saved your mother, and you didn't. So what makes you think you can save your husband?*

NINE

THE LOOSE BED RAIL AFFORDED John his first opportunity for escape.

In the iron bedstead, the framework for the headboard contained six rails about one inch in diameter which extended from the top rail of the headboard to the springs. The longest one was only twenty-four inches, but it was loose and that was all that mattered to John.

For hours he lay on his stomach on the cot and worked at loosening the rail further, until he could jiggle it with a fair amount of ease. The problem was that it fit like a towel rod into holes in the top and bottom rails of the headboard. Those rails were fixed; there was no way to just pull the thing out.

He tried anyway.

The chains which bound him to the steel post at the foot of the bed only stretched far enough for him to crouch on the floor at the head of the bed. There he braced himself, wrapped his fingers tight around the rail, and pulled until rivulets of sweat dripped down the sides of his face.

The solid iron bar bent slightly in the middle, but not

enough to pull free of the anchoring holes. Exhausted, he flopped back onto the thin mattress, panting, and examined the blisters that were forming on his fingers.

There had to be a way.

When his heart had stopped thundering and the sweat on his face and under his arms had dried, he got to his knees on the mattress and studied the headboard railing. After a moment, he tossed the pillow to the floor and rolled back the mattress. Balancing his feet on either side of the iron bar where it met the frame of the headboard, he stood, wrapped his fingers around the top of the railing, and stretched his body out as far as it would go, pulling upwards with his hands and pushing down with his feet.

A long, tortured groan erupted from him as every muscle in his back, shoulders, arms and legs protested. Just when he thought he must surely be ripping something loose inside somewhere, he heard a hollow *clang* and glanced down to see the rail rolling across the hardwood floor, where it came to a stop against the wall underneath the bed.

With a loud shout of triumph, John jumped down from his perch and grappled around beneath the bed until his hand closed over the metal bar.

He laughed. It was an odd sound in the little prison; one he hadn't heard for a very long time.

Still panting and sweating from the exertion, John extended himself as far as his body would reach from chain to wrist. Grasping the bar at the bottom—like a relay runner passing the baton—he stretched out the bar to the telephone which was perched on the old desk and began pushing it to the side.

Closer, closer he inched it to the edge of the desk.

Almost there. Careful. So close.

The phone tumbled to the floor and fell . . . just a half-inch out of the reach of John's iron bar. No matter how excruciating the pain to his wrists as he flung himself against the chains and groped with the iron bar, all he was able to do was tap the phone with impotent rage. For the life of him, he could not get his hands on it to call for help.

All he could do, it seemed, was live with his frustration . . . and fight a growing sense of fear.

Ghosts haunted Gypsy in every room of the old house.

Her mother's presence was everywhere; in the kitchen, upstairs in her old bedroom, in her mother's old bedroom. The furniture in the house was heavy, dark, and old-fashioned. It had belonged to Gypsy's grandmother and had once been beautiful, the mahogany and cherry wood gleaming after her mother rubbed it with lemon oil. But a generation of careless renters had left it scratched and scarred, stained and faded. The mirrors were chipped and clouded, like sad memories.

Everything cried out for repair and renewal: time-dulled wallpaper, split in places, yellowing paint on ceilings, dust-choked area rugs, dry and creaking hardwood floors, rusty bathtub and sinks. It took a little time and patience to get the ancient window-unit air-conditioners to work, but they weren't terribly effective and Gypsy was at least grateful that they wouldn't have to endure the smothering heat of summer. In fact, late autumn on the Gulf Coast meant rain, fog, and hurricane warnings.

She and Annie spent the entire first day just trying to make the house liveable. They pulled frayed and holey sheets off the furniture, balled them up, and stuffed them in a downstairs closet. Gypsy ran a crotchety old vacuum cleaner over the area rugs, scrubbed down the bathroom and kitchen, stocked the cabinets and stuttering refrigerator with food, and made up the guest room downstairs for her and Annie to sleep in.

Too many ghosts upstairs.

Outside, the day was cloaked in gloom, forcing Gypsy to turn on lamps, but it didn't help. Heavy mist dripped from the gnarled, leaning oaks and pressed against the windows like a malevolent specter.

The fog made Gypsy increasingly uneasy. Stone-tired from her all-night drive, she had no patience to deal with power struggles instigated by her daughter—who had slept soundly all through the trip. Annie's original enthusiasm about the place had turned to a whiny restlessness. Housework was boring; she was eager to go outside and explore. Unlike her mother, she found the fogginess to be mysterious and enchanting and couldn't understand Gypsy's reluctance to let the child out of her sight.

Frequent arguments drained what little energy Gypsy had left, and by dark, she was more than ready for bed. To her surprise, Annie did not protest. The change in climate alone had made her more tired than usual. Add to that the new environment, her mother's stress level, and the fact that the old television set received only a few fuzzy channels, and she was asleep by nine.

Lying awake in her mother's house, it took Gypsy a little longer.

She was running, running, her hands straight out in front of her in the velvet fog-shrouded darkness. The evil trees were trying to stop her, trying to grab her—they were snatching at her hair and plucking at her clothes. There was blood running from her ear down her neck and her head was filled with thick cotton and it was like a dream because she couldn't hear herself screaming. Screaming. Silent, deadly screaming.

"UHHH!" Heart jackhammering, Gypsy sat straight up in bed, chest heaving, hands clawing in front of her.

She glanced at the sleeping child beside her, her little face porcelain-peaceful in the gray shadows.

So it wasn't a scream, then. It just felt like one.

But it was so real, God help me. She yearned to turn on the bedside lamp, let the gentle pool of light chase away the spooks, but she didn't want to wake Annie, so she took some deep breaths in a valiant effort to calm herself and tried very hard not to look out the window.

This creepy feeling had hold of her deep down inside: *Someone is out there. Look.*

She kept telling herself that it was foolish, but then, why couldn't she look?

She looked.

Standing in the shadows just outside the window was the silhouette of the Jigsaw Man, watching.

Gypsy's breath died in her throat. For a moment, her body froze, then, with a second glance at her sleeping child, she dove under the bed for the shotgun. Because she'd been unwilling to keep a loaded gun within reach of a child, Gypsy had to fumble for shells. Under the cloak of darkness, her hand was shaking and she dropped half of them, but she finally managed to get the gun loaded and snap the breech back into place.

Holding the heavy weapon close with ice-numbed fingers, Gypsy padded barefoot around to the back door. Shotgun braced in front of her, she cracked open the door and peered into the damp dark. After a moment, she stepped out into it.

Gypsy knew she was at a distinct disadvantage because she would not be able to hear footfalls, a breaking twig, or even the noise she herself was making, whereas the Jigsaw Man could hear and see everything.

Just as on that night so very long ago, fog obscured the sea and moon and stars, and cobwebbed the spooky old trees.

This was no dream.

If anything, it was a nightmare, a *reliving* of a nightmare that she now realized must have been more a series of flashbacks to the night of her mother's death.

Only now, it was not Gypsy who lay sleeping while the Jigsaw Man stalked.

Now it was Annie.

There was nobody to protect her if Gypsy somehow gave in to the terrors which mesmerized her. If her child was going to survive, Gypsy was going to have to cast off the spell of that other night.

She could do it too, *would* do it. Clutching the shotgun fiercely, she thought, *This time I will not run.* She would be Annie's valiant protector, too.

But she was afraid. So very afraid.

Tiptoeing through the mist and the silence made eerie by the spooky fog-shapes, Gypsy tucked up her little bag of bravery beneath her heart, and went in search of the Jigsaw Man.

TEN

Deputy Chief James Fitzgerald reminded Parker Jefferson of Ichabod Crane, the character in the old ghost story, "The Legend of Sleepy Hollow." In this case, Jefferson figured Fitzgerald might do better without his head. It set perched atop a long skinny neck over stooped shoulders, the hair swept back like Dracula, the skin stretched over it skull-thin, dark, glittering eyes sunken into alarming hollows. His complexion was hopelessly pock-marked, now mottled with advancing age. The crooked beak-nose had obviously once been broken, and his parents had apparently not been able to afford braces, because his teeth were overlapped at odd angles to each other.

How the man had ever found a woman to marry him was beyond Jefferson's ability to imagine. What was not hard to imagine was why she had left.

They were sitting in the deputy chief's new office on the fifth floor of the Dallas Police Department headquarters at Main and Harwood downtown. There was no evidence of the office's former occupant, nor were there any sentimental mementoes of Fitzgerald's former wife or children. Fitzgerald's life seemed to begin and end with his job.

Jefferson had no problem with that. What he did have a problem with was Fitzgerald's sarcasm.

"So let me get this straight. You feds were tailing Halden's wife, and she got away?"

"According to the agents involved in the surveillance, Mrs. Halden used evasive tactics to elude them."

A mirthless grin stretched Fitzgerald's thin lips over his crooked teeth. "I wish you could hear yourself talk, Jefferson. You feds act like life is an Academy textbook. The point is, she shook the tail. Pardon me. I just have to laugh."

Jefferson scowled at the loathsome man.

"So now the only known connection we have to the prime suspect in Abe's murder has flown the coop, and nobody has the foggiest notion where she could have gone. Jesus. I guess it's time to call up *Unsolved Mysteries*. Maybe a TV show can do your job for you."

"We've got leads, Chief Fitzgerald. We're following up on them." Jefferson got to his feet. "We'll keep you apprised."

"I'm sure you will. I know I'll sleep easier at night, knowing that little fact."

Jefferson suppressed the urge to punch the guy right in the nose. It wasn't hard to figure out how he'd gotten it broken. What *was* hard to figure was how in hell he'd risen so far in rank.

He'd have never made it in the FBI.

More than ever, Jefferson was convinced that Fitzgerald was out to get him. He wondered why. Maybe the guy had tried to join the Bureau at one time and hadn't been able to make the grade. Or maybe they'd rejected him for being a creep. Whatever. It was obvious from his behavior that he was jealous of Jefferson and eager to take him down a notch.

In the end, they'd see who got taken down.

As Jefferson took his leave and walked down the corridor toward the elevator, his thoughts turned to Gypsy Halden, and the kind of smarts it had taken for her to successfully elude two FBI surveillance vehicles.

They had underestimated her.

He was going to have to be careful that they did not do so again.

Night winds fanned in off the Gulf, ruffling Gypsy's hair and sending chilly fog-fingers down the back of her neck. She couldn't see more than five or six feet in front of her. She kept feeling this . . . presence . . . behind her, but when she'd whirl around, all she could see were tendrils of shadows and mist, swirling slightly in the breeze.

There.

A man-shaped darkness, fathomless in the fog-shadows. Not six feet away.

Gripping the shotgun like a strong rope in heavy rapids, Gypsy froze, her heart expanding, or so it felt, to fill her ribcage. Pulling the hammer back, she raised the shotgun to her shoulder, hooked a finger around the trigger, and rested her trembling cheek against its smooth wooden stock.

"Stand right there," she commanded, willing her voice to be strong, "or I'll kill you, I swear to God I will."

Had he said something? Was he speaking? Without being able to see his face, she couldn't know. Gypsy moved first one, and then the next quaking foot in front of the other.

Closer. Closer.

"Don't move," she warned. "I've got a shotgun and I

know how to use it." Sensing a touch of hysteria lurking just beneath the surface, she added, "It's not like the other time, is it? I'm not that terrified little girl you chased through the trees. Not any more, you son of a bitch."

With a sudden lurch, the man-shape lunged at her and in the blink of an eye she'd yanked the trigger and the shotgun *boomed* against her shoulder, punching her in the cheek like a fist and sending her staggering backwards, heart slamming painfully against her breastplate like a hostage trying to escape and she found herself babbling to the Jigsaw Man as the first seconds' shock wore off and she realized she'd killed him, oh dear God, she'd killed him before he could tell them where to find John.

Flinging the shotgun aside, Gypsy plunged through the jabbing boughs of the encroaching twisted live oaks toward the Jigsaw Man in a bizarre, almost instantaneous flip-flop of purpose: she had to save him, had to keep him alive long enough to find her husband.

But when she emerged to the place where he had been when she blasted at him with the .410, she found only shattered tree limbs . . . and one shredded head-high bunch of mistletoe.

This time, John was waiting for him.

He'd been waiting it seemed, for days, lying stiffly on the cot, the pillow propped up hiding the headboard with its missing bar, the bar in question gripped in the crook of his left hand, snug against his body. The room was too soundproof for John to hear his captor's approach, but he was alert the instant the false door swung back from the false wall.

He'd planned this moment for hours, going over it and over it in his mind, and now he was ready, so ready. His nerves were coiled, muscles tensed.

"God, it stinks in here," said the creep Gypsy had always called the Jigsaw Man. To John's surprise, he didn't walk past the bed, but stooped at the foot of it and hoisted up the putrid yellow bucket that contained several days' worth of human waste.

He left with it, and John waited, the delay bringing on an unwelcome attack of nerves. He willed his heart to slow its racing, reassured himself with the cold hard feel of the iron bar in his hand, practiced the scene in his mind like an Olympic athlete before an event.

Arrogant son of a bitch didn't even bother to close the false door after him.

Which meant that nobody would be able to hear John even if the room weren't soundproofed.

Don't think about that now. Focus.

This time he did hear steps on the hardwood floor in the next room. The Jigsaw Man emerged into John's cell and put the yellow bucket—which now reeked of disinfectant—at the foot of the cot. He pulled shut the false door.

And, just as John had known, headed straight past the cot for the surveillance monitoring equipment at the end of the room.

With one catlike leap, John sprang from the bed, swinging the iron bar like a golf club, but something was wrong—the chains slowed him down just a fraction of a second. It was all the Jigsaw Man needed to duck and whirl, bringing up his forearm defensively. Rather than bashing in his head, the bar glanced off the Jigsaw Man's collar bone and slammed against his raised forearm. His other hand shot up and grabbed the bar.

The two men went down across the bed, John splayed back against the wall, the bar now suspended between them in an isometric exercise of death as each man pushed with all his strength against it. Under normal circumstances, it would have been a matched battle, but John's ordeal had weakened him more than he bargained for. In despair, he felt his arms give way as the bar began to press against his windpipe.

John's face was inches from the man who would kill him. He had wrestled to the ground many, many criminals in his day, but he had never looked into eyes like these, had never confronted such demonic hatred in his life. With a desperate surge of adrenaline he shoved the man to the side and jumped to his feet to escape, but the chains caught him fast and yanked him back down again.

The Jigsaw Man arched over John like the Angel of Death, his savage puzzle-face looming, the iron club swinging down toward John's head even as he screamed, *"You wanna fuck with me? You wanna fuck with me? I'll show you nobody fucks with me!"*

Even as he covered his head with his arms, John's thoughts scrambled to Gypsy, to Gypsy as a little girl called Annie, Gypsy cowering before this maniac just as he—a grown man—was doing now.

But the solid iron bar did not strike John in the head. Instead, the Jigsaw Man began a frenzy of blows—*slam* to the wall by John's right ear—*slam* to the wall by John's left ear—*slam* to the right—*slam* to the left—*slamslamslamslamslam*—each blow whizzing by so close John could feel the wind left in its wake—*slamslamslamslamslam* until finally, exhausted, the monster-man flung the iron bar across the room and stood, heaving and panting over his prisoner, blinded to the almost total splintered destruction he had left behind.

ELEVEN

SPECIAL AGENT BROOK CORRUTHERS, ASSIStant director in charge of the criminal investigative division of the Federal Bureau of Investigation, met Jefferson personally when his plane landed at Washington National Airport. Corruthers was big and balding, and spoke with the soft drawl of the small-town Georgia boy he once was. Only the sharp blue eyes and keen expression he usually wore betrayed what he did for a living. To Jefferson, Corruthers had always resembled the actor Gene Hackman.

The two men greeted one another with a warm handshake. They had been trainees together more than thirty years before, and Jefferson had held Corruthers's current position at headquarters before requesting the Dallas office, where he was made special agent in charge. A crewcutted, square-jawed young agent trotted along behind the two men and loaded Jefferson's luggage into a navy-blue Saturn. He drove as the two men swapped Bureau gossip.

"After your interview with the president," Corruthers said, "the director is taking you to dinner at the Willard Hotel." He grinned. "Nothing but the finest for our Golden Boy."

"The Grand Ballroom or the Willard Room?" cracked Jefferson.

Corruthers rolled his eyes.

Jefferson said, "Anyway, dinner with the director does not a new director make. The job is hardly in the bag yet."

Corruthers was not so sure. "The president and the director go way back," he said. "This cancer thing has them both shook up pretty bad. If the director thinks you would be the best replacement for him as director, then that's about all it will take to put your name at the top of the short list."

Jefferson gazed out the window as they crossed the Potomac at the Fourteenth Street Bridge. He'd traveled this route so many times, and yet somehow it seemed so different this time. Or maybe it wasn't the trip that was different. Maybe it was him.

After a moment, he said, "How bad *is* this cancer, anyway? All I've heard so far are Bureau rumors."

"It's bad, man," said Corruthers. "Get this. They only discovered it four weeks ago, but they don't think Kellerman'll last 'til Christmas."

"Shit. That's . . . how many weeks?"

"Well, Scrooge, if you had kids—or by now, I guess I should say *grandkids*—you'd know it's only eight weeks away."

Jefferson's stomach constricted with excitement, but he made only sympathetic noises to his old friend.

Traffic was light and the young agent delivered them to headquarters in record time. Jefferson and Special Agent Corruthers got out in the underground garage at the mammoth 2.5 million-square-foot J. Edgar Hoover building and entered on the ground floor of the Pennsylvania Avenue level. Even though Jefferson had top-secret clearance, he dutifully collected a visitor's pass at the escort desk and walked with Corruthers through the small lobby which looked out over an ivy-covered courtyard. A carved bronze inscription quoted the great man himself: "The most effective weapon against crime is cooperation . . . the efforts of all law enforcement agencies with the support and understanding of the American people."

Jefferson knew that former FBI director William Webster had chosen the mild quote to reflect the "new" FBI—as opposed to selecting any of a hundred more radical statements their old demigod had said.

He found that fact disappointing.

They took the elevator to the fifth floor, where the criminal investigative division directed the work of some eighty percent of the Bureau's 10,400 agents. There they stopped at the Strategic Information Operations Center (SIOC) briefly so that Corruthers could check the status of an ongoing counterterrorism case.

Corruthers entered a special code and then turned a lock on the vault door, which was marked with a red RE-STRICTED ACCESS sign. In the room, which was specially shielded against electronic emissions—both to and from—Corruthers spoke to an agent while Jefferson gazed through the glass walls to the several command rooms and conference rooms containing numerous clocks for different time zones, a large-screen TV, various satellite monitors, and a map of the world. Agents worked at a number of computer terminals.

With a thrill of remembrance, Jefferson thought of the time he had held Corruthers's job and the Persian Gulf War was going on. The SIOC had been a hotbed of activity then, keeping an eye on places all over the United States that might be vulnerable to terrorist attacks.

When he was appointed director, he reflected, he would

oversee all such operations. The special agents in charge of the fifty-six field offices, who themselves coordinated the resident agents at four hundred satellite agencies, would report *directly to him.*

He would have personal access to the Justice Department's Sabreliner jet, its MU–2 Mitsubishi turbo-prop, his own limousine, and a personal security detail of twelve agents. Over his desk would cross some of the most sensitive information in the world, provided not only by the FBI, but by other super-secret agencies such as the CIA, NSA, and, nowadays, sometimes even the KGB.

Each week he would have provided for him a rundown on all the major ongoing priority cases in each of the seven sections of the organization—civil rights, counterterrorism, drugs, investigative support, organized crime, violent crime, and white collar crime.

He'd sacrificed so much, worked so hard, made so many tough decisions to get here . . . and now it was payback time.

God . . . he could hardly stand it.

Corruthers finished his briefing with the agent and they walked together down the hall to his office, which overlooked the Justice Department. Corruthers led Jefferson past his work-piled desk to an inconspicuous door in the corner, leading to a smaller, more modestly furnished office which contained a secure phone. From a corner cabinet he withdrew a bottle of scotch.

"We celebrate," he said, pouring them each a drink. They toasted to the future.

The scotch burned just right, and Jefferson was feeling mellow as he reminisced with his old friend.

"Hoover was right, you know," he said. "Image is everything."

"Oh God," said Corruthers, tossing back his drink with one swallow and pouring another. "The good old days."

"Never embarrass the director," said Jefferson with a laugh.

"Hell no, or you'd wind up in a two-man resident agent office in Butte, Montana, copping the credit for stolen car recoveries from local police."

"Oh, it wasn't all bad," said Jefferson, holding out his glass for a refill. "In those days, the G-man was everybody's hero." He took a slow, satisfying swallow. "The FBI could do no wrong and a strong tradition of discipline kept everything under control."

"Yeah," said Corruthers, "and the Man was chief of the thought control police. Black bag jobs—"

"I prefer to call it surreptitious surveillance."

"If that's what you call illegally entering citizens' homes to bug them and wiretapping their phones. Geez, he *sanctioned* it. People were harassed just because of their political views, and top quality agents spent their days digging up dirt on celebrities or congressmen for Hoover to blackmail."

"Say what you will. If Hoover were here now, we wouldn't have any of the malarkey that's been going on lately. Agents getting busted for attending group-sex clubs. An agent sleeping with an informant—*an informant!*—and getting her pregnant. It's disgraceful."

Corruthers gave him an odd look. "You forgot to mention that that same agent murdered the woman after she threatened to expose him."

Jefferson, under a fog of scotch, shrugged and said, "He could have gotten away with that murder if he'd just kept his mouth shut. Nobody found the body. If he hadn't spilled his guts, nobody would ever have had any concrete evidence connecting him with her death. But the *preg-*

nancy—she'd already blabbed that all over town. And him a married man with kids of his own."

Corruthers lapsed into a thoughtful silence. His eyes took on a guarded cast.

This bothered Jefferson. In his single-minded clambering up the career ladder, he'd learned long ago that you couldn't trust anyone. The bottom line was that people were inherently users; everyone was out for himself, so the trick was to learn how to use rather than allow yourself to be used. Corruthers was one of the few agents Jefferson knew whom he felt he could trust. Now he was beginning to wonder.

Maybe he wasn't making himself clear. Jefferson said, "You see, image and reality are one and the same. If people perceive the FBI as being a bunch of sleazy little spies, then that is how we are going to operate. But if the public sees us as honest, hardworking, dedicated law enforcement officers protecting them from evil, then that is how we will be."

He leaned forward, sloshing his drink a little in his enthusiasm. "It's like when I was a kid. My daddy always told me not to hang around with punks, because I would be perceived as a punk myself, even if I hadn't done anything wrong. He was very strict with my brother and me. We stayed out of trouble mostly because of him."

"So you're saying—"

"That that's what I miss about Hoover. He was like this great father, you know? And we were all his sons."

He took another drink and glanced at Corruthers over the rim of his glass. Through the pleasant fog of scotch, he couldn't tell if he was getting through to his old friend or not. It was important to him that Corruthers understood. Being director would be a lonely job indeed if he didn't have at least one agent under him whom he felt he could trust.

After a moment, he shook his head and said, "And to think I was almost a bastard child."

"What do you mean?"

With a slight chuckle, Jefferson drained his glass. "You know how Hoover valued conformity."

Rolling his eyes, Corruthers nodded.

"Well, first time he saw me was when he shook my hand after completing training. For some reason, he took an instant dislike to me. He took one look at me and told his infamous assistant, Clyde Tolson, to throw me out."

"What'd Tolson say?"

"He said I was a hero, and that the FBI could always use a hero."

"A hero? Oh yeah. That time you pulled your brother from a burning house. Pretty gutsy."

Jefferson shrugged. "The Hoover days were the glory days, I'm telling you. We were a family—you didn't hear all this crap about civil rights violations or sexism or whatever. Our father maintained tight control, and we obeyed. He wouldn't allow us to fight each other, see. And the whole world looked up to us because of it."

"But I think it's much better now," insisted Corruthers. "Nobody, but nobody, deserves to have that much power to meddle in other people's lives—certainly not people outside the *family,* as you call it, like civilians."

"There's nothing wrong with power," argued Jefferson, "as long as you know how to use it." He gave Corruthers a smug smile.

Jefferson had given a lot of thought to the power he would wield as FBI director, and he couldn't wait to get at it. It seemed so unfortunate, somehow, that he wouldn't have anybody with whom he could share it.

*   *   *

On the morning following Gypsy's shooting ordeal, Annie awoke balky and fussy. She longed to go outside and play—preferably down by the water—and she had a natural desire to see if there were any other children around. She was simply too young to appreciate her mother's overprotectiveness and resented it mightily.

By way of compromise, Gypsy hid little treats throughout the house for the child to seek, while she herself ransacked all the old furnishings of the house for the letters.

Rain moved in off the coast, contributing to the gloomy cast of the house. Annie soon tired of their game and begged to at least be allowed to take her Barbie dolls and play on the screened-in front porch, where it was cool and the rain smelled heavenly. Gypsy reluctantly relented.

Knowing that there were some boxes of junk in the attic, Gypsy headed that way, and spent a couple of dark and dusty hours—punctuated by frequent checks on Annie—sorting through them.

In one old bureau drawer stuck almost hopelessly shut by the humidity, Gypsy came across a large brown envelope with a string clasp. Heart pounding, she opened the envelope and withdrew a copy of her birth certificate.

At least, she thought it was hers. But the name on the certificate was not "Gypsy." It was "Annie."

And the last name was not Martin.

A memory flashed across her mind, as clear as if it had just happened the day before: *"Let's make up some new names,"* her mother had said as they drove away from their Dallas home.

"Why, Mama? I like my name."

"Oh, I know you do, darling, but wouldn't it be fun to have a new one?"

"Like what?"

"Oh, I don't know. You're such a little gypsy now, aren't you?"

"Can that be my name?"

"What? Gypsy? But that's not . . . Oh, don't look at me that way. Okay. You can be Gypsy. From now on, you'll be Gypsy. Won't that be fun?"

But it wasn't fun. Not really. Gypsy had pretended that it was because she so wanted to see her mother smile again. But it felt . . . wrong somehow, not to be Annie anymore.

Gypsy rocked back on her heels, the birth certificate pressed to her chest. *She must have been hiding us from the Jigsaw Man,* she thought. *Poor, terrified woman.*

The sight of the name *Annie* on the birth certificate was such a surreal experience to Gypsy. To think that, apparently, after the trauma of that horrible night, she had completely blocked out her old name. Or so she thought. And yet she had given her "old" name to her own child.

What a strange thing the human mind is, she thought, and then a new realization brought her almost to her feet: *The Chief must have known that my maiden name wasn't Martin, after all. How could he have known about my father's murder? My father's last name was not Martin.*

It was all so confusing.

More digging finally revealed a marriage certificate for her parents. Stuffed behind the marriage certificate were several black-and-white snapshots: her parents on their wedding day, her grinning father in uniform beside his patrol car, and a formal portrait of her mother. Gypsy was amazed to see how much she resembled her mother, and gazed at that photograph for a long time.

But it was the picture of her daddy that brought the tears. It had been so many years . . . and now here he was in front of her as if he'd never left. Grief clutched at her and she struggled not to give in to it. Her parents were gone, that much was tragically true, but she couldn't afford to be sidetracked by that now.

She had to find the letters.

For the entire day, Gypsy dug through an almost overwhelming array of junk and renter leftovers, but no matter how industriously she looked, she could find no letters.

In mid-afternoon, Gypsy went to check on Annie and found her lodged in front of the TV, watching cartoons, a bowl of cereal on the floor in front of her. The sight gave Gypsy a stab of guilt; she'd forgotten lunch. She forced herself to eat a quick sandwich and spend a little time with Annie, then trudged back upstairs to continue the search.

It was exhausting. The rain had not let up all day and little driblets of moisture dripped from the roof in places. She had to set out some old bowls to catch it before it bled through to the ceilings beneath her. The atmosphere was close and dust-choked, and it aggravated her allergies. Once she started sneezing she couldn't seem to stop, and she was reluctant to take an antihistamine because she didn't want to get sleepy.

Kleenex tissues sprouting from her pockets like stuffing, Gypsy dragged herself over to another cardboard box of paraphernalia, but it would not lift easily. When she examined it, she found that it was a cover of some kind, fitted carefully to the floor.

When she finally pulled the covering box away from the wall, she discovered a video camera, rigged so that a cable of some sort snaked down between the wall studs.

Gypsy had been married long enough to an intelligence cop to know surveillance equipment when she saw it.

At first, Gypsy was stunned more than scared. It had

never occurred to her that the place could be bugged. Not here anyway, so far from her Dallas home and the insinuating presence of the bumper beeper.

For the first time, she began to give serious thought to the nature of her adversary. Before, he'd just been a frightening phantom from her childhood, a terrifying apparition come back to haunt her. Now she wondered just who he might *be,* and what relationship he could have had with her mother that would have caused him to track her down in hiding and murder her.

Her mind seized with a thousand thoughts, all shooting in different directions, Gypsy slowly descended the stairs. After absently checking on Annie, she took a feather duster from the kitchen and started pretending to fluff it around. While she fluffed, she searched. Inside one dusty lamp she spotted a tiny wire snaking from the metal branch of the lamp shade down into the workings of the lamp itself. Without bending down, she could see it running alongside the plug of the lamp and underneath the outlet plate.

She made a noisy business of taking down light fixtures in the ceiling, dusting them, and putting them back up. In the meantime, she noticed several insignificant wires running up into the ceiling through the hole where the fixture was attached.

Keeping a bored look on her face, she spied a hole no more than an eighth of an inch in diameter freshly drilled into a bookcase, just above the book line. She figured this was where the video camera must be attached by the cable she'd seen in the wall of the attic.

Heart pounding, mouth dry, Gypsy washed her hands in the bathroom, trying not to look for bugs everywhere. Were there more video cameras? Through the years, John had told her of some of the latest methods of electronic surveillance—most of which the police department could not afford. But she knew that most bugs required batteries to operate, which only allowed for short-term surveillance, say, ten to twenty hours, before the batteries would need changing or the operation could be called off. The fact that the bugs she had found were located near and wired to electrical outlets meant they were intended for long-term use—by the days or weeks, not by the hour.

Heart icy, she thought, *Maybe I didn't see the Jigsaw Man outside my window after all last night. Apparently he doesn't need to hang around in the dark and peer into windows.*

He had no need to, Gypsy now realized, because the Jigsaw Man already knew every move she made.

TWELVE

JOHN LAY ON HIS BED, staring at the demolished wall next to him, and thought about Chief Strickland and their last conversation.

"What was Gypsy's maiden name?" the Chief had asked that pivotal day.

"Reason I ask, is I had a partner many years ago—back in the early seventies—when I was still on the beat. As good a man as ever walked this earth, and one of the finest officers I ever had the privilege to serve with.

"Anyway, he had the loveliest wife you ever saw. Name of Anna. Gypsy is a dead ringer for that lady. I never saw anything like it."

John had assured him that Gypsy's maiden name was Martin, and that her parents were dead. At that, the Chief's brows crinkled together and he said, *"You know, my partner was murdered. We split up that day because we were short-handed. President Nixon was in town and half the department was down maintaining crowd control. Anyway, Mike marked out to go to lunch and he never marked in again. We found him in a dump three days later, just beat all to hell and back. Godawfulest thang you ever saw. And it wasn't two weeks later that Anna took their little girl and disappeared. I always wondered what happened to her."*

When John asked what had been the child's name, his heart skipped a beat when the Chief said, *"Annie."*

Chief Strickland continued, *"We never closed the case, either. Rousted out every low-life we could think of who might have crossed paths with Mike that day, but to tell you the truth, I always had my own suspicions, but there wasn't no way I could back them up with anythang concrete, so I had to let it go."*

By this time, John's heart was pounding. With awful clarity, he could see that "Anna" had to be Gypsy's widowed mother, Anna—who was murdered in front of her when she was a little girl. Whoever had strangled the woman had also walloped the child so hard that it deafened her.

From what Gypsy had told him, she and her mother had been living in the small fishing/retirement village of Rockport on the Texas Gulf Coast at the time of the assault. She had never mentioned living in Dallas, but if the Anna that the Chief knew had moved with her child after her husband's murder, then it would dovetail with Gypsy's account.

Yet why had Anna changed their names? Who was she hiding from?

Her murder had never been solved, either.

"What suspicions?" he asked.

"Man had a brother," the Chief said, the memory making him at once appear uneasy. *"They had a bad history, going way back. In fact, Mike says his brother was going with Anna while he was away in the Army. Anna took to writing to Mike, and he wrote back, and one thang led to*

another, and next thang you know, he's out of the Army and they're elopin'.

"Anyway, he hadn't seen his brother in ten years, see. And now he was back in town, hanging around Anna, and Mike was worried about him. He told me the guy was psycho."

John remembers how the Chief's eyes clouded over then, how he glanced over his shoulder as if somone could be listening.

John asked him why he hadn't followed up on those suspicions, why he hadn't thoroughly investigated the brother.

The Chief looked ill then, and in a voice heavy with the years, he said, *"I'm an old man, John. I've been in law enforcement thirty years, and I've enjoyed every one of 'em. But I swear to God, to my dyin' day, I'll regret that I pulled back. You see, at the time, I didn't thank I had any choice—you cain't imagine how hard it was to investigate this guy. See, there's more to it that I haven't told you. It has to do with these letters Mike had. They were addressed to his brother, see, and his brother had given him the letters for safekeeping. Thing is, those letters could have changed history."*

At first, John looked doubtful, but then the Chief told him who his old partner's brother was, and who the letters were from . . . and he could feel his jaw drop.

Now, here he was, held prisoner by a man called "psycho" by his own brother, completely unable to protect his family.

The Chief was dead. John knew that. His captor had been only too eager to brag about that, and about how he had set up John as the killer.

Dear God, Gypsy must be out of her mind by now.

Did she still believe in him? The thought tormented

him day and night. After all, she analyzed crime scene data for a living, and the evidence against him was pretty convincing, especially in light of the fact that he had disappeared from the face of the earth just before the Chief died.

John knew that his gun had been used in the murder and conveniently left where law enforcement could find it. There was no telling what other incriminating evidence had been planted. How could his wife possibly continue to trust in him?

If the situation were reversed, would you believe in Gypsy? he wondered.

Yes, of course he would.

For how long? Be honest. You know how suspicious and paranoid cops are. For how long would you be able to continue to trust her?

He thought about that.

I would believe in her always, because I know her, and I know she could never do anything to deliberately harm another human being.

But was that true? A couple of days before, he'd been ready to kill a man.

That's different.

How different was it? How threatened did a person have to feel before resorting to violence?

In the face of a staggering amount of evidence indicting John in the Chief's murder, how long could he expect his wife to believe in something intangible? But then, wasn't love a tangible thing? Couldn't they see it every day in the face of their child?

On the other hand, lots of people fell out of love with each other, even though they had children. How long could he expect her to hold on to their love when he wasn't even there to reassure her?

Around and around, like a cat chasing its tail, John would follow his thoughts to the same miserable conclusion: he honestly didn't know if his wife still loved him, or even if he could expect her to. And if she didn't, he could not blame her. Maybe someday she would understand. Like, when his rotted body showed up.

Even more worrisome was the question of the letters. He had no way of knowing if Gypsy even had any idea what letters he meant in that all-too-brief phone call. Why had that son of a bitch cut them off so quickly? How could he be sure that Gypsy would even know what he was talking about?

The guy was crazy. Stark raving.

And there was nothing any of them could do about it.

The Saturn pulled up to the visitor's entrance at the Northwest Gate, where uniformed Secret Service personnel carefully checked Jefferson's credentials and those of his trainee driver and phoned the White House to make sure his appointment did exist.

Although Jefferson had met a couple of previous presidents, this was his first visit to the oval office and his first time to met this president. In spite of his nervousness, he got a little patriotic chill down his spine at the sight of the Marine Guard, posted at the entrance to the West Wing, all decked out in his spiffy Marine dress blues.

Inside, Jefferson stopped at a desk just to the right of the entrance, where an attractive White House liaison called again to double-check his appointment while a granite-faced Secret Service agent looked on.

An official-looking woman in a dark blue suit who was possibly another Secret Service agent escorted Jefferson down the hall to the Oval Office.

Jefferson had thought he would be prepared for this

moment, but he couldn't help being simply awestruck. The great, arresting presidential seal, boldly rendered on royal blue carpeting chosen by this president was a glorious statement of muted power not overlooked by Jefferson.

President Bill Clinton was much taller than he seemed on television. He was also surprisingly handsome and the understated power of his charismatic charm put Jefferson at ease even though he'd voted a straight Republican ticket his entire adult life.

Clinton crushed Jefferson's hand in his own and chatted for a while about how overwhelmed he had been also, the first time he stepped foot in the Oval Office.

"Special Agent Jefferson—"

"Please, call me Dash."

"Dash?"

"It's a nickname I got in high school," Jefferson said.

"Oh—you were a track star, right?" asked the president.

"Well, sort of," said Jefferson, pleased that the man remembered that fact from reading his file.

While an aide served coffee, they exchanged a moment's pleasantries, and then the president got right to the point. "Director Kellerman's illness has been a devastating blow, not just to me personally, but to the country. As you probably know, I've caught some flak from the press for being slow to name appointments to important positions. I want to give them a name by the end of this week." He sat back, fixing Jefferson with a thoughtful gaze. "Tell me, Dash, what is your philosophy of life?"

The president's Southern unpretentiousness, coupled with such a piercing question, threw Jefferson momentarily off-guard, but he recovered quickly. The president was known for being widely read, a deep thinker. It was said he quickly bored of anyone he did not consider his intellectual equal. His administration had also been plagued by a series of scandals in its first years that had left him somewhat gun-shy. The word was that now, if he so much as sniffed even a whiff of a scandal within his staff, that person was out before he could clean out his desk—no matter how long he'd lived in Little Rock.

An FBI director's appointment ran ten years, Jefferson knew, but the president had the option to remove him or her at any time if there appeared to be just cause, as when President Clinton himself had sacked William Sessions.

All these things ran through Jefferson's mind.

After some thought, Jefferson said, "I've always been fascinated by the biblical story of Cain and Abel. Cain killed his brother, the Bible says, because his brother had more to offer than Cain. In other words, Cain couldn't stand it that his brother had the favor of everyone around him. He was jealous and envious of his brother, and he resented him."

The president, who was known as a devout Baptist, seemed intrigued. Encouraged, Jefferson went on.

"Whenever a carjacking occurs, or a tourist murder, or even war crimes such as we've seen in Bosnia, I think this ancient human drama is being played out, again and again. Violent crime—indeed, most crime of all kinds—is committed by people because they want what they perceive they can never have. Or they fear losing what they already have. Or even because they think they are personal favorites of God and everybody else deserves to be excluded."

"So what is the answer?" interrupted the president. "Do you think social programs, aimed at evening out the discrepancies between the haves and the have-nots, is the solution?"

Jefferson had read thoroughly of President Clinton's positions on various issues, and fashioned his answer accordingly. "Some of them have proven to be very effective," he said, "such as the Head Start program, which reaches at-risk children before kindergarten and gets them intellectually and emotionally ready for school." He shook his head. "Sadly, most of them do not. They are simply manipulated by cons who have no intention of ever doing the right thing. You see, they don't really *want* to be like Abel. They despise their righteous brothers."

"Tell me then. As FBI director, what would you do about this problem as you see it?"

Jefferson was ready for this question. He'd been ready all his life. "Well, the last thing we need is law enforcement brothers squabbling between themselves. I would engineer programs within the Bureau which would facilitate the task force concept as it already exists. In other words, I would see to it that regional police departments and competing agencies such as the DEA and NSA would dovetail smoothly with FBI investigations in such a way that efforts are not being duplicated or contradicted, and see to it that all our special agents get training which would help them learn to cooperate with local law enforcement with a minimum of rivalry and jealousy. Much the same way a father might handle quarreling between two brothers." Knowing the President's feminist, politically correct beliefs, Jefferson added, "and I would instigate sensitivity training for all our agents in the area of sexual discrimination and race relations."

The president's eyes lit up, and Jefferson knew he had him.

They discussed various problems now faced by the Bureau, both administrative and investigative, and the president skillfully felt out Jefferson on each issue.

"Your career has been most distinguished," he said, pointing at a thick dossier on his famous desk—the same desk under which John F. Kennedy, Jr. had played while his father worked. "You spearheaded several crucial investigations, including the one that brought down several high-level congressmen and senators for taking bribes from lobbyists. And it was you who brought in Cindy Lacey."

Jefferson nodded. Actually, it had been an entire team who'd been responsible for the arrest of the famous anti-war activist, but Jefferson was more than willing to take credit for it. "I believe her when she says she was unaware that the janitor was in the school administration building when she planted the bomb back in '69."

"I could hardly believe she'd been a save-the-whales activist all these years while she was underground."

Jefferson shrugged. "It's reasonably easy to change appearances and identities."

The president continued. "You have been given several incentive awards, plus I understand you received the Meritorious Achievement Medal for saving another agent's life."

"I couldn't leave him in that biker bar once his cover was blown. The whole thing came down before we were ready." *We* meaning the other agents Jefferson had postponed calling in so that he could be first on the scene and look the hero.

The president's probing had a direction which Jefferson had been dreading. He looked past the president's shoulder and out the long window behind his desk to the broad manicured expanse of the south lawn, the burbling fountain, and in the distance, the Washington Monument, stark against a flag-blue sky.

"You took part in the investigation of the assassination of President Kennedy, didn't you?"

Jefferson held up his hands modestly. "There were many of us, just trying to discover the truth." This time he was more than willing to spread the credit around.

The president nodded. "And what do *you* consider the truth, Dash? What do you think about all these conspiracy theories?"

Without hesitation, Jefferson said, "I believe Lee Harvey Oswald was acting alone."

The president considered this, and then said, "I guess there will always be an aura of mystery surrounding that terrible event—even when all the documents pertaining to the investigation are released by the FBI, there will still continue to be unanswered questions."

"Yes."

To Jefferson's great relief, President Clinton changed the subject. "I understand you were something of a child hero. In the house fire that killed your parents, didn't you drag your brother out?" he asked.

As though it had been no big deal, Jefferson shrugged and indicated his face. "Gave me these scars," he said.

"I can see you are a man of great personal courage," said the president. "We need people like that in positions of power. Our society has become cynical and jaded toward its goverment. Our young people think that they have no one they can look up to." He smiled. "There just aren't enough heroes anymore."

Without a blink, Jefferson smiled back. "My feelings exactly."

The heart of the interview seemed to have been concluded. President Clinton engaged Jefferson in conversation long after his aide's discreet insistence that he had other appointments waiting.

At last, he said, "I will be making my final decision in a day or two, Dash, after I've interviewed a couple of other candidates on the short list. Now, I don't want you to leak this or anything, but as far as I'm concerned, I've found my man. Keep your mouth shut about it, and wait for my call."

With that, he gave Jefferson a handshake and escorted him all the way down the corridor of the West Wing to where the young trainee agent had been waiting. There the president dazzled the rookie with a handshake and a little small talk.

And Jefferson, suppressing his jubilation, knew that if there was one thing he could handle, it was keeping his mouth shut.

Certain that secret eyes were watching her every move, Gypsy upturned her mother's old house, but there was no sign anywhere of any aged letters. She wasn't even sure what these letters were supposed to be, and so searched through every old envelope, read every scrap of paper she could find.

Nothing.

Again and again she searched her memory for any indication that her mother had mentioned these letters to her when she was a little girl, had shown them to her or maybe even told her their hiding place. But she could remember nothing.

When the search virtually ground to a halt, Gypsy loaded Annie up into the Blazer and went to the supermarket for groceries. She'd forgotten her list. Since her ability to concentrate was snuffed by her worries, Gypsy wandered the aisles aimlessly, allowing Annie to toss in pretty much whatever she wanted. As they headed toward the bakery area, Annie skipped on ahead gleefully, anticipating all sorts of normally forbidden treats, while Gypsy dragged along behind.

Just to the side of the bakery department was a newsstand stuffed with day-old *Corpus Christi Caller Times* facing out through a grill.

And there, staring at her with hooded eyes through the wire prison, was the Jigsaw Man.

Time stopped.

Trapped in a sort of twilight zone, Gypsy stared at the newspaper photo, her knees suddenly very weak. *It was him.* Even though his dark hair was now salt-and-pepper, there was no mistaking that face . . . those eyes.

Stomach churning, Gypsy fumbled for quarters in her bag and inserted them in the slot with unsteady fingers.

The headline read: TEXAS-BORN FED ON THE SHORT LIST FOR DIRECTOR OF FBI.

Abandoning her cart in the middle of the aisle, Gypsy herded a protesting Annie out the electronic door of the store, where she sank behind the wheel of her car and read through the article twice.

The whole world seemed to close in on her, narrowing itself all the way in to the suffocating cocoon of the warm Blazer and the hot, hazy Gulf sun. Sweat dripped off Gypsy's face. Annie kept touching her, trying to get her attention, but she ignored the child. She was numb to everything but the newspaper she held in trembling hands.

It all began to make perfect sense—everything: the phony bank accounts and credit cards in her husband's name, the planted evidence, the bug on her car in Dallas and the surveillance on her house in Rockport.

Not just any fed could pull off such an operation. But a special agent in charge of a major field office, one with almost thirty years experience, one who had held major administrative positions at the headquarters in Washington . . . such an agent would have many ways to do it.

He killed my mother.

The thought turned Gypsy's mouth to cotton and set her heart to racing. One thought then naturally led to another.

He must have killed Chief Strickland, too.

And the next thought, even more powerful.

He s got John.

But the last thought made her woozy.

Could this man have killed my father?

She remembered the brutality and complete callousness of that murder, her daddy's battered body tossed onto a dump like so much trash . . . her mother's screams and her godawful final gurgling gasps as she fought for her life . . . the crime-scene photos someone had shown her of the Chief, his blood-drenched face practically blown off . . .

And that dark and misty night, so vivid in her dreams . . . where she, a terrified little girl, had run like the wind for her life from the man with the jigsaw-puzzle face who wanted her dead.

Forcing herself to think rationally with her lab-tech mind, she began to consider the fact that these crimes were not just connected, but they were viciously hate-filled.

The rule of thumb in any unsolved murder was to consider first the family and close circle of friends. The more heinous the crime, the more likely it was committed by someone known to the victim, someone consumed with rage and resentment toward them.

Only in very recent years had that level of hostility been widened to include so-called "hate" crimes.

The family of man, it seemed, was consumed by sibling rivalry.

Jefferson. The Jigsaw Man's name was *Jefferson.*

Her real maiden name.

Dear God, she thought, *could this man be my uncle?*

Maybe that explained the brutality of the murders— that, and everything he stood to lose if these people crossed him on his way up.

Annie finally forced herself through her mother's pre-occupation. Forgetting all about the groceries left behind in the shopping cart, Gypsy drove the little girl down to the harbor.

The rains of the previous day had moved on, leaving a sun-spangled, scrubbed-clean indigo cast to the sky and the reflecting water. Parking nearby, Gypsy and Annie got out and walked past a jumble of bait shops and seafood markets. Aged wooden docks sheltered boats with names like *Second Mortgage* and *Lucky Day.* Graceful sailboats showed off amidst the bulky crowd of shrimp boats, their masts spiking the sky like a willowy group of ballerinas.

They paused beside a giant pier support sporting a peli-can standing on one leg, and Annie carried on a brief, se-rious conversation with it. Gypsy took her into a bait shop to buy some day-old bread, and while the little girl threw chunks of bread up in the air for a squabbling mob of seagulls, Gypsy focused all her considerable skills of con-centration on the situation at hand and how she could best handle it.

She knew for certain now that she could not go for help, not from John's old department and certainly not from the FBI. No one would believe her, not unless she could show them some kind of proof.

She needed evidence.

There wasn't much time. The article mentioned that

Jefferson had gone to Washington, D.C., to interview with the president. But the paper was a day old. Who knew when he might get back?

And when he got back, who could imagine what he might do next? The surveillance equipment in her house served notice to her that Jefferson wasn't spending all his time in Dallas. Somebody had to monitor the equipment.

Other agents? She considered it for a few minutes, then rejected the idea. What Jefferson was doing was illegal. He dared not risk exposure at a time like this. No.

With a sudden rush of heat through her body, it occurred to Gypsy that Jefferson . . . *the Jigsaw Man*— might be hiding John captive somewhere nearby. It made sense. Why would he keep John holed up in Dallas somewhere while he was monitoring her in Rockport?

As Gypsy saw it, it would just be a hell of a lot more, well, *convenient*—for lack of a better word—to have everything together in one place. But *where?* God, it could be anywhere, from the house next door to an abandoned warehouse miles away.

She couldn't find those blasted letters, and that was a fact. If she didn't do something, and do it fast, John was going to die.

She couldn't, she *wouldn't* let that happen.

He was depending on her.

A soft little hand intertwined with Gypsy's fingers, startling her out of her reverie. She managed a smile for her beloved child. Annie. She'd almost forgotten about her.

What in the world was she going to do about Annie?

Gypsy was afraid to let the child out of her sight. On the other hand, the idea she was formulating in her head could be very dangerous. Surely she dared not take the little girl along.

She even toyed, briefly, with asking the leather-faced lady behind the bait shop counter where she bought Annie a Coke, for the name of a reputable baby-sitter or day care center in the town.

Then she thought about calling John's parents, who lived a couple of hundred miles away in the hill country community of New Braunfels. They would come for Annie in a minute.

But what could they do if the FBI demanded they turn over the child?

Watching Annie skip with delight each time a seagull snapped up a piece of bread, her little face alight with joy, Gypsy seesawed. *Oh God,* she thought, *Is there no place where my child can be safe?*

No doubt about it, she had to give very serious consideration to this man, this *Jigsaw Man,* who had the resources and the training to find most anybody he needed to, anytime. Anywhere in the country.

No, she thought, her lips pursed in worry and fear. *If he can get his hands on my baby whenever he pleases, I will not be separated from her when it happens.*

They would stay together, come what may.

Briefly, she considered the possibility that he had engaged a squad of shady types—or even just one or two—to assist him in his crimes. Informants, maybe. Or criminals who owed him a favor.

In the end, she rejected that idea. He would never risk letting even one other person in on his nasty secrets. Not with the directorship up for grabs. He should know as well as anyone how quick suspects were to turn state's evidence on each other. Even if he planned to kill them, he couldn't count on them not to blow the whole thing in the middle of the plan.

No. He had to be working alone.

So that was it, then. It was going to be her against him.
Talk about your uneven match-ups.

How could she, a deaf woman dragging around a
seven-year-old, ever hope to outwit a trained, experi-
enced, powerful FBI agent? It was hopeless.

She couldn't think like that. If she did, John would die.
With a powerful concentration of will, she forced herself
to decide what to do next: *Find the Jigsaw Man's hideaway.*

From there, she could maybe track down John's whereabouts.

Trying not to shiver as her sweat dried in the warm afternoon sun and the full nature of what she was about to
do sank in, Gypsy gathered the reluctant Annie up and
drove out to the chalk-white house on the edge of the dazzling ultramarine bay where her realtor did business.

Frank Overton had the butterscotch complexion and the
crinkle-eyed grin of a man who spent most of his time
outdoors and loved it. He had sold, rented, and leased
homes of all sizes and shapes in the Rockport area for
thirty years and took a genuine pleasure in the idea that he
had personally helped to develop the area as a popular va-
cation/retirement spot. In all the years he had handled
Gypsy's mother's house, he had never questioned her
wishes and had seen to it that the house was in no way
vandalized or burgled. Gypsy was profoundly grateful for
that and they got along well.

Frank was, as always, glad to see her. "It's Gypsy Rose
Lee herself!" he cried, using the teasing name with her
that he'd adopted early on. "And her beautiful daughter,"
he added, handing Annie a piece of candy. "This is a
pleasant surprise, indeed." He showed them into his office. "How are you enjoying your stay in Rockport?"

Gypsy smiled at the realtor. It had not occurred to ask

him *if* she was enjoying her stay, only *how*. "It's really quite pretty down here," she said.

"Well, I'm very sorry it's been raining so much," he said, as if he were personally responsible for the weather. "But this is one of those perfect days, isn't it? You should hire a catamaran, take Annie sailing."

"Oh, Mommy!" cried Annie. "Could we?"

"One of these days," said Gypsy. "We'll see."

Disappointed, Annie concentrated her attention on unwrapping her candy.

"I just thought I'd drop in, let you know how much we appreciate everything you've done for us through the years."

"My pleasure, I assure you. I remember your mother. She was a very sweet lady."

"Yes." Gypsy swallowed. "Is this a very busy time for renters?"

"Oh, indeed. Snowbirds, escaping the weather up north."

"Well, I thought I saw an old friend of mine the other day—a single man I once knew long ago. I'd love to drop in and surprise him. I wondered if you had rented him a home."

"Well, I can sure find out for you. What's his name?"

Gypsy hesitated. No way Jefferson would use his real name. "To tell you the truth," she said, "my friend is an author, and when he travels to do research, he doesn't use his real name because he doesn't want to draw attention to himself. I'm not sure what name he's using now."

" Really? Wow. A real live author. Do I know him?"

Gypsy gave what she hoped was an enigmatic smile. "Probably."

He waited, as if hoping she would come forth with this famous author's real name, and when she didn't, turned with a sigh to his computer and clacked awhile on the keys. "You say he's single?" He looked over his shoulder at her as he spoke.

"Yes. In his fifties."

"Oh! I bet I know who that is. Feller came in here, had a full beard, wore sunglasses and a hat. Now I know why. It was a disguise!"

"Very possibly."

Grinning happily, Frank said, "Here it is. He's going by the name of Dick Saxton. You want the address?"

"Please. And if you don't mind, I'd appreciate it if you'd write it down, just so I'll be sure I got it right."

"No problem." He jotted down the address on a piece of scratch paper and handed it to Gypsy. The house was located only a couple of blocks away from her own.

Gypsy thanked the man for his trouble and took her leave as quickly as she decently could. Butterflies swarmed in her stomach. The Jigsaw Man—just a few blocks away. Maybe John was being held captive in that very house.

For a long moment, Gypsy sat in the hot car, trying to focus her tattered, terrified little thoughts.

She couldn't do this. It was crazy. He was a dangerous man. She could get them both—and John—killed.

But she had to do it! What choice did she have?

What choice?

Annie was growing tired and cranky. There were a number of long fishing piers nearby—they ringed the bay like snaggle-teeth—and Gypsy lured the child out onto one of them for a chat. They sat on the very end of the warm splintery boards and hung their feet over the edge, watching glistening silver fish jump up out of the water in seeming defiance of Mother Nature.

"Would you like to play a game with me?" Gypsy asked in sign.

Annie clapped her hands together in delight.

"Okay. Here's what we are going to do. Remember the friend I was talking to Mr. Overton about?"

"The author friend?"

"Yes."

"Uh-huh."

"Well, I thought we might drop in on him and surprise him, you know?"

Annie kicked her feet back and forth. "Okay."

"And a surprise must be very, very secret."

Annie nodded.

"We must not make any noise."

Blue eyes dancing, Annie made the motions of zipping up her lips, locking them together, and tossing the key out over the water.

As she wrapped the little girl in her arms, Gypsy held her close for a long moment, staring blindly out over the bay with bleak and fearful eyes.

THIRTEEN

THE CESSNA TOUCHED DOWN ON the remote landing strip like a feather floating to earth, and Jefferson guided it to a slow, uneven halt just to the side of the strip in a small clearing, next to the old Buick he had left parked there. Scrub brush and a few wind-stunted trees were the only vegetation. The soil was loamy and salt-encrusted. A couple of miles south stretched the endless salt marshes, and beyond that, the flat gray Gulf, protected along this part of the coast by a barrier reef which formed a series of islands. Spring break kids liked to hit the islands, where turquoise vistas and crashing surf provided the kinds of recreation that an ocean was expected to provide.

But Jefferson was not here for entertainment. That made the quiet, barrier-sheltered village of Rockport, popular with retirement-aged fishing enthusiasts, perfect for what he needed to do. Most tourists flocked to the glamour city of Corpus Christi and the surf-sculpted Padre Island, with its rippling white sand dunes and upscale condos. Too many crowds. Too many people who might recognize him, in spite of the disguise.

Even the isolated landing strip seemed designed for his personal convenience, although the Bureau had confiscated it from a drug-runner years ago and used it for their own business from time to time. His call numbers and make and model of plane were registered at the Houston and Corpus offices, so that if any agent should happen upon the Cessna parked here, a quick check with the field office would remove all suspicion.

Nobody questioned the movements of an SAC from a major field office.

Jefferson had bought the Cessna from the Bureau for next to nothing after another drug-related confiscation some years before. He kept it in a private hangar at Love Field in Dallas and preferred using it to fly to various business metings around the country, rather than taking the commercial airlines (although he'd flown commercial for the Washington interview). Since he usually took other agents along on the four-seater, or otherwise used it in related business, the Bureau always reimbursed him for fuel.

But for these little side trips, he was sending in no requisitions.

So far he'd been able to juggle it all: Halden, the demands of the Dallas office, the interview in Washington, but he was growing increasingly exhausted and knew he couldn't keep up the pace much longer. It had been a lucky break for him that Annie had managed to evade his agents and get out of town. They had all since been assigned to other cases, and as far as they knew, other agents were now hot on finding her. And so far, the Dallas PD seemed unaware of the house in Rockport.

Still, he hadn't come this far in the business without making some enemies along the way. They were always watching him, he knew, just waiting for him to make some kind of mistake. Especially now. They would do anything to sabotage his chances at the directorship.

And that Fitzgerald . . . Jefferson had no doubt that if the shrewd cop could find some way to destroy him, he would do it.

That was obviously what Strickland had been trying to do, when he set his sniff-dog, Halden, out snooping around. All those years Strickland had apparently had it in for Jefferson, and he'd seen the perfect chance to make his move. Now it was Jefferson's turn.

With a slight smile on his face, Jefferson jiggled through his key chain for the Buick's key, unlocked it, and started the car, idling for a moment so that it would run smoothly when he needed it.

If there was one thing the Bureau had taught him, it was patience.

God, it was all such a delicate string of dominoes! One false move and the whole string would come toppling down.

Pulling the Buick out onto the landing strip and heading it toward the intersecting two-lane road, Jefferson thought once again about the dominoes. While in college, he had once watched a competition in which a bazillion dominoes were lined up in incredibly complex patterns. If one domino were touched, the entire row would collapse in upon itself in a dazzling display of the true chain reaction.

His life, Jefferson reflected, had been a hell of a lot like that.

Somehow or another, he had to stop the dominoes from collapsing.

He wondered if he should have made Halden phrase the phone call differently. There was an outside chance that Annie wouldn't realize *which* letters he meant.

But remembering that night twenty-five years before, he couldn't see how she could *not* realize which letters.

She was smart. She would understand. He was certain of it.

He just hoped to God she could find them. God knows he'd tried hard enough.

Forget about it. Water under the bridge.

As he turned the Buick onto the two-lane highway toward Rockport, Jefferson marveled at how much like her mother this grown-up Annie was. It was like seeing a ghost.

A ghost from a past he didn't much like to think about. It all seemed like another planet to him now, so foreign from the self he had since invented.

They had started calling him "Dash" in high school, back before he received his terrible scars, when it was discovered that no one else in the state was faster at the hundred-yard event.

In the beginning, he'd hoped that such a fact would impress his parents, but Texas was a football state; as far as they were concerned, what was the point of running the hundred-yard dash in ten seconds flat if you had no intention of using that speed on the football field? Mike played quarterback. Mike was the captain of the team. Mike was dating one of the cheerleaders. Mike was the star in the family.

So even though all his friends—and even the beknighted Mike—took to calling him "Dash," his parents refused. *"If we had wanted to name you 'Dash,'"* said his mother drily, *"we would have."*

Fuck her. And the horse she rode in on.

If those goddamned dominoes had just been set in some other pattern, he might even have been part of Annie's life from the very beginning, as he should have been.

After all, they *were* related. And she had Anna's blood in her.

Just the memory of that woman had the power to stir him. Once, a few years back, he had caught a whiff of her perfume on a crowded street in New York and almost got himself arrested trying to find the possessor of that intoxicating fragrance.

Oddly enough, to this day he still missed her.

Why did she have to be so treacherous? Why did she have to betray him, lie to him, and break him—not just once, but *twice?*

The first time, she didn't even say good-bye. Just vanished in the night. Didn't even have the nerve to give him back the engagement ring. He'd had to get it from her mother.

Her mother!

It galled him, even now, just to think about it. It wasn't enough for her to break his heart; she had to humiliate him, too,

He tried to forget her. God knew he had tried. For ten years he stayed away from her, launched a career . . .

He never should have seen her again. One of those fateful dominoes.

He should have known she would tell Mike.

The bitch.

And Mike. He never should have trusted him in the first place with something so valuable as those letters. Never.

And now . . . if it hadn't been for the child, standing there like some skinny little specter, watching . . . if she'd just stayed in her room . . . if he hadn't lost her in the fog . . .

He'd kept low for the first few years, certain that she would give him away to the cops. But she never did. He just always assumed she'd blacked the whole thing out of her mind somehow. He'd heard kids could do that.

Twenty-five years, for God's sake!

Of course he'd known that Anna knew about the letters. Mike told him that much. *"Anna knows about the letters, Dash,"* Mike had said. *"She's seen them. She knows how you screwed up, and she's scared of you, man, can't you tell? I'm telling you—stay away from my family or I swear I'll see to it that those letters go public. And that'll be the end of your precious career, you got that?"*

Dash had gotten it, all right.

Those goddamned letters. The miserable truth was that he didn't know if they even still existed. For all he knew, they'd long since been lost.

If Mike hadn't threatened him with those letters . . .

After all this time, he had been certain that the situation was under control. It hadn't occurred to him that Mike would have said anything to his partner, Abe Strickland. Even in the years just after Mike's death, that possibility hadn't entered his mind. Why should it? Nothing had come of it.

Not for twenty-five years, it hadn't.

But Mike *had* said something . . . and twenty-five years later, Strickland had blabbed it to, of all people, the man who married the little girl on the stairwell.

Another goddamned cop. Who just had to go snooping around.

Jesus, he'd left them in peace all these years—*why* did they have to go stirring things up now?

Because *now* his career was all he had in the world. And there was far too much on the line now—everything he had ever worked for or dreamed of, everything he had sacrificed for, everything Anna could have had—*would* have had—if it hadn't been for Mike.

He had no desire to hurt these people just for the hell of it. He'd had every intention of leaving them alone. If only they had just left *him* alone.

He'd come too far now. Those letters must never get out. Ever. Because if they did, he would be destroyed.

He didn't know how much longer he could keep it all up, either, and so this was it. This trip was going to be his last. He was sick and tired of playing games with the Haldens.

In a couple of days, he'd be flying back to Dallas, and the whole thing would be all over. Hard to believe, after all these years, that he would find himself squaring off with his brother.

Mike, taunting him once again.

This time from the grave.

Gypsy parked at her house and she and Annie cut through the oak-choked property behind her own house as well as her neighbors, running lightly on sneakered feet as the sun dipped below the horizon, sending emerald-black shadows slanting across their path and turning the Gulf deep purple-blue.

The ramshackle old house was just as the realtor described it. There were no cars parked anywhere around. Gypsy and Annie slunk up to a side window and peered inside. The rooms were darkly shadowed and looked bereft in spite of a few pieces of flimsy furniture.

They peeked into every window.

All of them, as well as the doors, were locked, just as she had expected, but they did manage to find one at the rear of the house in which the old hasp had come loose from its moorings and hung free. They were able to push this one up and crawl inside.

Ignoring her own almost stark terror, Gypsy pasted a

thin smile on her face for Annie's sake and clung to the child's hand.

Nobody—and nothing—downstairs.

As they crept up the dark stairs, Gypsy had no way of knowing if their footfalls could be heard or not. She signed to Annie to let her know if they did, and the little girl, still excited with their game, nodded.

She searched two enormous old bedrooms with high ceilings, but the third was unexpectedly short.

Back out in the hall, she sought another room next door, but there was none. The hall dead-ended at the outside wall of the house. And yet, the corresponding inside wall was some sixteen feet down the hallway from the door to the last bedroom—but that room couldn't be more than eight feet wide.

Gypsy returned to the third bedroom. Squinting in the gathering dusk, she studied the walls. Her work, as well as her deafness, had long since taught her to be keenly observant. The wall, which should be nearest the outside wall, did not match the other three walls. The wallpaper was just a tad too new-looking.

Like a blind person in the darkening light, Gypsy began to examine it with her hands, running them smoothly over the surface of the wallpaper.

Suddenly, Annie gave her T-shirt a sharp tug. Gypsy glanced down.

The child's hands were signing frantically. She had heard a car pull up and the front door being opened.

Gypsy, of course, had had no such warning.

FOURTEEN

JEFFERSON PUSHED OPEN THE CREAKY front door with one hand, juggling the fried chicken bucket with the other. Let no one say he was a complete son of a bitch. Guy must be sick of bologna by now. Fried chicken would make a nice last meal.

Jefferson was tired of this whole situation. All the trouble he went through to install that surveillance equipment, and for what? Half the time he couldn't be here to monitor it. And the trip to Washington had been a complete surprise.

Granted, everybody in the Bureau knew the director was sick, and the rumor mill had been pretty consistent that Jefferson was to be the next Anointed One, at least, if the director himself had anything to say about it.

But nobody, apparently, knew just how sick the director really was.

Shit. Two months. Hell of a way to go.

But all the better for *him*.

Crossing the shabby little living room, he snapped on the overhead light. He'd let this situation drag out way too long. And every day added to the ever-present danger that he would somehow be found out. He simply could not take that risk anymore.

Annie didn't know it yet, but she had one more day to find those goddamned letters before he was forced to kill them all.

Granted, it looked as though he was going to have to kill them all anyway, but he didn't want some other relative to happen upon those letters afterward—*God, would this nightmare never end?*

Shoving the keys in his pocket, Jefferson started up the steps.

It wasn't that he really wanted to kill those people. After all, he was no depraved serial killer or anything. He didn't kill for the thrill of it.

It was just a matter of expediency.

But what was he supposed to do?

Once that old son-of-a-bitch Strickland got to shooting off his mouth, once John Halden got to digging into the past . . . it was just a matter of time before his whole career would be over and he'd wind up being the subject of yet one more slimy movie-of-the-week.

There was too much at stake. And not just for him, either.

For the entire free world.

At the top of the stairs, he turned right and headed down the hallway past the two empty bedrooms. As he stepped across the threshold of the third bedroom, the hairs on the back of his neck stood on end.

He stopped.

Listening with fierce intensity, Jefferson quickly glanced around.

Nothing seemed out of place.

He should have paid more attention when he left the house the last time. Should have put little security measures into place that would reveal if anyone had been inside the house.

Jefferson set the chicken on the floor and unsnapped the holster for his Smith & Wesson ten millimeter. On stealthy feet he entered the room, after first glancing to check if the wallpaper was out of place. It was not.

Then, he slunk over to the closet and shoved the door back.

Nobody.

Finally, he crossed to the window and looked down on the shady street below, casing it as far as he could see from one end to the other. There were no suspicious-looking vans that could be surveilling him. No cars parked there that didn't belong. No one sitting in any of the parked cars.

Satisfied, he reholstered his semi-automatic, retrieved the chicken, and pulled back a restickable strip of wallpaper to reveal the door cut into the false wall.

This whole thing, he decided, was just giving him the jitters. Making him paranoid.

He would be glad when it was all over.

Gypsy, her body wadded into a ball in the furthest edge of the closet behind the open door, her child squeezed into her lap, loosened her grip on Annie somewhat.

Her hand over Annie's mouth, Gypsy counted to sixty ten times, but the Jigsaw Man did not return to the bedroom.

Stifling a cry, she stretched out her cramped legs, pushing the door back out ever so slowly, terrified that it might make a loud creak that she would not be able to hear. Finally, when there was room for Annie to stand up next to her, she put a finger to her lips to signal quiet, and inched her way around to where she could see through the crack in the doorway of the closet.

Across the room, she could see a strip of wallpaper hanging down from an upper corner, revealing the neatly sawed edge of what must be a false door.

Her chest tightened, and she could hardly breathe.

John had to be in there!

Right now, this minute. Maybe hurt or starving.

At the mercy of the Jigsaw Man.

She cursed herself for leaving the thirty-eight at home. She was not a cop; carrying a gun was not second nature to her, especially not with a child beside her practically every moment.

On the other hand, what did she think she could do with it when facing down the Jigsaw Man?

He'd be armed, of course, he was an FBI agent. And though she knew how to handle a gun and had done her share of practicing at the police firing range, an FBI agent had to qualify with his weapon eight times a year.

Crouching there at the door crack, Gypsy was in a quandary.

What would happen if she went to the police and told them her husband was being held hostage in a secret room by a top FBI agent?

Okay. What if she told them that he was hurt and needed help and . . .

No. What if she told them that there was a family disturbance and her husband was being held . . .

No matter what scenario she came up with, Gypsy knew how cops thought. Especially in a small town, with an individual they did not know and had never seen before. They would take her name and address and run a computer check on her, and they would run a computer check on her husband and learn that he was wanted in connection with a slain fellow officer.

And there was nobody cops hated worse than cop-killers. Except maybe a cop who killed a cop.

Even if she persuaded them to come with her, they would not enter and search this man's home without a warrant. And they couldn't get a warrant without probable cause.

What they would do was . . . talk to him.

And he would show them his credentials and explain that he'd been deep undercover on a top secret surveillance job and would appreciate it if they'd butt out.

Which they would.

Leaving her exposed to the Jigsaw Man's rage, and John, most likely, dead.

Annie gave her an impatient tug and signed that she needed to go to the bathroom. *Bad.*

Nothing like kids to send a jolt of the here-and-now reality into a situation.

Okay. She'd withdraw, recoup, and think of something.

But first, she had to get her baby out of this death trap.

John had not wanted to give Jefferson the satisfaction of seeing him wolf down his food, but he couldn't help it. While Jefferson fiddled around with his surveillance toys, John gnawed on a bone and tried to figure out what this new development could mean.

He knew from reading accounts from such Iranian hostages as Terry Anderson, that the captors could show unexpected kindnesses completely arbitrarily. The next day they could beat you senseless.

But this was not Iran.

As the living room of Gypsy's mother's old house leapt

into view on the video screen, John had a hard time believing that this was actually the United States of America.

My God, we're in Rockport, he thought. Rockport, Texas in the good old U-S-of-A.

And this guy, a high-ranking FBI agent.

He couldn't get over the irony of it all. As an investigator with the Intelligence Division of the Dallas Police Department, John had occasion to work on various task force investigations in conjunction with the Dallas field office of the FBI. Naturally, in that capacity, he had met Dash Jefferson several times.

He just had to go asking questions.

Nothing accusatory, just curious and only slightly probing.

"My Chief tells me you worked in the Dallas field office before, twenty-five years ago. He says you could possibly help me find out what happened to my wife's dad, name of Mike Jefferson. The Chief's old partner back in his flat-foot days. I understand he was murdered."

"My brother," Jefferson had said, his face suddenly saddened. *"You know, I lost touch with Mike's wife after he was killed. She took their little girl and moved away. You mean your wife . . .?"*

An expression of wonder crossing his face, Jefferson shook his head. *"Hell of a small world, isn't it?"* Then, with a smile, he said, *"Sure, I don't mind talking about it, but let's get out of this office and go someplace for lunch. There are too many interruptions around here."*

And he did. Just like a true dumbass. He climbed into the car with a murderer and didn't even bother to unsnap his holster.

Now here he was, chained to the wall like a junkyard dog, gnawing on a bone and pitifully grateful for it.

Annie's voice suddenly echoed through the room, and

John started, dropping the bone, riveting his attention to the video screen.

And there they were, just as he'd dreamed of them countless times. Gypsy and Annie, big as life, walking around the living room of that old house and talking like nothing had happened.

She came to Rockport, looking for those letters, bless her sweet heart, he thought. *Just as the bastard knew she would.*

Stifling a cry of anguish, he squeezed shut his eyes, so that he didn't have to look at their sweet faces, but there was nothing he could do to block out their voices.

"Your kid deaf, too?" interjected Jefferson, forcing John to open his eyes and watch his precious little one signing like a little electric typewriter to her mother. Presently, her mother spoke back, followed by some signs.

"No," said John in a dead voice. "Her mother is always working with her on her signing. Annie helps Gypsy some when she can't understand what people are saying to her."

He closed his eyes again.

"Smart little thing. Reminds me of your wife at that age. I mean, I really didn't get to see her. I always visited her mom when she was at school. But that one night . . . well, this child reminds me of her."

The muscles in John's jaw clenched and worked at just the idea of this creep even talking about his family.

"Her mama never said word one about her being deaf."

"She wasn't," said John through gritted teeth. "She got the shit knocked out of her the night her mother was murdered. Deafened her in one ear. The other ear lost some hearing in a sympathetic nervous reaction." He glared at Jefferson.

"No kidding?" The loathsome man leaned forward,

peering at the screen. "I wondered why she could speak so well, you know, for a deaf person."

No remorse, Not one smidgeon.

I swear to God I'll kill him with my bare hands.

Gypsy's voice: "Did you enjoy your trip to the Aransas Wildlife Refuge today?"

Annie: "Oh yes."

Gypsy: "Even I've never seen a whooping crane. They are very rare, you know. This is where they come to spend the winter."

Annie: "How do they get here?"

Gypsy: "They buy a ticket at the airport and catch a plane for Corpus Christi."

Annie: "Mommy, that's silly."

Gypsy: "Well, you ask a silly question . . ."

Gypsy: "Can you keep a secret?"

Annie: "Oh, yes!"

Gypsy: "You know those letters I found in the old armoire from the back bedroom?"

Annie: "What letters?"

With a rattle of chains, John sat bolt upright and stared at his loved ones. *Shut up Gypsy,* he begged, willing her to silence with all his being.

Gypsy: "You remember. I showed them to you. Well, I hid them today, in a secret place. At the refuge."

Suddenly, John's attention focused on Gypsy's hands. In sign language, she was saying, *"You're doing great. Do you like our pretend game?"*

Annie: *"Yes. It's a lot of fun."* Aloud, she said, "Where is the secret place where you hid the letters?"

III

For this is the message which you have heard from the beginning, that we should love one another, not as Cain who was evil, and slew his brother. And for what reason did he slay him? Because his deeds were evil, and his brother's were righteous.

—I John 3:12
NEW AMERICAN STANDARD VERSION

FIFTEEN

IT TOOK EVERY OUNCE OF self-control John could muster not to concentrate too fiercely on the exchange, not to betray by one twitch of muscle what was happening on the video screen before him. He stole a glance at his captor. Jefferson was hunched over the screen, eyes aglitter, his fist opening and closing in an unconscious gesture of triumph.

Gypsy: *"You are such a smart girl. This pretend game is going to help us find Daddy."* Aloud, she said, "Remember when we climbed way high on the observation deck? Well, I hid them underneath it in a place where nobody will ever find them."

Annie: "Why?"

Gypsy: "Because a man I know wants them, but I'm not going to let him have them." In sign, she said, *"The man will go hunt for the letters, and while he is gone, we will go find Daddy."*

Annie: "I love you, Mommy." She said the same thing in sign language.

Gypsy: "I love you too, baby." In sign, she said, *"I love you too, baby, and I love your Daddy with all my heart."*

Hot, miserable tears sprang unbidden to John's eyes, and before he could hide them, Jefferson whipped around in his chair with a victorious gloat on his face. "I knew it!" he cried.

"Go get the fucking letters," John said, his tone wooden, "and then please leave my family the hell alone."

Jefferson sat back, regarding him. "No rush," he said. "It's dark now. I go poking around there, I'll get the park rangers after me, and I'm not ready to show my creds around here. I don't want anybody to think I'm here on official business. No. I'll go first thing in the morning."

He continued to stare at John with knowing eyes. John stared back equably, silently praying that the wild pounding at the pulse of his throat did not betray him. Predators were always sensitive to such signs of vulnerability.

He was thunderstruck at his wife's resourcefulness, amazed that she had found the bug Jefferson had planted in the old house. *Had* she found the letters?

On reflection, it didn't seem likely. Why would she tip her hand so early in the game? It must be some elaborate ruse then, but *why?*

As he ducked his head over the chicken bucket to hide the powerful emotions running rampant through his mind, John considered every possibility.

There was one . . . but no. Impossible. There was no way she could have found this house, no way she could know where John was.

Was there?

Hadn't she said, " . . .*we will go find Daddy. . . .*"?

Because if she was planning to send Jefferson on a wild goose chase so that she could get him out . . .

No way. Gypsy was good at her job—no doubt about that—but she wasn't a cop; she didn't have a cop's resources available to her. How could it be?

Intuitively and professionally, he was aware of Gypsy's situation, how difficult it would be for her to get the cooperation of local law enforcement agencies, how unwilling to believe her the FBI would be if she tried them.

She was so alone. So very alone.

But if she didn't know where he was, then what was she trying to do?

He wondered briefly if she were trying to lure Jefferson out to the remote spot so that she could cause him bodily harm, but rejected that possibility as well. Not his sweet, gentle Gypsy.

Still, she was up to something, and in spite of himself, John felt a little thrill of hope—the first real hope he'd known in all the desperate hours since being kidnapped.

Gypsy had given him that hope. And to think he had doubted her love and trust and faith in him.

Suddenly overwhelmed, he blinked away more tears from his weary eyes before Jefferson caught sight of them. God knew he was on the edge. Hope and fear warred within his soul in a wild jumble of conflicting thoughts.

On the one hand, he didn't want the family he loved to be put in any more jeopardy than they already were.

On the other hand, Gypsy was more alert and aware of her options—and lack of them—than a person who knew nothing about law enforcement would be. After all, she'd found the bug, hadn't she?

She was sharp all right, and so very brave.

He didn't want her in danger—and certainly not their baby, either—but on the other hand, if she could get him out of here, he would no longer be that chained-up junkyard dog.

He'd be free to track Parker Jefferson down and kill him with his bare hands.

The prospect excited him. He couldn't help that simple fact.

Jefferson chose that moment to turn away from the screen, where Gypsy was reading Annie a book, and stare at John, his eyes searching probes that seemed to ferret out every single one of John's murderous thoughts, which he made no attempt to hide.

For a long, tense moment, the men locked gazes. Neither man blinked.

It was Annie's laughter that broke the deadlock. Jefferson turned to look at the child's image on the screen.

Whether it was the greasy chicken, or the fact that this man was now privy to the quiet moments of John's family; whatever, his stomach seemed to turn over.

Watching his little girl's happy, unsuspecting face, and the bent head of his wife, her glossy hair falling down over her cheek, it was all John could do not to throw up.

Gypsy, my darlin', he silently pleaded, *please, please be careful.*

The rain returned that night. It tit-a-tatted at the windows, gurgled through the storm gutters, lashed against the trees, and plip-plopped through the bowls and pans Gypsy now had set out all over the house. And though she could hear none of these watery little sounds, she did feel the pervasive damp cold that came with the rain, which forced her to turn off the clattering old air conditioners and light the cantankerous gas space heaters instead. She hadn't had time to clean them—hadn't expected the need to—and the dust within them burned, giving out a frightful odor of fire that kept her constantly vigilant lest the whole house go up in flames.

It was just as well. She could never have slept anyway.

She kept thinking about that afternoon, the sheer panic

which had gripped her when Jefferson returned to the house, the terror of those long minutes in the closet, the cold horror of the moment when he had shoved open the door and stood only inches away from her, the feel of her daughter's trembling little body in her arms.

Pacing the old house from one end to the other, watchful of the ever-present video camera, she questioned her judgment, again and again, of keeping Annie with her. Dare she risk her child's life to save her husband's? Was she insane not to ask someone—anyone—for help? Had she lost her freaking *mind,* going into the Jigsaw Man's house? With her child?

But who could help her? *Who?*

There was no one.

She'd been over it and over it, and she knew she'd never get local police to enter that house. Even if she were able to convince them to at least check it out, and even if they did, they'd never find the secret room. Not with a top-ranking FBI agent standing right there.

And how did she know for sure that John was in that room? How did she know that, even if they entered the secret room, they'd find her husband? How could she be certain that . . . wicked . . . man hadn't fashioned some sort of trapdoor or something to hide John? The possibilities were endless, but only one thing was unarguable: if she drew law enforcement attention to the Jigsaw Man, John would die. She knew that in the deepest fibers of her being.

She couldn't take that chance.

And what *about* Annie? Where could she possibly leave her little girl that the Jigsaw Man couldn't find her? She was too young to leave alone anyplace; she'd need an adult caregiver, and there wasn't a caregiver she could think of who could not be forced to hand over a little girl to the Federal Bureau of Investigation if they demanded it. Even Annie's beloved grandparents.

So what if she found John, and helped him to escape, only to have the Jigsaw Man steal away their child?

He will probably do it anyway, she thought, *if you don't handle this thing right. One false step and you could all wind up dead, just like Mama and Daddy.*

Back again where she started.

Okay, she mentally told herself. *Enough. You're going to do it. You know you are. So be prepared. Plan for every eventuality. Think through every single step. Make sure there will be no surprises. Never forget that you are being watched. And make damn sure you're well armed.*

There would be one more thing. Something she dreaded almost more than anything else.

She was going to have to tell Annie the truth.

So close.

God! He was so close!

As darkness crept over the Gulf, Dash Jefferson paced the threadbare living room downstairs. Gypsy and her daughter had gone to bed, so there was no more monitoring to be done for the night. He'd locked up his prisoner, checked again for signs of surveillance, and now all his paranoid little doubts were edging closer as the shadows gathered.

There was always a crucial moment in any undercover operation when you ran the risk of being found out. This was that crucial moment, and Jefferson was excruciatingly cognizant of it. It scared the hell out of him. So many things could go wrong.

After all, the woman was married to a Dallas intelligence cop. How did he know she didn't have some of Halden's buddies down here, setting up a trap for him? Or maybe Deputy Chief Fitzgerald. Jefferson knew Fitzgerald was gunning for him. Maybe she had called him, told him something.

Maybe Fitzgerald had helped her slip the tail Nicky and them—

Or wait. Nicks *definitely* had an axe to grind against Jefferson now. Or maybe he'd had it all along. Maybe he had *allowed* Gypsy to get away!

There had always been something about that guy Jefferson didn't trust. After all, he'd gone and blown an investigation. A sure sign of disloyalty if there ever was one.

Now that he'd made the short list, Jefferson knew there were plenty of other agents who were jealous and envious, agents who didn't appreciate his methods, agents he'd crossed through the years for one reason or another on his way up the management ladder. Some in his own office. Any one or more of them could all be in on this.

Maybe even Corruthers. Jefferson had sensed a definite difference in Corruthers's attitude toward him during their talk at headquarters. A cooling of sorts. It wasn't much— a flicker of an eye, a quiet in the middle of a conversation. It was obvious that he didn't agree with Jefferson or Jefferson's ideas.

He might not be very loyal when Jefferson was made director. Might even talk about him behind his back. Criticize him. Diminish the respect he should be receiving from the other agents at headquarters.

A sudden flash of fear strobed through him: *Could Corruthers actually know about the letters?*

No, he decided. No way. He'd have to have known about it from somebody years ago, during the early, crazy days of the investigation.

Okay. Fine. With a sigh, Jefferson thought it so obvious

that his own ideas were right, whereas Corruther's were so glaringly wrong.

Pursing his lips, Jefferson considered Corruthers. An FBI director had to maintain a strict hand in the organization. Punishments for rule infractions must be clearly spelled out and swiftly dispensed. Not only that, but anyone *not* an agent had to be considered a potential lawbreaker. To that end, the FBI must be prepared to deploy any means necessary to maintain law and order.

Why, in the Old Man's day, civilians didn't dare criticize or humiliate him publicly. If they did, they soon found a couple of agents at their door, looking into their own miserable lives.

Now *that* was respect.

The director of the FBI could not be undermined by members of his own staff. Either they were loyal to him or they weren't. It was that simple. Hoover had understood that. And he'd built the greatest law enforcement agency in the world because of it.

Jefferson knew that he had what it took to restore the agency to its former glory.

And the first thing he would do was some serious housecleaning. As civil service employees, even the Director could not arbitrarily fire agents unless they were caught breaking the law, no matter how disgraceful their antics might seem. The two agents who had belonged to the group sex club had not lost their jobs.

And there was no longer a satellite office in Butte, Montana.

But that presented no real problem, because there were places—oh, there were places—where an FBI agent could spend the remainder of his career rotting. For one thing, there were stacks of files as high as a skyscraper, since the FBI continued to conduct all its in-house business on paper well into the nineties. It would take a hundred years to transfer Bureau business to computer disk.

Oh, there were graves for the living dead agents, and he knew just where they all were. Nicky had found one. There were many, many more.

And Dash Jefferson had a long, long memory.

He checked every room of the house for bugs, and surreptitiously examined every parked car on the street to make sure he was not under surveillance. And as he stretched out on the rickety couch beneath a ratty blanket for a few hours' catnap, the ten-millimeter secure at his side, he lay awake a long time, remembering.

SIXTEEN

THEY HAD BROUGHT ANNIE'S WINNIE-the-Pooh night-light from home and plugged it into the wall not far from the bed where she and her mother slept, so that she could see it and be comforted. The morning was still black out when Gypsy sat on the edge of the bed and studied her little girl's face in its milky glow: the soft outline of her cheek, the tangled, tumbled mass of curls fanning out over the pillow, the loyal long-suffering Pooh-Bear still clutched tight after hours of sleep.

The vulnerability of sleep rendered Annie's face even more innocent and trusting than it was in the harsh, cold light of day, and Gypsy was so possessed with terror for her child that it was all she could do not to bundle Annie up and drive far away from this threatening place.

If anything happens to this child, I'll surely die, she thought, and doubts vexed her again. Heading back to Dallas was the most tempting thing to do; just abandon John to his fate and try to build a new life back home.

But the Jigsaw Man would never allow her to do that.

She knew that now. He had already demonstrated his power: he had killed a law enforcement officer and very convincingly framed a man he had also successfully kidnapped. Who knew what havoc he could wreak in her life if he chose. He could even see to it that Annie was taken away from her.

But was she crazy to think she could outsmart such a clever and powerful man? Was she insane to think she could actually rescue her husband from his clutches and somehow save the day?

The answer was yes. Of course she was nuts to attempt such a thing, but she had to try, she *had* to, for Annie's sake, if nothing else. After all, that was her daddy being held captive. How could Gypsy face her daughter through the years, knowing she'd had an opportunity to save him and had let it pass?

How could she face *herself*?

Not very well. She'd already demonstrated that. In all those years since her mother's death, she'd never once probed into what really happened that night. She'd allowed the horror that had left her frozen on the stair landing that terrible night to continue to paralyze her all the way into adulthood.

All her life she'd hidden from the difficult questions, hidden from her own stark fear of the Jigsaw Man. She'd hidden behind her deafness, behind her husband, behind her work. And while she had been hiding, he had slipped out of the phantoms of her nightmares and stalked her in real life, committing more evil acts for his own twisted purposes, destroying the life she had so carefully constructed for herself.

No. She would stop him this time. She would risk everything to stop him, even if it meant she had to die trying.

But all the same, as she watched her child sleeping, Gypsy sent up more than one frantic prayer that *this* little girl could somehow be spared from the rampage of the Jigsaw Man.

Then she tiptoed from the room, shouldered her backpack, and melted outdoors into the fog-shrouded black.

John's watch told him it was four o'clock. He assumed that meant in the morning, but he couldn't be sure anymore. Jefferson had told him he was going to the refuge to search for the letters in the morning. That must mean dawn would soon approach.

John had slept very little. All he could think about was his family. He would fret himself to sleep about them. Fear-tossed dreams would rack his restless doze, and he would awaken fully alert, still worrying about Gypsy and whatever scheme she was cooking up, and Annie and the dangers they were both in, and their aloneness and his own *frustrating* inability to do a damn thing to protect them.

He was beyond tears now, beyond escape attempts, beyond anything but obsessing endlessly about what was going to happen when Jefferson left for the wildlife refuge.

Then he would doze off for a few more minutes, and it would start all over again.

The first opaque fingers of mist-smothered light were just beginning to part the heavy living-room drapes when Jefferson awoke. Rubbing sleep from his eyes, he crossed the room to the window and peeked around a side of one of the curtains to make sure no one was watching the house. Satisfied at last that there was no surveillance, he took a shower and then fastidiously applied the fake beard. He could never be too careful. Could never allow himself to be seen without his disguise; the burn scars on his face were entirely too distinctive, and his picture was all over the papers.

Applying and removing the beard were extremely painful processes for his hypersensitive facial skin. Plastic surgery had made remarkable advances in the forty years since the fire that had ravaged his face. He'd even considered submitting himself to some of it, to try to repair the damage made long ago by doctors with an insufficient grasp on the delicate procedure of skin grafting. Who knew what they could do now with those fancy lasers and stuff?

But in the end, he'd rejected the idea. He liked terrorizing the underlings with one fierce and horrible glare. In his younger days, he'd even practiced it in front of the mirror. It was especially entertaining to focus it on young trainees—particularly those who were laying eyes on him for the first time. Sometimes it was all he could do not to laugh.

The morning was chilly and wet. He dressed in a black turtleneck and dark blue Levi's and black Reeboks, and set the floppy-brimmed fishing hat he favored out on the kitchen counter along with the sunglasses. Then he made himself some coffee, but made no attempt to carry any upstairs for Halden. Why bother? It would only make him piss more, and Jefferson was sick to death of dealing with that damned bucket. Only one more day, and he could wash his hands of the whole mess. Literally.

There was so much that had to be done. He couldn't leave anything to chance. Everything had to be meticulously planned out and every detail attended to. Then, as soon as he got his hands on those letters, the final plan would be set in motion: the "murder-suicide" of the fugitive, John Halden, and his family. It shouldn't be too hard to set up, and the local cops would accept it easily enough, considering Halden's past, murdering his boss and all.

And by the time the bodies were found, Jefferson would be far, far away.

After a quick breakfast of English muffins and jam, Gypsy dressed herself and Annie in sturdy jeans and boots and jackets. In spite of her lack of sleep, Gypsy's thoughts were clear and calm. While Annie brushed her teeth, Gypsy loaded the thirty-eight and jammed it down the waistband of her jeans, pulling her sweatshirt and jacket over it and pocketing extra bullets. Then she checked the contents of her trusty backpack, added a few items, then shouldered it for the second time that morning.

With the car parked in front of the house as a sign that they were still at home if Jefferson should happen to drive by, they vanished into the fog-blurred trees and brush behind the house. When they had traveled what Gypsy judged to be a safe distance, she stopped and had a talk with the child.

"I wasn't entirely honest with you yesterday," she said, "when I told you we were going to pay a surprise visit to a friend." She hesitated.

"I know," said Annie. "You were scared in the closet, and you wouldn't have been scared of a friend." She regarded her mother with huge, solemn blue eyes.

The mist gave them an eerie sensation of being entirely alone in the world. Gypsy picked Annie up and set her down in a bough of one of the wind-crippled oaks, so that they would be at eye level to each other.

"I'm going to tell you something, and you need to be a very big girl for Mommy now, because I'm going to need your help."

Annie nodded.

Gypsy bit her lip, then said, "The truth is that the man we went to see is a bad man, honey. And I think that he kidnapped your daddy."

Annie's eyes saucered, and her mouth formed a little "o".

"And I think Daddy may be in that house where the bad man was. Tied up or something."

"Shouldn't we call the cops?"

This was the hardest part. How could Gypsy make this child understand that the "bad man" *was* the police? How could she make her understand that in such a way that she would still trust police officers afterward?

"Well, honey, we could, and maybe we *should,* but this man is a very important man, and I don't think the police would believe me if I told them what I think."

Annie considered this for a long moment, then nodded. "It happens on Scooby-Doo all the time," she said, referring to her favorite cartoon program.

Gypsy didn't know what to say. "It does?"

"Oh yeah. And then at the end, see, the man everybody thinks is a nice man pulls off the nice-man mask he was wearing, see, and everybody can see that he is *really* a bad man!"

Gypsy smiled, shook her head, and said, "Maybe I should have been watching those cartoons with you more often."

Annie grinned. "Mommy, do you think we could try to save Daddy ourselves?"

Gypsy's breath caught in her throat. "Well, I was kind of hoping that. I mean, that's sort of what we were doing yesterday."

Suddenly the child jumped to the ground, put her little fists on her waist, and glared up at her mother. "Well, gosh, Mommy, why didn't you just say that in the first place?" And she turned and stomped off ahead through the trees, her mother staring dumbfounded after her, wishing with all her might she could call on Scooby-Doo himself to help her catch the masked man.

The soupy morning fog was difficult to drive in, and Jefferson was so worried that somebody could be following him that he almost missed the entrance to the wildlife refuge, located some thirty miles from Rockport in a remote rural area of salt marshes, alligators, twisted scrub oaks, and ramshackle farmhouses.

After parking the car, he waited for some time to see if anyone was going to pull in after him, but no one did. Finally he got out, peering nervously around, and followed a path and signs to the ranger station nearby. The ground was white and crusty underfoot. In the distance, he could hear the soft silky hum of the Gulf waters, not the wave-throbbing one would hear, say, around Padre Island, where the surf crashed powerfully against the silky dunes; but a gentle soothing presence, nonetheless. There was a heavy, moist scent to the air.

After checking in at the ranger station and paying a nominal fee, he followed the path to the observation deck. On this fog-cloaked day, it was deserted. Here—closer to the water now—towered gigantic oak trees whose trunks must have been six feet in diameter and had been here, as the Ranger had helpfully explained, since the days of Coronado's explorations. Bearded with Spanish moss and cobwebbed by thick vines, they pressed jungle-close and produced a misty green arc overhead.

Against his will, he shivered.

At the observation deck, he waited again, straining to hear the slightest sound above the hush of the Gulf and the dripping of mist—anything that could alert him to the presence of watchers. From time to time he patted the ten-millimeter in his shoulder holster, concealed beneath a jacket. As he trudged up the many switchback steps of the observation deck, he looked down through an earthborn cloud to the tops of the great oaks. Then, he began a slow, methodical search of the board railings, the deck, and as far underneath the deck as he could safely reach.

Frustrated, he started down, one step at a time, and hunted vigorously for anything that might conceal or contain a couple of thin letters.

Jefferson had not yet reached ground level before he realized that he was not going to find those letters. Either she had buried them someplace, or he'd been had.

But that problem could be easily remedied. He'd drag her out here—by the hair, if necessary—and make her show him the letters.

If she couldn't—or wouldn't—he'd just kill her quick and get it the fuck over with.

Hell, nobody would ever suspect the special agent in charge of the Dallas field office—the one on the short list to make director—of having anything whatsoever to do with the murder of a deaf woman in the twisted, thick, live-oak forest and chest-high salt-marsh grass of the Texas Gulf Coast.

SEVENTEEN

AFTER THE BUICK PULLED OUT of the drive, Gypsy forced herself to wait a full fifteen minutes before sprinting through the trees and across the street, Annie's little hand clutched in her own. It wouldn't do for the Jigsaw Man to forget something, turn back to the house, and discover Gypsy and her child inside.

In the dreary light of a wet, cold morning, the house looked forlorn, uncared-for, its lawn shaggy and paint job unkempt; a crash-pad for a sporadic and mysterious renter who didn't spend much time there.

In no way did it look as if it could harbor a hostage inside, a prisoner whose life was seeping away daily. On the other hand, neither did it appear welcoming, and Gypsy's heart thudded dully in her throat as she pushed up the broken window, catapulted Annie through, and clambered through herself.

For a long moment, she paused, her hand on Annie's shoulder, struggling to get her heavy breathing under control and waiting just in case there could be anyone else inside. But the place had a deserted air about it, and after a minute they hurried up the stairs and down the hall to the short bedroom. The fog had draped the house in gloom, rendering Annie jumpy and Gypsy more than a little nervous.

As they entered the third bedroom, Gypsy stopped, and Annie's head banged sharply against her back. While Gypsy studied the freshly papered wall in the dim light, Annie stood so near to Gypsy's elbow that it was all she could do not to bark at the child to back off. She reached above her head and slowly unstripped the wallpaper, revealing the makeshift door.

She turned to the child. Annie's eyes were round with fright. Gypsy stooped down and cupped the little girl's chin in her hand. "Now honey, don't forget what we talked about. You be Mommy's eyes and ears, all right? Stand here to the side of the window and watch for the bad man's car to come back, and listen to hear if anybody is coming into the house."

Annie suffered a failure of confidence. "Can't I go with you Mommy? *Please.*"

"Sweetheart—"

"What if the bad man comes back and I don't see him somehow? Mommy—what if the bad man *gets me?*"

Her small chin shook in Gypsy's hand. She took the child in her arms and squeezed her tight. How could she possibly reassure this little one about what was her own worst nightmare?

Her heart melted, but she had to stand firm. She needed Annie's help, but it was more than that.

The truth was, she dare not let that child see what was on the other side of the door.

At least, not until she had seen first.

If John was dead . . .

She wouldn't think about that.

"I know you're scared, baby. Mommy's scared too. But

Daddy needs our help right now. He needs us to be very, very brave. Do you think you can do that? For Daddy?"

After a moment, she felt Annie's face nod slowly against her shoulder.

"Okay. I'm so very, very proud of you. Wait 'til your Daddy hears what a big strong girl you were."

Annie stepped back then and finally positioned herself like a brave little soldier by the window. Gypsy blew a kiss to her daughter.

Then, chest aching, blood rushing through her ears, Gypsy pushed open the door.

Thoughts of revenge preoccupied Parker Jefferson as he headed the Buick back down the empty rural highway toward Rockport. So the old gal thought she could fuck with him, eh? Thought she could one-up him, did she?

Well, he hoped she was enjoying her little triumph, because it was the only one she was going to get. Nobody, but nobody, fucked with Dash Jefferson.

He pressed his foot harder on the accelerator. Even with the false ID he carried, it wouldn't do to get a ticket, but he didn't care anymore. All he wanted to do was get back to Rockport, get his hands on that woman, and get this whole tiresome charade over and done with.

He was in a hurry anyway. There was a lot that needed to be done. The surveillance equipment had to be dismantled and packed up. All traces of John Halden had to be removed from the house and everything put back as it was. He even had plans for the secret room, should anybody happen on it at any time in the future.

No questions. It was important that he leave behind absolutely no questions. Should anyone check, the only possible connection Parker Jefferson could have with south

Texas at all during this time were the flight plans he'd been forced to file each time he made the trip.

But there would be no reason for anyone to check those flight plans. He'd had good reasons for being out of the office every time he'd had to leave, and he'd checked in frequently so that nobody had to search for him. Some of his trips—down to Rockport and back—were completed in a matter of hours, so that he could be seen in the office morning and evening on the same day.

Everything was covered, but things were getting busier now in the Dallas office and he had things to do as he readied himself for the announcement he was sure would come any time now that he had indeed been selected to succeed Jim Kellerman as director of the FBI.

This whole mess had to be all cleaned up by then. No loose ends. No questions.

Without warning, the power suddenly disappeared from the Buick. To Jefferson's amazement, it cruised to a stop, while he struggled against the lost power steering to get it over to the side of the road before it finally came to a halt.

"What the f—"

Mid-curse, his gaze dropped to the fuel indicator.

Empty.

"No way!" he shouted. "I filled this fucker up before I left for Dallas last time. It was sitting at the landing strip with a full tank!"

Consequently, in his increasing paranoia that he might be followed, as he had almost constantly checked the rearview mirror, it had never occurred to Jefferson to glance down at the fuel gauge. He'd just assumed—

"You bitch!" he screamed. *"You little bitch! I swear to God, I get my hands on you, I'll take* pleasure *in squeezing the life out of you!"*

His furious cries echoed back to him in the fog, mocking him.

He had underestimated her again.

In a raging temper tantrum, Jefferson slammed his palms against the steering wheel, beating it with all the frustration that consumed him.

The highway was absolutely deserted, and it was miles to the nearest gas station.

After the fruitless attempt to give vent to his rage, he yanked open the car door, climbed out, and slammed it shut, giving the tire a hard kick for good measure.

And as he started to walk, the weirdest feeling crept over him. It took him a moment to decipher it.

Pride.

Shit. That was it! She was Mike and Anna's child, after all, his own blood niece.

And she made a hell of an adversary.

John Halden, curled on his side in the fetal position, was startled awake when the door to his cell opened. Immediately, he sat straight up, as he always did when the asshole came to call.

It was the only piece of dignity he had left.

In spite of the light bulb overhead, the doorway was shadowed, and John was, after all, half asleep, so he didn't quite believe what he was seeing when Gypsy stepped dreamlike through the door.

But it was no dream when she flung her body across the room and into his chain-heavy arms, her tears wet on his neck and her scent in his nostrils and her glorious hair choking his mouth.

A gun, sandwiched between them, pressed heavy on his ribcage.

"What are you doing here?" he cried, "It's too danger-ous!"

And then he remembered that she couldn't hear him.

She felt so damn good it didn't matter anyway.

Finally, he pulled back so that she could read his lips. "Where's Annie?"

She pointed just outside the door and his gut twisted in on itself.

"You've got to get her out of here before Jefferson gets back," he said, slapping the heels of his hands together for emphasis as he signed the words.

"You're going with us," she said, stepping off his lap and standing back to examine the chains. "I didn't think to bring a saw!" she cried, upset with herself.

He gestured toward the gun. "Too slow, and we don't need one anyway." He pulled it out of her jeans and ges-tured in Annie's direction. "Go stay with her so she won't be frightened," he said. "I'll shoot the chains off."

"Wait," she said, holding her palm out. "Give me the gun back."

"What?"

"Just for a moment."

Mutely, he handed it to her. She jammed it back into the waistband of her jeans and shrugged off the backpack to the floor.

Dumbfounded, John watched her for a moment, and then stomped the floor to get her attention. "Annie's call-ing to you," he said. "She wants to know if everything is all right." He lifted an eyebrow quizzically.

"Everything's just fine, sweetie," she called, "Wait just a minute before you come in, all right? I'll tell you when it's okay."

Then she reached into the backpack and withdrew a small video camera, which she switched on.

"I am standing in the secret, hidden room of the house where my husband, John Halden, has been held hostage for almost three weeks." She gave the address of the house. Panning the camera over John, from his chains to the steel pole to the bucket, she left out nothing. Focusing to a close-up, she panned the camera over to the computer equipment. "This is where Parker Jefferson kept his surveillance receiving equipment which he has used to follow the movements of myself and my child in our own home, here in Rockport, Texas." She mentioned that address.

"What are you doing!" cried John. "We don't have time for this, Gypsy! Jefferson could be back any time now."

"Don't worry about that," she said, panning the walls of the room, including the makeshift door. "We've got a little time, and I'm gathering evidence." Finally, she switched off the camera, lay it on the bed, and withdrew a fingerprint kit from the backpack.

"Gypsy!" John touched her, shoulder. "Give me that gun now. We're getting out of here. *Now!*"

She turned to look at him. "I can do this, John. It won't take but just a few minutes. I intend to prove that Parker Jefferson held you hostage. I'm going to take every little shred of evidence I can, because as soon as he gets back, he's going to take this place apart and there will be no sign you were ever here."

"I don't care about that!" cried John. "I just want to get out of here!"

Still holding the fingerprint kit, she said, "Then I'll give you the gun and you can shoot off those chains and take Annie back to the house. I'll be along in just a minute."

"No way! Are you insane? I'd never leave you alone in this house, Gypsy!"

She gave him a long, level look. "Then you'd better help me collect this evidence while there's still time."

He stared back. For the first time in their marriage, Gypsy was taking control. After the ordeal of the past few weeks, it was the last thing he'd expected from her in all his fantasy-reunions. It was frustrating and confusing, but he didn't want to fight with her. Not now, anyway.

Dragging his fingers over his head with a rattle of chains, he said, "God almighty, woman! Do you have any idea whatsoever how *infuriating* you are?"

She gazed at him with eyes full of love. "Sure. You tell me all the time."

Finally, he heaved a heavy sigh. "Give me the god-damn gun. Then get out of the way before I *accidentally* shoot you."

She grinned. "I'll step out the door here and tell Annie you're all right."

As his wife walked out of the room, John had this sudden and unreasonable but powerful fear that he would never see her or Annie again. He shook it off. He'd been down that helpless road before.

Never again.

Eyeballing just how close he could aim the gun toward the chain without getting serious powder burns on his wrists or killing himself with a ricochet off the iron bedstead, he pulled back the hammer and slowly squeezed the trigger.

EIGHTEEN

WHILE JOHN FILMED HER WITH the video camera, Gypsy took Parker Jefferson's fingerprints from the telephone, the desk, and the steel pole, which she placed carefully in well-marked evidence containers held up to the camera for added insurance. John also filmed the bedstead with the missing brace and the battered wall by the bed, explaining about his foiled escape attempt as he did so.

Annie, subdued by her daddy's emaciated, bearded appearance and the full gravity of what had happened to him, sat cross-legged on the floor and watched with solemn eyes. She did not speak, and Gypsy worried about what might be going through the child's mind, but she could not take the time to deal with it. They would talk later.

Every move they made was stamped with a sense of urgency. Gypsy wasn't sure how much gas she'd siphoned out of Jefferson's car at four A.M. that morning. She didn't know if she'd taken out too much, so that he would run out before he got out of town, or if she hadn't taken out enough, enabling him to return sooner than she'd hoped.

And she didn't like to think what would happen if he'd actually thought to check the fuel indicator before leaving town.

There were so many variations, so many things that could happen, and she rushed much more than she would ever dare to do in a real criminal investigation. Still, she knew her business, and was able to gather a couple of very clear prints from the telephone receiver.

Finally, they packed up her crime kit and fled, grateful for the fog which helped to hide their escape out of the house and into the brooding trees.

Back in the temporary shelter of her mother's house, Gypsy led John to the bathroom, which she had thoroughly screened for bugs earlier. Annie did not want to be left out. She was naturally clingy and more traumatized by the day's events than Gypsy had expected. Finally she allowed the little girl to wait just outside the door with her Pooh-Bear and Barbie dolls so that they could talk in private but she could still be near to pound on the door if at any time she grew frightened.

"We don't have much time," she whispered. "What are we going to do now, John?"

"I don't know about you, but I know exactly what I am going to do."

She didn't like the expression on her husband's gaunt face. "What?"

"I'm going to track the man down and kill him with my bare hands."

"John, no—"

"It's all that's kept me going, Gypsy. That man has destroyed so many lives—yours, more than anyone's—and he's gotten away with it. My God, who knows what he's capable of doing?"

Impatiently, she shook her head.

"When I think of what he did to you, and what he's done to me," John continued, more urgently this time, "the hatred inside of me . . . it just threatens to consume me. I've got to do something, Gypsy, before it eats me alive."

Gypsy placed her hands on her hips, mimicking Annie. "So tell me, John. Where does it all end, huh?"

He shrugged.

"This man hated my father for some reason, and he killed him. He acted upon that hatred and rage with violence. If you do the same thing, you are not only the same as him, but you are continuing the circle. It will just go on and on and turn back upon itself."

"I don't care. I—"

She grasped his arms which hung at his sides, the chains still dangling toward the floor. "John! Listen to me. It's got to stop! The hatred, the killing . . . it's got to stop someplace, don't you understand? You can hear what I'm saying but you're just not listening!"

He gave her a baffled look. "I hear you, Gypsy. I just don't understand. I thought you, of all people, would want to see this man dead."

For a moment, she was thoughtful. "Let me put it this way. If this guy gets smushed by a Mack truck, I'll dance in the street next to his body. But John, if he dies at *your* hand, if *you* are the cause of his death—no matter how justified it may seem to you—then you are no better than he is."

He started to protest, and she said, "And where will it end, then? When you get gunned down during a police chase somewhere? When the state puts you to death with lethal injection for murdering an officer of the law? Keep in mind, you are still wanted for the Chief's murder. You'd be killed for killing, one way or the other."

"Are you saying we should turn the other cheek and *lo-o-ove* everybody?" He rolled his eyes, and the bitterness of his experience hardened his words. "That's a little lame for you, isn't it? You are hardly a child of the sixties."

"Maybe not, but I heard that we should love our neighbor as ourselves, that we should forgive someone who has wronged us seventy times seven." He started to turn away from her, and she took his arm. "I don't hate this man, John. I pity him, because he does not know what it means to be truly human. He knows hatred, but he does not know love. He does not know joy. He does not know the freedom of simply doing the right thing. He is a man without soul."

She stopped to think a moment, then said, "If you stoop to his level, you stand to lose all those things that set you apart from him. You stand to *become* him. After all your years of upholding the law as a cop, you should know this better than anyone . . . The more the killing and the violence continues, the less in touch we all are with our humanity."

He stared at her. "You really mean all that, don't you?"

"I've had a lot of time to think about it."

For a moment, he was quiet, then he said, " I don't know if I can accept everything you say, not right now anyway. But I do know that you are right about the death penalty in this state for killing a law enforcement officer, a penalty that has been enforced many times. If I were to kill Parker Jefferson, I'd be a fugitive for the rest of my life—for the rest of yours and Annie's lives—until they finally caught me."

He sat on the edge of the tub and looked up at her. "In fact, the more I think about it, the more I realize that there are ways to punish this man far, far worse than taking his life."

"Such as?"

"Such as *ruining* his life."

She sat on the toilet seat. "But we've collected all this evidence already. In the secret room. I'm proud of that, John. It's the first time in my life that I refused to hide from the Jigsaw Man."

Stroking her cheek softly, he said, "Video tapes are not always effective in court. It's too easy to doctor them. Besides, he can always claim you set the whole thing up."

"Not the fingerprints!" she cried, setting her jaw.

He shrugged. "Even those."

Crestfallen, she said, "Then why the hell didn't you just stop me?"

He grinned. "*Stop* you? Like I could stop a hurtling freight train."

She did not return his smile. "Still. This evidence will be worth something to somebody, I'm sure of it."

"Maybe so, " he said doubtfully. "It might buy us some time. But I'm thinking of something a little more damaging."

"Like what?"

He locked gazes with her. "Like a confession."

She laughed out loud. "Now *you're* the crazy one."

"Crazy like a fox," John said, getting to his feet and lifting her up. "I've got a plan—at least, the beginnings of one. We can work out the details later."

Gypsy looked at her husband, so haggard and thin, bearded and dirty, and she knew she had never loved him more.

Dash sensed something wrong as soon as he stepped foot in the door of the rental house. Though nothing appeared to be out of place, there was a void to the atmosphere, an emptiness different from its usual silence.

"No," he whispered under his breath. "She couldn't know—"

Gun drawn, he sprinted up the stairs. Glancing around the corner before quickly pulling back, he then headed down the hallway, repeating the movement, gun held low at his thigh, with each doorway, until he reached the last bedroom.

The doorway to the hidden room was standing ajar.

For a moment, he froze, then cautiously entered the makeshift room, even though he already knew that no one was there.

It was easy enough to tell that the chains had been shot off.

The breath momentarily sucked out of him, he collapsed onto the edge of the bed. *That bitch!* How could she have known? How could she have *possibly* known?

A flash of rage was quickly doused by the cold, wet fear of what was going to happen next.

He could be exposed.

Feeling suddenly very weak, Jefferson clenched his teeth to avoid throwing up. All his effort had been for nothing. *Nothing!*

It took a few moments for the shock to wear off and his brain to unscramble. Then the federal agent mentality took over and Jefferson dove for the phone, intending to tip off a statewide hunt for a cop-killer in this area.

Trembling hand in midair, he stopped short. Black powder filmed the receiver.

Fingerprints.

Jesus, they took fingerprints!

His focus clearing, he began to look more closely around the room. Fingerprints had been taken in several places.

The veins in his forehead began a slow, steady pulsing as his heart started pounding heavily in his chest.

What the— Confused, he began to wonder, *Were the cops already in on this? His enemies in the Bureau?*

Then something more chilling caught his eye and yanked his full attention front and center like nothing else could.

A crude, hand-drawn sign glared, slightly out of focus, from the video terminal where he had surveilled the woman's house. Someone had deliberately placed it within view of the camera hole in the living-room bookcase. It said:

WILL TRADE LETTERS FOR FREEDOM. DO NOTHING & WAIT TO HEAR FROM US OR WE WILL GO TO THE MEDIA. LOVE, JOHN. P. S. FUCK YOU.

Nineteen

THERE WAS SO LITTLE TIME and so much to do; every decision they made, every move, was torched with the fire of urgency. They had no idea what Jefferson's reaction to John's escape would be—if he called in the feds and the local police, they were almost sure to be caught before they could arrange a meeting with him.

It was John's sincere hope that their little "message" would prevent that from happening.

Still, there was little time to pack or even to think; John was operating almost solely on instinct and experience from his own days of tracking down runaway felons; mainly, he wanted to do the last thing Jefferson would expect. Consequently, they fled not to the open road or even to a different city, but to a run-down old fishing lodge on the water less than a mile from Jefferson's rental house.

There wasn't time to ditch the car, so they just parked it around back of the long, one-story edifice, which was constructed of ugly but hurricane-resistant cement blocks, painted a pukey green. A faint mildewy smell clung to everything and the furnishings were cheap fifties cast-offs. But it had a small kitchen—complete with plastic dishes and worn pots and pans—a sofa bed in the living room, an air conditioner that worked, cable TV, and a landlord who asked no questions when proffered cash.

And the view—if they were careful only to peek through the cracks in the vinyl drapes—was splendid.

It also had its own private fishing pier, sturdy and well-lighted extending a full half-mile into the bay. John hoped to be able to put it to good use in the plan which was formulating in his mind as he and Gypsy hurriedly carried in their things through the back door of the little apartment.

John knew better than to believe the illusion of safety that the little place provided, but there was something about being surrounded by his family—at long last—that made him think he could accomplish anything.

Once he had the toolbox from the back of the Blazer open in front of him on the Formica table in the kitchenette, it didn't take John long to figure a way out of the chains which still hung from his wrists. Considering the rush they were in, Gypsy had worked miracles with a few empty cardboard boxes and the supplies she'd stored away in her mother's house; while John labored at the chains, she loaded the small refrigerator and the cabinets.

He ate a whole bag of Oreos. With milk.

When the locks sprang open at last and the chains lay like dead snakes on the table, John yanked his arms away from them as if they were hot. His wrists felt weird without the weight of them. He reached for them, intending to jerk them up and hurl them across the room, when he felt a soft hand on the back of his neck and the vaguely flowery scent of his wife's perfume and, for the moment, his rage was soothed.

She said, "I brought some of your big T-shirts to sleep in. When I left Dallas, I mean. It made me feel close to you."

He reached up and covered her hand with his.

"Why don't you take a shower and you can change into one of those shirts," she said. "You'll have to wear the same jeans—I'm sorry."

He signed, "I don't suppose you packed any underwear?"

She stepped in front of him, dismay all over her face, and something about it struck him as hilarious. He started laughing, great gales of laughter, laughter that hurt his sides and made him weep. At first, she looked bewildered, and then she started laughing too.

It wasn't that funny, and they both knew it. Still, they guffawed.

But it was just so goddamned good to be alive, and together.

Gypsy broiled some chicken breasts in the old gas cooking stove, tossed a salad, and boiled some corn on the cob in butter. When the chicken was done, she stuck some brown-n-serve rolls under the broiler and set the rickety little table for three; it felt so odd, such a habitual, homey thing to do in this strange place and under these impossible circumstances.

Even weirder than that was the fact that none of this mattered; all that mattered to her was that her husband was *alive* and they were together. Nothing else—not even the danger they were in—seemed to make any difference.

He wasn't dead. And he wasn't a murderer, a liar, a cheat, and all the other things the media had insinuated. He was her John, just as he had always been, and he was here, now, with her. She couldn't seem to stop touching him, sneaking glances at him through her lashes, standing closer than she needed to. He was alive.

He was alive!

They could face whatever else happened. As long as they were together, they would figure out a way to fight it. They were going to find a way out of this; she just knew it.

He seemed to take forever in the shower and emerged at last, looking damp and exhausted and wan. But he had shaved, using her razor, and he gratefully wolfed down supper like a teenage boy.

Annie, hyperexcited by the day's events, hardly touched her meal, and giggled when her father ate most of her plate, too. He was very tender with the little girl, and while Gypsy washed the dishes, he splayed himself out over the living room floor and played Barbies with her. Every now and then, Gypsy would sneak glances at them, then sob a little, her tears dripping down into the dishwater. It was such a comical sight, and so dear, and she had come so very, very close to losing it forever.

Finally, they settled Annie into the sofa bed and let her watch TV until she fell asleep, while they sat at the kitchen table under the glaring overhead light and made plans together, signing and murmuring softly.

At some point in the evening, Gypsy caught her mind drifting. She found herself staring at her husband's masculine forearms, at the dark hairs and the big hands, and suddenly she wanted him with a fierceness that almost frightened her. She looked up into his eyes. They were red-rimmed with fatigue, and even as she gazed into them he blinked and rubbed them again with the heels of his hands.

"If I don't go to bed," he said, "I'll fall asleep right here."

Hiding her disappointment behind a quick smile, she nodded and turned away. Of course he was worn out.

She'd been selfish to think of anything other than his obviously desperate need for sleep.

John staggered off to bed and Gypsy busied herself, straightening things that didn't need straightening. Then she took a long shower, trying to forget the burning inside and the urgent need she felt to connect with her husband. Finally, she tiptoed into the bedroom, nude and hot from the shower, where he was sprawled all over the double bed, and crept in next to him. There wasn't much room for her, so she curled onto her side and stared into the darkness.

She tried very hard not to think about the Jigsaw Man.

Then she felt a caress along her arm, and she shivered.

Gooseflesh broke out all over her body. For a long moment, she lay perfectly still, savoring the thrill of her husband's touch, and then she turned to him, where he took her with the kind of passion that not only defies death, but laughs in its face.

Dash spent one whole nerve-wracked day disassembling all the surveillance equipment from both houses and removing all traces of John's recent captivity from the false room. When he was finished, there was nothing left in the room but a few boxes of junk he had found in the rental house attic, and the wallpaper had been permanently sealed over the door-cut in the fake wall.

Inwardly, he was screaming with frustration that he had lost control of the situation and was now at the mercy of two people who had the most to gain by destroying him.

He knew a simple phone call could spread a dragnet from which they could never escape, but as long as the letters were out there, he didn't dare do anything that could provoke them to turn the letters over to the media or the FBI or whoever they pleased.

He must have the letters!

He couldn't eat, couldn't sleep, couldn't do anything but obsess about his situation. At night, he paced the floors, talking to himself. The fake beard was beginning to itch, but he left it on anyway, fearful that his distinctive features might stand out in the small town; someone might remember him later.

The Dallas office was clamoring for his presence and his attention on a thousand duties associated with his job, but he took a few days vacation time—it would be a good cover in case his presence in Rockport was ever revealed. He could always say he'd only come down for a little fishing, some downtime while he awaited word from the White House. In fact, he'd used vacation time to build the secret room in the first place. There was a similar setup in Dallas. He'd done it as soon as the rumor mill began bandying his name about as a possible replacement for Kellerman. Gypsy and her family represented a skeleton in a closet Dash Jefferson had wanted to keep forever locked. During the past several months, a strong hunch had warned him that if he did not get his hands on those letters, they would come rattling out to haunt him when he least expected or needed them to.

And they had.

As far as the needs of the office in his absence, Dash knew that, when it came to the rank and file, the FBI generally considered each unit of the bureaucracy to be interchangeable; no one was supposed to be indispensable. In his absence, the ASAC (assistant special agent in charge) would supposedly take care of things. Since he was often away from the office on business anyway, he wasn't worried about it.

But he knew he had to get this thing under control soon, before it ate him alive.

One frantic message finally reached him from Doris. The White House had called. President Clinton had definitely chosen Parker "Dash" Jefferson to be appointed as director of the FBI. It would soon be leaked to the press, and Dash had been invited to the White House for a press conference on the day the President was to make his formal announcement, to be held in two days.

Then would come the Congressional confirmation process, sure to be a rubber stamp, unless . . .

It was all so breathtakingly close! He could see it, he could *smell* it . . . so excruciatingly near at hand.

And the only thing, the *only* thing standing in his way was one deaf woman from out of the mists of his past . . . and those letters. The goddamned letters.

He should have burned them the first time he set eyes on them. He damn sure never should have trusted his brother with them.

Thirty-some-odd-year-old letters, letters that could crack open history like a ripe melon, and lay it bare for the whole world to see . . . what a fool, what a blind, stupid fool Parker Jefferson really was.

Funny, he thought with bitter ruefulness, *If I'd acted on those letters in the right manner in the first place, I could have changed history, and nobody would have ever known.*

His own brother would probably still be alive, and Anna. None of those dominoes would have fallen.

He'd have been a hero, though. Just like he always wanted.

"Tell me about the letters," said Gypsy as she lay entangled in her husband's arms in the pre-dawn hours of Gulf-gray light and mystic silence. Her head rested on John's chest, and she could feel the *thu-thump* of her husband's heart against her cheek; nothing could be more soothing or reassuring to her.

His chest rose and fell in a long sigh.

"Who wrote them?" she persisted.

After a moment, he reached his arms around her and held his hands in front of her face so she could read the name he spelled out with his fingers:

L-E-E-H-A-R-V-E-Y-O-S-W-A-L-D

IV

Show me a hero and I will write you a tragedy.

—F. SCOTT FITZGERALD

VI

TWENTY

GYPSY SAT STRAIGHT UP IN bed and stared at her husband. "Are you kidding?" she said aloud.

He shook his head.

Too thunderstruck to think what to say next, she pulled the sheet up around her naked breasts and waited.

"Some of this I got from the Chief," John said. "The bare-bones details. A lot of it I got from good old-fashioned library research after he talked to me, and the rest I filled in with common sense."

"Superior intelligence," she said, giving him a ghost of a smile.

"Kidneys," he replied, tapping the side of his head. For a long moment, he stared at his hands. Then he said, "Have you ever stopped to wonder what might have happened if the Secret Service—or even just the FBI—had known ahead of time that Oswald planned to kill Kennedy?"

"Sure. They could have stopped him."

"Exactly. They could have prevented the assassination of the President of the United States."

"Lyndon Johnson might never have been President."

"Kennedy may not have escalated the Vietnam War like Johnson did."

"So there wouldn't have been all those anti-war demonstrations."

"Maybe not."

"Oliver Stone would have had to think of something else to make a movie about."

He grinned, then grew sober. "Who knows what would have been different."

"You could go on forever, thinking about it."

"Right."

"So. What does that have to do with Parker Jefferson?"

John shifted position in bed, pulling his underwear on and flipping the sheet over his legs, in case Annie should walk in on them. "What do you know about Lee Harvey Oswald?" he asked.

She shrugged. "Classic loner. Defected once to the then-Soviet Union. Married a Russian wife. Worked at the School Book Depository. Not much."

"Well, he was a certified nutcase. Got court-martialed while he was in the Marine Corps for shooting himself in the elbow when his unit prepared to ship out to the South China Sea. Served time in the brig and came out even weirder than he was when he went in. By that time, he was already a loud supporter of Fidel Castro. He left the service early and they were pretty much glad to get rid of him."

"Is that when he defected?"

"Tried to. Even the Russians didn't want him. See, here's the thing: Oswald was a letter writer. He was forever spouting off to embassies and various government officials, both in our country and in theirs. Just an all-around nuisance and general weirdo. In fact, when they tried to deny him Russian citizenship, he slashed his wrists."

"I didn't know that!"

"Yeah. Actually got thrown into the mental ward of a Russian hospital. They didn't know what else to do with him, so they gave him a job and an apartment and hoped that would make him happy."

"But it didn't."

"Not for long. See, what Oswald was looking for was attention. He thought he'd be this big-time hero in Russia, especially after he offered to tell them everything he knew from his stint in the Marine Corps. He was expecting newspapers, TV—the works. He was even planning to write a book."

"But they weren't interested."

"Not really. Oswald made them nervous. There was tremendous tension between the two superpowers at that time. They didn't know what the United States would make of this whole situation and they didn't really want to find out. So they just made him fairly prosperous by Soviet standards and hoped it would satisfy him. Even let him marry a Russian woman."

"But it wasn't enough."

"He got bored. The factory was drab, and Russia didn't sport all the sinful nightspots you'd find in the U.S. at the time. Before long, he started pestering the U.S. embassy to let him return home— at their expense."

"You're kidding!"

"No kidding. He was just a little shit, really."

"So he came back, and . . ."

"Again, he expected this great folderol from the press. Figured everybody'd want to interview him."

"But nobody did."

"Well, the FBI did. But no media."

"What happened next?"

"He bounced around from job to job and house to house for a year or so. Sending off letters to U.S. based Communist newspapers. Started buying guns from a mail-order house."

Gypsy rubbed her arms vigorously. "I'm getting goose bumps," she said.

"There was a right-wing political figure living in Dallas at the time; man by the name of General Edwin Walker. Walker was a leading advocate for militant action against communists, civil rights activists—any kind of liberal, in fact. He had a thing going called Operation Midnight Ride, a sort of anti-Castro crusade with a pretty obvious reference to the Ku Klux Klan."

"I'm getting confused."

"Hang in there with me. Okay. To make a long story short—in April of 1963, Oswald stalked, planned, and attempted an assassination of General Walker."

"What? Did the FBI know? Wait—" she smacked her hand upside her head. "Of course they didn't know, or they'd have arrested him."

"Right. They knew somebody tried to shoot the general through his dining room window as he sat figuring his taxes, but they didn't realize it was Oswald until after the Kennedy assassination, when they went through his house and found evidence for the Walker shooting."

Gypsy was silent for a moment, thinking. "Was Oswald trying to be some kind of left-wing hero or something?"

John shrugged. "Who can say what he was trying to do? But his widow now says that he expected to be caught and written up in all the papers, and seemed disappointed that they didn't realize who had shot at the general."

"Not to mention the fact that he missed."

"Well, yeah, and that's where good old Parker Jefferson comes in."

"I was wondering if he was ever going to figure into this saga."

"Patience, my dear Watson. Patience." He smiled at her.

Impulsively, she leaned over and kissed him, just because he was there and she could do it.

"Don't distract me," he teased. "Now, where was I?"

"Shooting at General Walker."

"Right. Okay. Over the next six months, Oswald was a busy boy. He walked around for a while in downtown Dallas wearing a sign around his neck saying *Viva Fidel!* You know, subtle stuff like that."

"A *sign* around his neck?"

He grinned. "Then he traveled to New Orleans and tried to start a branch of a communist organization—writing letters right and left, here and there, announcing his intentions. Stood on street corners and passed out *Hands Off Cuba* leaflets."

"I knew about that. I've seen pictures."

"Right. He tried his best to get to Cuba—again, he must have thought old Fidel would embrace him with open arms and set him up with medals and women or something, but he only got as far as the Russian and Cuban embassies in Mexico City."

"Why wouldn't they let him go to Cuba?"

"Because, as I explained earlier—were you listening?"

She smirked at him.

"Most emissaries of the Evil Empire knew a nutcase when they saw one, not like our own government representatives. "

"Well, it's a free country, you know. You can be crazy here if you want to." She was laughing.

"But can you write letters threatening to assassinate somebody?"

Gypsy stopped laughing. "Say again?"

"When Oswald got back, the FBI was beginning to wonder about him. They sent a couple of agents to question his wife, but those same agents claim they were not made aware of his Mexico City trip."

She shook her head. "Bureacracies."

"Their little visit pissed Oswald off. He left a note at the FBI Dallas office for one of the agents, threatening to blow up the Dallas Police Department and the FBI field office in Dallas if they didn't leave Marina alone."

Gypsy's mouth suddenly grew very dry. "Those agents . . ."

"One of them filed his notes away. They've only been released for public viewing in recent years. The threats were hidden from the public in order not to embarrass the Bureau."

She was watching her husband very closely. "And the other agent?"

"He was a rookie. A kid, as eager to please as a puppy. In a hurry to make a name for himself. He had a theory that Oswald had been the shooter in the Walker case."

"Jefferson?"

John nodded. "According to what Jefferson's brother, Mike, told his old partner Chief Strickland way back in the early seventies, Jefferson had a hunch about Oswald. As early as October of 1963, he was convinced Oswald was going to try again to kill Walker. In the days leading up to the assassination of President Kennedy, Agent Jefferson received two letters from Lee Harvey Oswald, letters threatening to do something drastic, something so momentous the FBI would never recover from it, if they didn't leave him and his family alone."

"So he didn't specifically threaten to assassinate President Kennedy."

"Not in so many words. But Jefferson had no doubt from the tone and content of the letters that Oswald was going to kill *somebody,* and he was convinced it was General Walker. See, it was Walker's people who had spit on Adlai Stevenson during his trip to Dallas that fall, Walker's people who had taken out those hostile ads in the Dallas papers against Kennedy—they were very, very visible in those days leading up to Kennedy's visit. Since they were so blatantly anti-communist and anti-Castro, Agent Jefferson felt sure Walker was going to be Oswald's target. Especially since the first attempt had failed."

"Why didn't he show the letters to his superiors?"

"That, my dear, is the sixty-four-thousand-dollar question. What he did was, he followed Walker around. I don't even know if his colleagues at the Bureau knew what he was doing, but I doubt that his supervisor would have okayed such a plan since they were all busy getting ready for the Kennedy visit. Anyway, apparently—and this is the guessing part—he thought he could spot Oswald in the crowd, maybe somehow stop him, and be a big hero to J. Edgar Hoover, who hated communists probably more than anybody else in the country. By saving the life of the biggest right-winger in the country next to Hoover himself, he'd be guaranteed some kind of promotion—maybe even to the exalted seat of government itself."

"The seat . . ."

"Headquarters in Washington. Pay attention."

She smirked at him again, then asked, "Why didn't the guy follow Oswald around instead?"

With a heavy sigh, John shook his head and said, "Why

indeed? Why didn't he do what he was supposed to do in the first place? I can only guess inexperience, Gypsy. Just plain rookie stupidity combined with blind-dumb-and-deaf ambition."

"Question."

"I am here to serve." He bowed.

"If Oswald hated Walker, and Walker hated Kennedy, then why would Oswald kill Kennedy?"

"You know, that's interesting. In one of the studies I was reading about Oswald, he once said that he admired Kennedy."

"You're kidding."

"Well, don't forget, the guy was a nut. That's for starters. Nothing a certified nutcase does has to make sense. But I think that basically, it was a matter of sheer opportunity, for one thing, and for another, Kennedy was a much, much greater target. More prestige, see, in Oswald's twisted little mind."

"Opportunity . . . you mean the motorcade route?"

"Exactly. See, they found evidence in Oswald's home that he had given extensive planning to the assassination attempt on General Walker, but there was no such evidence that he'd gone to such lengths to plan the assassination of the president. It seems the guy was a cheapskate, and one of the things he did at work every day was read the day-old newspapers his coworkers had bought, read, and discarded."

"And the motorcade route was published in one of the Dallas newspapers."

"Right. A couple of days before Kennedy arrived. It is believed that Oswald saw the motorcade route in the paper, like, the day before. He had to go to a friend's house to dig out the gun he had stored there. That morning, he left his wedding band in an ashtray on his dresser, along with about a hundred bucks. He didn't figure he'd be coming back. Either they'd catch him after the shooting, or he'd be killed in the attempt. Didn't seem to bother him either way."

"So. He must have left the threatening letters for Jefferson just a day or two before Kennedy was killed. No earlier."

"Probably not."

"Okay. The president is killed. Jefferson's got these incriminating letters. What does he do next?"

"He sent the letters to his brother Mike for safekeeping. Couldn't bring himself to destroy them—they were just too valuable, even then."

Gypsy ticked nine years off on her fingers. "Daddy was killed in 1972."

"That's when his brother, Dash Jefferson, started hanging around your mother again and bothering her. He'd been sent to Dallas for a few months to help out on something or other. Anyway, nobody knows what happened, but it could be that your dad threatened to go public with those letters, and Jefferson freaked. Beat his brother to death."

After a moment, Gypsy said, "That would have been about the time the Warren Commission report came out."

"Actually, no. The Warren Commission report had been out for some time by then, and of course, there were conspiracy theories all over the place since the FBI documents were sealed."

"Okay. Let me think this through. If letters from Oswald to an FBI agent, dated just days before the assassination and threatening some sort of violent act, were released to the media, then even if the publication of those letters would absolutely lay to rest all those conspiracy theories that bothered Hoover so much—still the agent to whom the letters were addressed would look sinister, or at the very least, amazingly irresponsible."

"Exactly. And remember—J. Edgar Hoover was still alive in 1972, still ruling with an iron fist. Hoover had been especially determined that Oswald be portrayed as the lone assassin by the FBI. He rushed the investigation and announced Oswald as the shooter just hours after the assassination. If Hoover found out that Oswald had actually *warned* the FBI that he was going to do something momentous, just days before Kennedy's scheduled—and controversial—trip to Dallas, and that the FBI agent in question did nothing on that information, didn't even pass it on to the Secret Service, then think how bad the entire organization would look as a result."

"And think how short-lived would have been the career of that selfsame agent. Shit. No wonder my ambitious uncle hid the evidence."

He stared at her. "It blows my mind, thinking of him as related to you."

"Think how I feel."

For a while, neither spoke. Finally, John said, "So."

"So," said Gypsy. "Now here he is, about to be announced the next director of the FBI."

"A man who not only hid valuable evidence which could have changed the history of this country, but murdered to keep it hidden."

Gypsy felt suddenly very tired, and very, very sad. She met her husband's eyes and said, "A true hero for our times."

TWENTY-ONE

TWO DAYS. JEFFERSON HAD TWO days to find and dispose of the Halden family before they brought ruin and devastation upon him. He became increasingly worried that they were not in this alone, but had recruited help from any of a number of sources, most particularly his enemies, who did not want to see him appointed director. Repeatedly, he checked the house for bugs and kept a watchful eye on the streets, front and back, for any sign of surveillance vehicles. He could never be too careful.

Skin problems forced him to remove the beard, and he was so paranoid about being recognized that he never left the house in daylight after that. Even as he paced and fretted, he knew he'd done all he could.

Now there was nothing for him to do but wait.

Pacing one end of the shabby house to another with restless nervousness, pausing at each window to glance outside, he thought about growing up in a small, dusty Texas town miles from nowhere, with nothing to do and nobody to do it with. Everybody knew everybody else, and everybody's parents had been born and raised there too, as had *their* parents. And nobody—except Dash Jefferson—seemed to want to change that fact. They graduated high school, married their high school sweethearts, went to work in the family business, and started families of their own. Their kids went to the same elementary school they'd gone to—sometimes even had the same principal.

To Dash, it was like being incarcerated in prison, with no possibility of parole.

Dash did his time like a true lifer, minding his own business and staying out of trouble. At home, he barely existed. Mike was the boy wonder, his parents' pride and joy, the town football hero and high school golden boy. Since they never seemed to notice anyway, Dash quit competing with his brother early on, making average grades in school and staying away from the football field.

There were only two things that kept Dash going in those days . . . well, three: the local cinema and Saturday afternoon G-man movies; running track; and Anna Powell. In the movies, he could lose himself—or what there was of himself. Sitting in the darkened theater with a big tub of popcorn—extra butter—he could imagine himself as one of those square-jawed, straight-arrow investigators who never stopped until they had their man. Most families were acquiring television sets in those days and kids were staying away from the movies to watch cartoons at home. Not Dash. He was there every Saturday without fail, paying his fifty cents and eating his popcorn. One day, he knew, he would get out of this jail and go be one of those men.

When he wasn't at the movies, he was at the track. The dirt oval around the football field was the only place where Dash Jefferson could excel—all on his own, and in his own way. When the starter pistol cracked, it was as if Dash himself would fade away and a different person would inhabit his soul, someone who touched his feet with fire. The crowds would blur and all he would know was the spring of his feet and the pumping of his heart until he broke through the ribbon. Only then would he become aware of the explosive pain in his chest, the burning in his lungs. Sometimes he would collapse from the effort; sometimes he would vomit in the grass. But always, always . . . he won.

His parents never managed to make one of his meets.

But Anna was there. Anna was always there. He'd be able to look up at last and see her on her feet, cheering him, the wind tousling her dark hair all around her face and her beautiful smile shining through.

When he ran, he ran for her.

After the house fire that killed his parents, Dash was praised in the newspaper for being a hero and pulling his brother Mike from the flames. For once, he had achieved the recognition he always craved, but it was a dark victory. Sometimes, when he'd look into his brother's eyes . . . he would think that maybe Mike knew . . . but he could never be sure.

As soon as he got out of the hospital, Mike dropped out of school—in the middle of his senior year, no less—and joined the army. Dash remained in the hospital for months. In all that time, Anna stayed loyal to Dash, visiting him in the hospital through all his surgeries and skin grafts. But they didn't know as much about reconstructive surgery in those days forty years ago, and Dash soon became aware of a difference in Anna.

He blamed himself. Of course, he must look hideous to her; she must be repulsed by the sight of his face; he could understand that. She insisted that was not the case. She even accepted his engagement ring.

Everything should have been great then. Mike was out

of the picture; Dash had the most beautiful girl in the school on his arm; and he didn't even have to put up with his parents anymore. He was so grateful to Anna for staying with him in spite of his ugliness; he felt so blessed, so fortunate.

If only he could have figured out what was *wrong*. He knew there was something, but Anna kept denying it. There was just a . . . coolness about her, a dampening of the fire.

He thought it might be his running. After he recovered enough from his burns to return to school he no longer won any races; in fact, he had trouble even finishing them. Eventually he dropped out of track. School was harder than he'd expected. Granted, he was regarded as a hero, but he could see kids staring at him out of the corner of his eyes, pointing and whispering, looking away when he turned around. Even the teachers did it.

He had been so proud of Anna in those days. She'd walk straight down the hall with him at school, her head held high, making certain everybody knew she was his girl and proud of it.

Little liar!

The whole thing was a lie! The whole goddamned thing!

God, how could anybody be so blind and so stupid? What an *idiot* he had been!

He just *thought* Mike was out of the picture. He damn well should have known different. What a fool she made of him, in front of the whole school. The whole town.

Two years after Mike left town, he came back, and the very next day Anna was gone, Dash's engagement ring handed over to her mother. Eloped with big brother Mike, the golden boy.

Naturally.

All those days when Anna was walking down the hall at school with him, she was sitting in study hall, writing letters to Mike. Falling in love with him, just like everybody else.

She'd only stayed with Dash out of pity.

Pity!

Even after all these years, the bitterness galled him.

He'd done it, though. He'd shown them all. And now, here he was, about to become director of the FBI.

Too damn bad they couldn't be around to see it. He'd have loved to rub their smug faces in it.

One thing, though. He'd learned a good lesson, and he'd learned it well: Never trust *anybody*.

People were liars. Liars and selfish bloodsuckers. Everybody was out after himself or herself and what they could get. Users. He'd spent more than thirty years making sure he never got used again, and it had served him well.

He wasn't about to blow it now.

Pacing, pacing, his thoughts running amok through his mind, Dash paused yet again to peer out the window, and his heart stumbled. A white piece of paper fluttered from beneath the windshield wiper of the Buick.

Bolting outdoors, peering left and right, he yanked at the note. It read:

MEET ME AT THE END OF PIER #1530 AT MIDNIGHT TONIGHT TO DISCUSS THINGS. GYPSY.

A light drizzle was falling as Gypsy stood—too nervous to sit—at the end of the pier and waited for the Jigsaw Man. The waves were choppy, and a moist wind tugged at her hair. In spite of the closeness of the atmosphere and the tension of the occasion, the fresh rainy air felt good after being cooped up in the little apartment with a seven-year-old for more than two days. *Still,* Gypsy thought, *if I had a choice, I'd jump into the water right now and swim forever.*

She hadn't expected to be this scared. After all, she and John had rehearsed the encounter that afternoon, but she hadn't counted on the changes that took place after darkness fell. For someone who depended so much on her eyes to make up for the deficit in her hearing, the cloud-curtained night and heavy atmosphere were a blindness of sorts.

Even the boards on the pier seemed to have vanished, only coming into view directly under the night-fishing lights which were strung along, straight and even, every fifty feet or so, before disappearing on shore. The faint mist gave them a soft focus and wrapped her body in a velvet chill.

There was no one about.

She didn't know if she would be able to stand still and face down the Jigsaw Man.

The murderer of her parents, the thief of her hearing.

The phantom of her nightmares.

The things she had told John back in the bathroom of the old house the day she'd rescued him were high ideals, to be sure, but she didn't know if she would be able to walk the walk nearly as well as she could talk the talk.

The damp, splintery boards begin to vibrate in rhythm with a man's footfalls.

Heart pounding, she grasped a wooden rail support. It took all the courage she could muster just to turn around. She was startled to see that the Jigsaw Man was halfway down the pier already, approaching at a quick clip, in and out of the shadows like a specter, in and out.

He could kill her so easily, she knew.

Her heart was clanging about in her ribcage like a pin-ball in a game machine. She realized how completely trapped she was; there was nowhere to go.

He came to a stop just beneath the last light. An electric shock of recognition gripped her body. He did not stand still; he rocked on his heels slightly, and the effect was an almost macabre flashback to the first night she ever saw him, blinking up at his backlit jigsaw face through the swarming dark dots and the high-pitched ringing in her ears as his mouth moved at her like a fish but she could not hear.

She had run back then.

Now she was forced to stay.

Gypsy felt very faint and took a few deep breaths to stabilize herself. *She must not blow it now!*

Before she could say anything, he withdrew a small de-vice from his pocket which resembled a transistor radio with a short antenna. Pointing the antenna in front of him, he began poking it into every nook and cranny of the pier. A staticky noise emitted from the device.

Finally, he pointed the antenna toward her shoes and worked his way up her body.

Even though he did not touch her, she found herself shivering and clasped her hands together to prevent it from showing.

When he reached her head, the device set off such a fierce feedback squeal that even Gypsy could hear it. She swayed back in instant pain, grasping her left ear.

"What is it?" he screamed. She could tell he was screaming at her from the veins popping out in his neck. She could even hear him slightly. *"Where's the bug?"*

"It's not a bug!" she yelled back. "It's my hearing aid!" She pulled it from her ear to show him.

"Oh." Subdued, he stuffed the bug-detecting device

back into his shirt pocket. "Open your jacket," he ordered, "and let me see if you are armed."

Dreading the thought of his hands on her body if he should feel the need to frisk her, she opened the jacket and even pulled her shirt loose from her jeans, pirouetting before him so that he could see for himself that she was unarmed.

Giving her a cursory nod, he pulled a pair of binoculars from around his neck and peered out into the quilt-like dark. Finally, he appeared to come to some sort of uneasy satisfaction. "Okay. We'll talk." Glancing over his shoulder as he replaced the binoculars, he stepped back, slightly, into the dark.

She did not. Mouth so dry she could hardly move her tongue, Gypsy said, "You will have to speak clearly and distinctly and not look away when you are talking to me."

"I refuse to shout."

"There is no need. But you can't mumble or I won't understand you. And you need to move closer to the light."

From the suspicious look on his face, it was obvious he did not like the conditions. After a moment, he gave a reluctant nod and took a small step closer to the light.

"I'm ready to make you an offer," he said.

Stifling a shudder at just the very sight and smell of him, just his *presence* so close to her, she said nothing. Her mind was racing.

Maybe John had been wrong to trust her with this. Every instinct, every nerve ending in her body screamed at her to flee. She was too frightened, too horrified by this man to think clearly. It was all she could do not to brush past him and run blindly down the pier. Anything to get away.

She forced herself to watch his lips closely, to listen carefully. Her heart was pounding against her breastbone and it was hard to breathe.

She tried not to think of her mother.

"You give me the letters, and I'll give you $100,000 in untraceable cash and a boat passage from the Rockport harbor to any coastal South American country which does not extradite. Your choice."

"How do I know I can trust you?" she asked.

He smirked. "And how do I know I can trust *you*?"

They glared at one another. It *was* a little easier, it occurred to her, being all grown up now, and no longer a petrified little girl. Finally, she inclined her head in agreement and said, "Fine."

He studied her face. "I need some time to get all this lined up."

"You must stand under the light, because I can't read your lips."

He shook his head. There was a brief stand-off between them. Finally, glancing nervously all around, he stepped into the light.

"I need some time to get all this lined up," he repeated.

"When?"

"Midnight tomorrow. At Rockport harbor. Look for the *Sink or Swim*. The skipper will be ready to take you wherever you want to go. Bring the letters and I will have the cash."

"Tomorrow night, then." A strange, reckless bravado suddenly possessed her. With a defiant lift to her chin, she added, "If you set us up—the way you set John up for the Chief's murder—we'll see to it that the whole damn country hears about your blatant disregard for FBI procedure, your arrogant attempt to hide your mistakes, and the murderous things you did to cover them up."

His eyes narrowed in alarm, but it was too late, she couldn't stop herself and went on in a rush. "We'll release Oswald's letters to the press—I should think they'd be very excited to receive them. The president would be interested too, I bet. I hear he's squeamish about being associated with another scandal."

His face flushed. She was beginning to make out the scar-lines that had paralyzed her with such merciless terror as a child and through many a heart stopping nightmare. The thin white patches in his skin burned crimson.

She gave him a hateful smile. Maybe that was it, then. Maybe she was moving past the fear and straight into hatred. "How does it feel," she asked wickedly, "to know you could have prevented the assassination of President John F. Kennedy, and *you blew it?*"

For a long, terrible moment, he stared through her with deadened eyes. Instantly, Gypsy regretted her impulsiveness. This was a very dangerous man, and she must never, ever forget it.

When he answered her, it was in a fast, incomprehensible mumble. But Gypsy felt certain he said, *"Don't fuck with me, girl. I'll cut your heart out."* Her eyes widened.

He turned to go.

Trying valiantly not to stutter, knowing she must be mad, Gypsy had to ask him one more thing.

She had to.

"Why did you kill my daddy?"

He froze. Then, turning slowly back, he stared at her with unblinking eyes. The eyes of a snake.

"And why did you kill my mama?"

With slow, deliberate movements, he folded his arms across his chest and said nothing.

"You murdered Chief Strickland, too, and you took my husband hostage and framed him for it. My God—why?"

He raised a hand—she wasn't sure why—but something about the gesture triggered a rush of passionate grief and she found herself screaming at him, *"Why? Why? WHY?"*

Gypsy felt her throat closing and she choked back tears, ashamed at her outburst but desperate, nonetheless, for some kind of explanation that would make sense of the whole long tragedy of her life. Wild emotion threatened to undo her, making her appear hysterical in the presence of this unfeeling man. With herculean efforts, she brought herself under control, all but the trembling.

After a long excruciating moment, he shrugged and, as if it were an afterthought, simply said, "They got in my way."

In that instant, Gypsy thought she understood what true, core-deep hatred really meant.

She wanted to kill him, hurt him, make him suffer. Avenge the deaths of all the innocents he had heartlessly slain. Maybe then she could have some sort of closure. Maybe then she could sleep nights.

More than anything, she wanted to make him sorry for what he had done, but she knew that wasn't possible.

But the thoughts and impulses that raged through Gypsy were foreign to her. She was a gentle soul, after all. Revenge was not her way. Not like this.

I will not stoop to his level, she forced herself to remember. *I will not let hatred run my life. It all stops here.*

With inscrutable eyes, he studied her face for a long time, almost as if he were memorizing it. His gaze lingered on her hair, curling madly now in the damp.

A shudder possessed her, but she did not look away.

At last, he said, "I loved your mother, you know." Then, pivoting like a soldier on parade, he strode briskly away, the vibrations fading behind him.

Shaking so violently her teeth chattered, she watched his receding back until he no longer looked like anything more to her than just a man.

TWENTY-TWO

"SO, EXPLAIN TO ME AGAIN why we've got a man named Fancy Fingers coming here to our very own home-away-from-home—a precarious hideaway at best, I might remind you."

Gypsy's tone was teasing, but her face betrayed her anxiety. Sunken half-moons exaggerated her dark eyes. Worry lines knit her forehead, and her normally glossy, thick hair was pulled back to the nape of her neck in a tired, dull ponytail. John knew that her meeting with the person she'd known all her life as the Jigsaw Man had taken a lot out of her. Her courage moved him deeply, and he was very proud of her, but he could see that emotional and physical exhaustion was making her raw and edgy.

John, on the other hand, felt energized. By seizing control of the situation from Jefferson, John now felt much the same way he did when working deep undercover; every move he made was charged with a certain intensity, and his own craft, cunning, and experience determined that most of his choices would be right ones.

Still, he wasn't up against some half-witted drug dealer

or lower-echelon gangster. This was an adversary not only clever and cruel, but powerful. And desperate.

Nothing made a man more dangerous than desperation.

Gypsy was right. He wasn't just doing a job, here. He was risking the lives of his family.

But what choice did they have?

"Come here," he said, patting the edge of the bed where he sat propped up against the wall. She crawled over next to him and leaned her weary head against his shoulder. He held her that way for a while, wishing he could talk to her while holding her and maybe reassure her that way. Finally, he gave her a gentle push and she sat up, watching him as he spoke.

"You've heard me talk about Mooch Myers."

She nodded. "Your best informant."

Grinning, he shook his head. "No, no, no. How many times do I have to tell you, dear? Cops don't have informants. Only FBI agents have informants. Cops have *snitches.*"

Her mouth smiled but her worried eyes did not.

"Anyway. Mooch is my best snitch, on account of how I saved his ass when he was the wheelman for a B and E that went bad."

"The owner surprised the other two guys, and one of them shot him."

"Right. Which boosted their little crime right on up there to capital murder. Mooch didn't even realize anything had happened until they came hauling ass out of the building."

"So you got the DA to cop a plea for Mooch if he'd roll over on his buddies."

"Even better. I told each one of his cohorts that the *other* one had ratted them out."

"So they were too busy threatening each other's mothers to think much about Mooch."

"Exactly. And he got out in six months and they're still in."

"I assume you are referring to the Big House?"

"The joint."

"Legal incarceration."

He smiled at her, but her returning smile still did not reach her eyes. "Okay. So I'm the one in trouble now, which sort of makes Mooch and me brothers, if you know what I mean."

"Soulmates."

"In a manner of speaking. So I called up old Mooch, who has been following my various publicized crimes with great interest."

"You mean Mooch reads the paper?"

"Absolutely not. But he hangs out down at the local Stop 'n' Rob and catches all the latest gossip."

"I see."

"Anyway, Mooch was delighted to hear from me and understood exactly what I meant when I said, *'Hey man, I didn't do it.'*"

"It's nice to have friends in low places."

"I told Mooch I needed the services of a first-rate forger, and it just so happens that our very own Mooch Myers has an uncle living right down here in Sparkling City By the Sea—"

"I assume you mean Corpus Christi."

"—The very same. Now, Uncle Fancy Fingers is of the old school of crime. From back in the good old days when there was honor among thieves. He's never used a weapon in any of his, er, jobs, and he has never hurt anybody."

"At least, not physically."

"And he stays away from them nasty drugs, but he has been known to take a nip or two."

"For medicinal purposes."

"And his rheumatiz does act up on occasion."

"Like when it rains."

"Or the sun shines."

"And he's coming here to our home."

"If you wanna call this home." He stretched out his hand to indicate the pea-green cement block walls, the flimsy furniture, the faint odor of mildew.

The light bantering expression faded from Gypsy's face as suddenly as firelight doused in water. "We don't have very much money to give him," she said. "And how do we know he can do the job? And what makes us think that it will work, even if he does, and—"

John put a finger to his lips to silence her, then folded her back into his arms and rocked her, like a baby, until the tension sagged from her body.

Even then, the fear never left her eyes.

Gypsy's heart plummeted when the grizzled old black man stepped through the back door and into their little kitchenette. She didn't know what she had been expecting, but certainly not this. Body odor and a faint whiff of cheap whiskey wafted behind him as he stood beneath the glaring overhead light, his short-brimmed straw fedora clutched in a gnarled, shaking hand. His faded brown jacket was frayed at the collar and cuffs, his white shirt stained and missing a button. He was the blackest black man she had ever seen, and the whites of his bloodshot eyes were actually yellow. When he smiled and shook John's hand, she counted three teeth missing.

Glancing around the small apartment nervously, he

licked his lips and said, "I never done nothin' for no cops before. I ain't no snitch."

John gave the man a solemn nod. "I understand, Mr. Myers. But right now, I'm not a cop. Right now I'm a man trying to save my family." He glanced over toward the nearby living area, where Annie sat swaddled in Barbies and Pooh-Bear, watching TV.

The old man turned his silver-haired head toward Annie and watched her for a long moment. "I gots a grandbaby 'bout that age," he said.

"Please, sit down, Mr. Myers," said Gypsy, standing back a bit to spare herself his pungent aroma. He pulled out a vinyl-covered kitchen chair and sat down at the Formica table. Groping through his pockets, he finally produced a grimy, much-folded piece of copy paper. "I wonted to brang the book," he explained, "but they wouldn't let me take it out since I didn't have no liberry cahd."

Gypsy exchanged a glance with her husband. They were both thinking the same thing: *He could have stolen it.* She was beginning to understand what John had meant by the old-style of criminal.

As he slowly unfolded the page, his hands shook so hard that the paper rattled. He licked his lips again. "You wouldn't happen to have a little shot o' Jim Beam, would you? I need sometin' to settle my hands."

Glancing once at Gypsy, John got up and rooted through the overhead cabinets in the kitchen. "Gosh, I'm sorry, Mr. Myers," he said. The old man's face fell. "All I've got is this Wild Turkey." He withdrew an unopened bottle of the expensive whiskey.

Myers's face took on the glow of a penitent at prayer. Gazing at the bottle with rapturous eyes, his voice squeaked as he said, "I couldn't axe it of you, Mr. Halden. Dat be da good stuff."

"Call me John." He held out the bottle and a plastic tumbler. "And it's all yours, Mr. Myers."

Myers's face broke into a beatific, toothy grin. "And my name be Fancy." He took the bottle from John and cracked open the seal. An orgasmic shiver passed over his body. As he sloshed a couple of fingers into the plastic tumbler, Gypsy stifled a feeling of profound despair, and tried very, very hard not to panic.

She looked over at John. Surreptitiously, his hands close to his chest, he signed, *"Trust me."*

The Wild Turkey bottle stood half empty. Wadded sheets of discarded paper littered the top of the kitchen table and spilled over onto the floor. Annie was asleep. John took a sip of the smooth brew and watched with fascination a true professional at work.

"The book at the liberry showed some letters Oswald had wrote in reg'lar handwritin', and this diary he kept where he printed. I decided to copy the diary, because if he was writin' a threatenin' letter to somebody, he would print, like this, pressin' down hahd on the paper wid a bold stroke. He would wont to be took ser'ously."

John nodded.

"See heah, he writes quick-like, and scribbles stuff out. He don't think thangs th'ough first. He like to use big words, but he misspells 'em, and when he prints, he mixes up the capital letters wid the small ones. Sometime he 'breviates words and sometime he goes back and sticks stuff in—he be lazy. Don't wont to recopy nothin'."

That would fit with the personality profiles John had read of Harvey Oswald when he did his research, prior to his little ill-fated meeting with Parker Jefferson.

"Look heah." John and Gypsy both leaned closer. "He be describin' a book he was give by a translator when he first got to Russia. See how he spelt it: *Ideot, by Destoevski*. Not only did this idiot not know how to spell 'idiot', but he couldn't even be bothered to look over at the book when he was writin' in his diary and make sure he spelt the author's name right." Fancy shook his head in disgust. "And see heah how he axes for *Sovite citizenship*. He thanks he's smaht 'cause he can spell 'citizenship', then he screws up 'Soviet.' Some communist he was." He made an emphatic snorting sound.

John glanced down at the backless, well-thumbed dictionary the old man had pulled from a jacket pocket, and felt a deeper respect for him.

"He be paranoid, too," continued the forger with another satisfying gulp of Wild Turkey. "Over heah, after he say he cut his wrists and they th'ew him in the loony bin, he complains that an American at the hospital is suspicious of him—see how he spells it? *Suspious*. Then he states that he is 'generally evasive' to the man's questions. And he wonders why the guy's *suspious* of him!" He threw back his head and guffawed.

John and Gypsy laughed, too.

"Then, over heah, he say the nurses are 'suspious' of him. He thanks ever'body suspicions him, which means he suspicions ever'body else."

John found himself marveling at the man's simple grasp of complex psychology.

"So. Here's what I thank he would say: *If you don't leave me and my wife alone, I will do something so moentous the FBI will never get over it. Never!!*"

Gypsy said, "You left the 'm' out of 'momentous.'"

He gave her a gap-toothed grin. "I know. It's da kind of thang he would do."

"And you scribbled out 'FBI,' then stuck it back in," said John admiringly. "Then you underlined the second 'never' and used two exclamation marks."

"Yeah. He like them exclamation mahks. Now, the second note would be stronger: *Stay away from my wife, or someone important will die, and it will be you're responsiblty.*" Tapping an arthritic finger over the missing "i" in the word "responsibility," the old man said, "He was always leavin' off little pahts of his words."

As he noticed the deliberate misuse of the pronoun "you're," John gave the old forger an approving nod.

"Notice how sometime he uses a small 'e' and sometime a capital 'e', and the capital 'e' looks like a backwahds 'three', but all his 'i's are small unless he's talkin' about hisself." He tapped a pen onto the copied page. "See heah, how he uses the word 'weather' when he mean 'whether.'" He rolled his eyes. "Kind of embarrassin' for our country, when you thank that such a moron could git away wid killin' the president of the U-nited States."

Even worse, if you could have prevented it, thought John. He glanced over at Gypsy. From the look on her face, he could tell she was thinking the same thing.

"Now. It was hahd to pick out the right paper. From the pitures in the book, it was hahd to tell, but I didn't see none that was wrote on lined paper. Plus, he was always whinin' about how he never had no money, so I bought some cheap old tablet paper wid no lines, and soaked it for a while in tea bags." He fished around in another jacket pocket.

"Why?" asked Gypsy.

Finally he pulled out a yellowed sheet, which had been folded once. "Make it look old," he said, tossing back another slug of whiskey. The more he drank, the surer he became of himself and the steadier his hand. It was remarkable to watch. From a shirt pocket, he withdrew a ratty, blue-splotched handkerchief, from which he unrolled, with a flourish, an old fountain pen. "Didn't have no ballpoints or felt-tips back then," he informed his surprised observers. "And from the way the writin' on the page is light and then dahk, see, it look like he be usin' a fountain pen."

And then, in front of their astonished faces, Fancy Fingers Myers proceeded to jot down a note which, from all appearances, could have been written—and signed—by Lee Harvey himself.

Later, with a dignified bow, the old man refused all offers of payment, saying only, "Mooch is fambly."

He did, however, take the near-empty bottle of Wild Turkey with him.

TWENTY-THREE

A LIGHT, COLD RAIN DRIZZLED down the windshield of the Blazer, putting a star-filter on the few anemic lights which strung along the harbor as John pulled up to an empty parking lot across the street. It was eleven-thirty. Clouds shrouded the moon, veiling the MOM'S BAIT SHOP sign and the chunky shrimp boats at dock. Not a soul stirred, and he glanced over at Gypsy, shielding his uneasiness with a smile.

Her wan face was freckled with shadow-dimples made by rain droplets on the passenger window; her dark eyes were unreadable in the gloom. The damp air had sprung her hair loose from its imprisoning clasp, and wild tendrils corkscrewed around her face in a glossy black cloud. Her mute beauty broke his heart. He fought the urge to slam the car into gear and take off in a skid of tires, taking her away from danger just as fast and as hard as he could.

But take her where?

Her mother hadn't been able to escape the Jigsaw Man twenty-five years ago, and neither would he now. If they ran now, he'd be forced to drag Gypsy and their little girl from town to town in a mindless attempt to hide from a relentless pursuer who would never give up until he'd found them.

And once they were caught . . . John didn't like to think about that.

For now, all he should be thinking about was the plan and how they were going to implement it. How he wished—with all his heart and mind and soul—that he could do it without Gypsy; that she could stay behind in some temporary safe place with Annie until it was all over.

John glanced over the backseat at the child, curled up in a cozy puff of pillows and blankets, sleeping peacefully with Pooh-Bear clutched close. He dreaded waking her, dragging her out into the rain and the wild night, but there was nothing for it. Even though she would probably continue to sleep through the whole thing, he could never risk leaving her alone in the Blazer. The Jigsaw Man knew their car; she would be as exposed in it as a target on the firing range. They could not leave her alone, period.

But could he protect her? Placing his hand on the grip of the thirty-eight which was stuffed into the waistband of his jeans, John gave it a reassuring stroke. He longed for his nine-millimeter with its fourteen-shot clip, but Jefferson had taken it soon after his capture. Still, he had the thirty-eight and the shotgun, thanks to Gypsy's clear-headedness. It would not have occurred to most women to bring the weapons along on the search for the letters.

But Gypsy was not most women.

Reaching across the console which separated the two front seats, John took her small hand into his, holding it as if it were a lifeline and he, a drowning man. She turned her face and looked at him, her eyes full of unasked questions. She did not ask the questions because neither of them had the answers.

"There's something I want to say to you," he began, and immediately, his throat closed off, bringing him treacherously close to tears.

She squeezed his hand. "There's no need."

Clearing his throat, he nodded. "Yes there is. I want you to know that, no matter what happens . . ." He locked gazes with her, silently cursing his verbal ineptitude.

She started to shake her head.

"Gypsy." She stopped.

He pulled his hand free, knowing that the lyrical beauty of sign language would express what he never could on his own. He pointed at her. "You," he signed, "are my hero."

Her eyes widened and filled with tears.

Closing his hand over hers once again, he opened the fingers and kissed the soft palm. There was so much more he wanted to say, but they both understood that it had all been said.

Gypsy stood alone on the dock near a pier support, her back to the water, and strained to see through the droplets of moisture which beaded the night. Rain seemed to hang suspended in the clouded air, and her inability to hear the lapping of waves against the boat hulls made the night seem hushed and expectant, like a dark scene in a movie where the killer lurks in the shadows.

Her stomach was cold Play-Doh, her heart a thumping pressure in her throat. All her earlier bravado from their previous meeting had vanished with the light of day, leaving behind a greasy sensation of dread. The notes forged by Fancy had seemed so real beneath the spotlight of the overhead kitchen lamp, but as the appointed hour of her meeting with the Jigsaw Man crept ever closer like a cold-blooded reptile inching toward its prey, Gypsy's doubts had slowly turned her stomach to clay and her nerve to jelly.

She hid her doubts from John, who seemed so cock-sure. Did they have any choice? Was there a better idea? She couldn't think of one.

They were counting on the murk and the mist to buy them some time. That and the passage of the years. After all, it had been over thirty years since he'd seen the notes. How well could he remember the exact contents of them? And even if he did remember, would he not question the accuracy of that memory, if only for a little while?

He might . . . unless Oswald had written the notes in script, on lined stationery. Or if he had specifically mentioned the president by name, though John said even Oswald wouldn't have been that stupid. Or if the letters had been long and rambling, though Fancy had said probably not, since the other threatening notes he'd sent to the FBI were brief and to the point.

Wouldn't Jefferson glance at them, accept them for the time being, and leave?

Wouldn't he?

Gypsy glanced at her watch, but it was a dress watch and impossible to read even under a dim pier light in the stygian gloom. Folding her arms across her chest, she hugged her elbows. The lightweight windbreaker she was wearing kept her reasonably dry, but it wasn't warm enough, and her head was exposed to the moody, wet night air. She worried about Annie and John; disjointed scraps of worry that were disproportionate to the situation. Rather than worrying if they would get out of this alive, she fretted that they might catch cold. It was a coping tactic, but not a very successful one.

Then he was there.

She'd not had vibrations to warn her, as on that night

on the pier; the harbor dock was simply a paved extension of the parking lot. And she'd been looking in the wrong direction; he seemed to have prowled up on her flank, a sinewy cat creeping up on a fluttering bird.

Shivers possessed her from head to foot and she shrugged her shoulders to stop them.

He was carrying a zippered nylon athletic bag, which he set down on the wet pavement beside him. From the pocket of a trench coat, he withdrew the anti-bugging device and again traveled it over her body. As before, it set up a screeching in the vicinity of Gypsy's head, but he seemed satisfied that the cause of the warning was her hearing aid. Again, she had to prove that she was unarmed.

His movements were jerky, nervous. He kept glancing over his shoulder and peering into the shadows as if he expected to discover someone in hiding.

"Where's John?" he snapped.

"Taking care of Annie, our daughter," she said, hoping she'd projected enough volume in her voice to sound confident. Still, he poked into the corners of the bait shop doorway, lifted the lid on a large bait chest, and even thunked down a couple of nearby connecting piers, leaning over to peek into the darkened, mute shrimp boats.

"You don't think we'd bring her out here, do you?" she called as he made his paranoid way back to her.

He said something, but she couldn't hear and couldn't see his lips in the mist-cloaked night.

"You're going to have to stand under this pier light," she reminded him, "and speak clearly so that I can understand you. I can't read your lips in the dark."

Suddenly he brushed up close to her, so close she could see the madness lurking in the corners of his eyes. Her blood ran cold and she stifled the almost overpowering urge to run for her life. She tried to glance away, but was mesmerized by those eyes.

With a breathless shock of recognition, she could see her own eyes reflected back to her.

They were, after all, related.

Her tongue turned to sand and she stood, hypnotized.

"Read this," he said, his lips curling in derision, "I'm through fucking with you. Give me the letters or I'll kill you." In a flash, she saw the gleam of a semi-automatic pistol beneath the soft downy glow of the rain-shaded pier light.

Somehow, she managed to say, "The money first." Then, the blood seemed to drain from her brain; she stopped breathing; time poised—he could kill her right now and snatch the letters from her body. There was nothing any of them could do about it.

She did not blink.

After a few stand-off seconds, his face creased into a twisted grin. "You got balls," he said. "I like that."

Stepping back a pace or two, he reached for the bag and unzipped it, holding it open in front of her. She caught a glimpse of crisp bills, neatly stacked and wrapped in rubber bands resting inside before he yanked the zipper shut. Then he placed it on the tarmac next to her.

Ignoring the bag, she glanced around her. "Where's the boat? There's no boat here called the *Sink or Swim*."

"There was a problem getting it lined up. It'll be here at dawn."

She stepped back. "We had a deal."

Running the tip of his tongue over his scarred upper lip, he said, "All I want is the letters. As far as I'm concerned, the further away you get from this country, the better for me."

Searching his face for any sign of a lie, Gypsy hesitated. She didn't know what to do. After a moment, he gestured with the gun, and that decided her.

With shaking hands, she reached inside the windbreaker and pulled out the two notes. Shoving the gun into a shoulder holster beneath the trench coat, he snatched the letters from her hand, stepped closer to the light, and unfolded them, shielding them from the rain with his body. Tendrils of vaporous mist began tiptoeing in from the sea, curling around their bodies and masking the rain.

Gypsy felt a pulse throbbing in her head. She had a sudden, terrible urge to urinate, and her breath came out in jerky little clouds. The night hung suspended in the fog, like the memory of a dream, or the faded image of a loved one years after death.

Gypsy watched as the Jigsaw Man folded the letters and put them into the pocket of his trench coat. Her heartbeats were explosive, painful.

Then, with a rattlesnake strike, he had her, her head locked in a chokehold, the ten-millimeter jammed against her jaw. As he began dragging her backward across the slick pavement, he put his lips against her "good" ear and shouted, "I can't let you get away! You know too much."

She let her body go limp, forcing him to drag dead weight backwards toward his car, but he was strong and it barely slowed him. With every step, the gun barrel jabbed her throat.

Gypsy thought she heard Annie scream in the distance, but it might have been in her head.

All thought emptied from her mind.

They stopped. "Open it!" he yelled, shoving her body toward the driver's side car door. With numbed hands, she fumbled with the door handle. Pulling back his gunhand, he smacked her—hard—on the cheekbone with the flat grip of the semi-automatic.

With a staggering gasp, she opened the door. He pushed her down, heedless of her head, which cracked against the side of the door. Clawing at the car seat, she dragged herself into the car in unison with the Jigsaw Man, who slammed the car door and transferred the gun to his left hand long enough to start the engine and throw the car into gear.

The whole thing—from the pocketing of the notes to the breathless skidding of tires as they vaulted out of the harbor area—took seconds. Expertly steering with his left hand, he shoved the barrel of the ten-millimeter into her ribcage and commanded her to sit still.

Running red lights and stop signs in the near-empty streets, he headed the car for the highway leading out of town. Mirror droplets of mist reflected the headlights' glare back to them as he accelerated, flying over a dip in the road with such speed their heads banged against the ceiling of the car. Gypsy tasted blood.

This is it, she thought. *I'm going to die. The Jigsaw Man is going to kill me. I knew it. All my life I knew it.*

Then, clear as a summer day in her mind, Gypsy saw Annie's face, dimpling as she signed, *"I love you"* to her mother.

An electric current could not have given her a greater jolt.

"No," she thought. *No.* She glanced at the Jigsaw Man from beneath her lashes. *I will not let you steal Annie's mother away from her the way you stole mine.*

She would not leave Annie and John. *She would not.*

She braced herself—for what, she didn't know. An opportunity. Anything.

It came seconds later. A car, traveling on a rural crossroads and expecting the Jigsaw Man to stop at the stop sign, burst out upon them, forcing him to slam on the brakes. Gypsy's body was flung hard against the dashboard, her head barely missing the rearview mirror. The car fishtailed as he left-handedly spun the wheel, his gunhand instinctively swinging out and pointing upward as the car slowed.

Without thought, Gypsy grabbed the passenger door handle and bolted from the still-moving car. She hit the pavement on all fours and rolled, arms and legs flailing like a rag doll. Yet even as the momentum slowed, she sprang to her feet, forcing her staggering legs to run, heading straight for the underbrush like a fox before bloodthirsty hounds.

A tree limb exploded next to her. She had not heard the shot. She didn't stop. Twisted branches, shrouded in mist, snatched at her hair and snared her clothing. Her breath was hot in her throat as she plunged blindly through the night fog, clambering for a foothold, running, running . . . from the Jigsaw Man.

TWENTY-FOUR

"SHIT!" SCREAMED JEFFERSON AS HIS shot went wide and Gypsy scrambled from sight into the trees, the mist eclipsing her.

A man leapt from the other vehicle and came running stupidly toward Jefferson. "Is everything all right?" he cried.

Jefferson leveled the gun at the man. "Get the fuck out of here," he called, "before I blow your head off."

The man's feet skidded comically to a stop and he stared at the gun like a cobra before a snake charmer. Jefferson cursed his luck. He did not want to draw attention to himself in any way, and killing this local man—or allowing him to call the cops—would do it. Besides, he was no fucking mass murderer.

Reaching into the trench coat, he fished out his credentials and flashed them so fast that all the man could possibly see was a glimpse of badge.

"Police business," he barked. "Get out of here before you get hurt. *Now!*"

The spell was broken. The man rushed back to his car and took off in a spray of gravel. Jefferson plunged into the trees after Gypsy. Wet, crooked branches grabbed at him, while gnarled roots tripped him repeatedly. After only a short distance, he stopped, panting heavily and squinting into the ghostly dark. Cold water droplets smacked the back of his neck and drippled beneath his coat collar. He shivered.

Aside from the moist pattering of mist drops on leaf and earth, it was utterly silent.

He waited.

Nothing.

Bringing his breathing under control with great effort, he considered his primary advantage: he could hear her, but she could not hear him. His eyes had long since adjusted to the dark, but the fog obscured everything.

A rustling sound.

He whirled around, straining to hear over the cacophony of a million water drops hitting trees and ground.

Again. *There!*

Adrenaline pumping, he headed straight towards the direction of the sound. The *crack* of a broken tree limb urged him to hurry. It was almost over. He could taste it.

Visibility was only ten feet or so—the sudden shimmer of Gypsy's windbreaker just up ahead in the trees caught him by surprise. Still, he did not hesitate. Heart pounding, he drew a bead on the snatch of cloth and pulled the trigger. Even as the recoil yanked his hands upward and the windbreaker fell from sight, he was leaping forward toward his target, his *prey,* laughing maniacally that it was over, he'd done it, he'd finally gotten her, that all he had to do was call in a dragnet on John Halden and he would be free, *free* of them, of the whole mess—because nobody would believe Halden, a proven cop-killer—and the directorship would be his.

It came out of nowhere, whizzing from behind before he could even duck, whacking against his skull with a sickening *crack* that was the last sound he heard before he felt his body go limp and sink heavily to his knees. He never felt himself go down like a dying tree, hitting the rotting leaves face-first.

Gypsy's hands stung from the force of the impact of the heavy tree limb against the man's head. Chest heaving, she stood over him.

Kill him, said her own voice, from somewhere deep in her consciousness. *Do it. No one will ever know.*

The faces of her mother and father, of John and Annie, of Chief Strickland—broken lives, destroyed lives—flashed into the bloody haze that was her mind. The mist glowed red. She raised the jagged branch over her head. Her mouth twisted into a grimace, and a growl seethed up from the back of her throat.

She would beat him into an unrecognizable pulp. She would smash his filthy body until all the rage was spent and justice was done. She would do it for her folks, and for the Chief, and for her husband, and for the child Annie who died, too, those many long years ago.

She would do it.

A bloodcurdling yell erupted from her, a battle scream so primal she could hear it herself.

Her arms swung down with all her might and strength and power and glory.

"Gypsy!"

Cold shock hitched the momentum of the blow and threw off the aim. The branch thunked into the wet earth beside the man's head with a smacking thud that reverberated all the way up to her shoulders and left a small crater behind.

The voice had belonged to Gypsy's father.

She whirled around, hot-and-cold needles of fear and

wonder working their way over her body. Vaporous mists swirled at her elbow like ghosts. The deformed trees glowered at her from behind their menacing curtains of fog.

She had heard him. She *knew* it. Had she gone insane?

Her dry lips croaked out a single whisper, *"Daddy?"*

Panting, shivering, she waited in a sort of arrested madness, almost as if she expected him to step out from behind a distorted, fog-shrouded tree and scold her.

But he did not.

She glanced down at the inert form on the ground before her. The blood-red vapors in her mind faded to hot pink and then cleared altogether.

If you kill him, her own mind told her, *then he will have surely destroyed you.*

Gypsy flung down the gnarled tree branch.

She would not give him that satisfaction.

Instead, she turned and raced, stumbling and groping, through the tangled undergrowth until she reached the road. Emerging from the trees about a quarter mile from where she had entered them, she could see Jefferson's car where he'd left it in the middle of the road, headlights penetrating the fog, engine still running, doors gaping open.

She hurried toward it, limping now, as exhaustion and reaction set in. By the time she sank down behind the wheel, she was shaking violently from head to foot. It occurred to her that she could have killed him anyway with that first blow, but she was damned if she was going to go back and check. Slamming the car doors with trembling hands, Gypsy gunned the engine, spun the car around, and headed back toward town.

Controlled panic dictated every move John made.

It was his worst nightmare, everything he had dreaded

might happen but had prayed would not. Rowing with all his might, he bumped against the dock and sprang from the small boat, dragging a near-hysterical Annie behind him. Abandoning the video equipment and hoisting the child into his arms, he sprinted down the wooden pier, his frantic footsteps echoing hollowly, and across the dock parking area and the street to get to the Blazer which was parked on the other side. Skidding over a puddle, he almost went down, and grappled to keep from dropping her. She was too big to carry but too small to run fast enough.

As they reached the Blazer, Annie struggled from his arms and yanked on the car door, screaming, *"Hurry, Daddy! Hurry!"* over and over in a sort of panicked mantra. They leapt into the car and John took off in the direction he'd seen Jefferson take, almost donuting on the wet pavement.

Visibility was zero and the headlights were useless. John flew through one red traffic light but stopped at the next one, raking his fingers through his hair in frustration, trying to tune out the blubbering child.

Which way would Jefferson have headed? *Think.*

Not back to the house. For some reason, John was certain of that. Where, though? *Where?*

Annie was tugging at his jacket sleeve, screaming, "Don't stop, Daddy! Don't stop! The bad man has Mommy!" Her hysteria penetrated his fierce concentration and he glanced over at her. She was almost at the point of no return.

Grinding the gearshift into park, John reached over, unsnapped the child's seatbelt, and gathered her small body into his arms. White-faced, she could not seem to stop crying; her little heart beat wildly and she clutched at him almost as if he were not there. He held her shaking body tight against his. "It's okay, Annie," he said firmly.

"Daddy will find Mommy. It's all right. We'll get her back from the bad man. But you have to calm down and let Daddy think."

Precious seconds were being gobbled up, but John knew he had to do something before the little girl went into shock. He reached over the back seat, fetched Pooh-Bear, and handed him to her. She grabbed the bear in a suffocating hug and shuddered. After another endless moment, she seemed to gather her courage. Noiseless tears continued to stream down her cheeks, but she no longer screamed or clutched at him.

John strapped the child into the backseat amongst the blankets and her other toys, covering her cold, shivering body and stroking her cheek until she had curled up and gone into some miserable, silent place.

It was the best he could do at the moment.

Yanking the gearshift into drive, he churned out from under the traffic light and took the highway out of town, which was virtually empty this time of night, heading north in some sort of vague notion of pointing toward Dallas, squinting into the wet, dark cloak of night for any sign of crimson taillights up ahead. Doubts assailed him, tormenting him like a swarm of killer bees.

Even if Jefferson took the highway out of town, how could John possibly know which direction he was headed?

She's gone.

No, he argued, desperation pushing the car up to seventy, eighty—insane speeds in a heavy sea fog in spite of the fact that the road was deserted. *I won't let her be.*

The window fogged up. He turned on the defroster. It didn't help. The cloud was on the outside. Thinking of the child in the backseat, he was forced to slow down.

What will I tell her if her mother dies? She'll never trust me again.

Don't think about that. Just find Gypsy.

I can't live without her. I'll die.

Shut up. Don't think it. Just find her.

Twin beams of light, furry and dim in the fog, appeared on the road up ahead, coming towards him.

It wouldn't be Jefferson, coming back.

Unless . . . *Unless he killed Gypsy and dumped the body somewhere and was coming back for John.*

He eased the thirty-eight out of his waistband with his right hand and pointed it toward the driver's side door, just beneath the window, and slowed the car.

The other car flashed past.

Jefferson's car.

Nausea curdled John's stomach and gathered at the back of his throat. Stomping on the brakes, preparing to spin the car into pursuit, he glanced in his rearview mirror. Taillights glowed red, then, expanded as the other driver braked. Shouting, "Get down, Annie!," John whipped the car into a U-turn in the middle of the road.

Jefferson was armed. It would be a real shootout, and John didn't want to die in front of his daughter. Besides, there was a chance Gypsy could still be alive. He eased the Blazer behind Jefferson's car, ducked his head, and opened the driver's side door, dropping to the ground and using it as a shield.

"Get the fuck out of that car, Jefferson!" he screamed. *"Put your hands up or I'll blow your head off!"* Every nerve ending in John's body tingled with the power surge of adrenaline. The other car door opened.

His fingers itched to pull the trigger. John pulled back the hammer of the thirty-eight and drew a bead right where Jefferson's head would emerge from the car. Mists swirled around the two vehicles. Droplets of water dripped from John's hair and oozed down his face, clotting his lashes. He blinked and shook his head, tightening his grip on the revolver. He knew he didn't have as many shots as Jefferson did, so the ones he fired had to be dead-on accurate.

A moment of exquisite tension stretched between the two cars. It was all John could do not to start blasting away.

The driver got out of the car and turned toward John. He did not put his hands up; one, in fact, was hidden from view.

John tensed.

TWENTY-FIVE

CONSCIOUSNESS RETURNED TO DASH JEFFERSON in bits and pieces, like crazy half-understood dream fragments before dawn. The only certain consistency was the powerful, throbbing pain in his head. When he lifted it and turned it on his neck, the pain stabbed through the dark with strobe-flash brilliance, leaving him nauseated and weak.

He groaned. Sleep yawned at him, a beckoning cavern of forgetfulness. He yearned to give into it, but with each waking moment, memories flooded back. Humiliating memories of how he'd been outsmarted—again—by Gypsy Halden.

He rolled over on his back and the earth rocked. Involuntarily, he clutched at the ground to steady himself. A big cold drop of water splashed onto his face. It felt good. He lay still for a moment, letting the world settle back into place and the dripping trees wash his face. Then he pushed himself up to a sitting position, turned and retched, remaining statue-still for another few minutes until his stomach quit churning.

Probably had a concussion, but he would live. Exhaus-

tion soaked into his very bones. He was getting too old for
this shit. Should never have happened. He blew it. Reaching up, Jefferson probed delicately at the back of his head
and his hand came away sticky. He wiped it on some wet
leaves. The air was filled with the sound of dripping
moisture and the fog was still thick. You never saw fog
like this in Dallas. Never saw screwball trees like this, either.

He hated this place.

Hoisting his body up on one knee, Jefferson waited another long moment and heaved a heavy sigh. How could
he have dropped the ball so completely on this one? How
could he have been so fucking *stupid?*

Desperation. It had tripped him up before.

Finally, Jefferson lumbered to his feet and started pushing toward the road on wobbly legs. God, what an idiot he
was. He'd fallen for the old jacket-on-a-tree-limb trick.
He was losing it.

Shit, he'd been in management too long. Field agents
did all the investigating and rounding up of fugitives.
Guys like him stayed behind a big desk and supervised
things. An FBI agent had basically two routes he could
take in his career. He could either be a "mere agent" and
work the streets for the duration, or he could join the management program and get on the promotion-transfer track,
which basically removed him from the hands-on operation of most investigations.

In the beginning, Jefferson had worked the bricks, dis-
tinguishing himself for the media, looking for ways to in-
gratiate himself with management, jumping in whenever
there was a chance to take the credit or look like a hero.

But once he got on the management train, his destina-
tion was the top, and he never looked back. Somewhere
along the line he'd lost his edge, the instincts that warned

a field agent of impending danger and guided him away from it.

But so panicked was he to stop these people before they destroyed everything he'd worked for that he'd gotten sloppy.

It wouldn't happen again.

Stumbling a little, Jefferson emerged from the choked tree-line to the road and squinted in the direction of the car. Blurry headlights no longer pierced the fog.

She'd taken the car.

Bitterness boiling up inside of him, Jefferson began trudging down the road, head down. He was sick of Gypsy Halden, sick of her self-righteous husband, sick of the whole situation. It was time he brought it to an end.

It wouldn't be easy—he'd have to adopt a whole new plan. And it would be messy and very, very public. All the same, he had no choice. And anyway, all was not lost. After all, if there was one thing Dash Jefferson was very, very good at, it was damage control.

Dual beams of light permeated the fog and roamed across the trees in an arc behind and over Jefferson's head. The sound of an engine cut through the suffocating mist. Jefferson turned around, stepped out into the road, and began waving his arms.

The vehicle slowed and crept toward him, angling across the road so that he could lean into the driver's window.

He couldn't believe his luck. It was a sheriff's department car, sent, apparently, to check out a complaint made by the man Jefferson had threatened.

By the time the vehicle had slowed to a stop, Jefferson had his creds out and thrust toward the driver. "I'm with the FBI," he said, his voice ringing with authority. "And I'm chasing down a fugitive who's armed and dangerous.

I've been assaulted and my car's been stolen." He allowed a small smile to crack his face. "Am I glad to see you! I could use some help."

The cowboy-hatted deputy reached for his radio mike. "Get in," he said, "and tell me what you need."

Annie's shrill voice cut a path from John's brain down his spine to his toes: "It's Mommy!"

He almost dropped the gun. She stepped away from the car. Still, John hesitated. It could be a trick. Jefferson could be using his wife as bait to get him away from the car. If he reacted too quickly, he could get them both killed.

But Gypsy didn't stop or even slow down as she ran towards John. Confused, he stayed down, still blindly pointing the gun at her while his brain tried to decide what to tell his body to do. There wasn't any training for a situation like this. His eyes told him she had escaped and somehow gotten Jefferson's car, but his mind told him that was impossible.

At the last moment, as she reached the car door, it occurred to him to point the thirty-eight away from Gypsy. Slowly, he got to his feet.

"I got away from him," she said breathlessly. "He chased me through the trees, but I hit him in the head with a tree branch. I knocked him out. He might be dead—I don't know."

Before John could say anything, the rear car door flew open and Annie hurled herself at her mother, who gathered the child to her and suddenly burst into tears. The tension-releasing, womanly response snapped John out of his shock. Shoving the gun into the waistband of his jeans, he stooped down and lifted them both up in his arms, laughing and whirling them around in circles, shouting, "I love you!"

But the celebration was all too brief. In the next instant, he was herding them into the Blazer. "We've got to get out of here," he said. "We've got a head start now—let's take advantage of it. Did anyone see you?"

She shook her head, then hesitated. "Yes. I almost forgot. We nearly hit a man—that's how I was able to jump out of the car. Jefferson shot at me. The other man saw it."

"Did he shoot the other guy?" John struggled to turn his face so that she could read his lips, while steering the Blazer at breakneck speeds down the fog-curtained highway.

"I don't know. I don't think so. I was too busy getting away to notice."

"But you couldn't hear the gunshot? *Think,* Gypsy." He was hoping that she might have been able to hear a noise that loud with her right ear.

"I didn't hear the one aimed at me. I just saw the tree limb exploding."

The gun was fired at her from a distance, then. Thank God. "So you didn't look back. You didn't see any more shots."

"I don't know. I don't think so." John tried to mask the exasperation he felt. After all, she'd nearly been killed. She'd been smart and resourceful and brave and hadn't lost her cool. Still, it was frustrating not to know what happened to the witness. If only she could *hear* . . .

Forget about it. Wasted thought.

He reached for her hand and squeezed it. They were together again. Alive and well, so far. That was all that mattered. They'd think of something.

He looked over the seat at Annie. Sitting rigidly, straining against her shoulder harness strap, she was holding Pooh-Bear in a strangling grip and staring at her mother as if to look away would make her disappear. Her face was pinched but most of the color had returned to it. She wasn't crying anymore. She'd be okay.

Glancing back at Gypsy, he started to say, "We've got to ditch this car," but decided against it when he saw her. She was staring unseeing out the rain-spattered windshield, her drawn face stunned with the post-trauma realization that she was not dead.

She would need a little time to absorb what had happened to her. He decided to leave her alone for the time being. Besides, he needed to gather together all the silent forces of concentration he had, just to figure out how in hell they were going to get out of this one.

Deliberately calming his jumpy thoughts, he tried to make a blank of his mind, a clean screen that would soon spell out what they should do next. It didn't take long for a single thought to sting him bolt upright in his seat:

The video equipment. And then, *Shit, the money.*

They had to go back to the harbor, had to collect the tapes he'd made of the exchange with Jefferson, get the incriminating bag they'd all left behind. It was their proof, the final nail on the bastard's coffin.

And the first place he would think to look for them.

As the terrifying episode in the woods with the Jigsaw Man began to recede behind Gypsy, a numbing sensation seemed to follow along in its wake. Everything about their situation was still in crisis and yet she seemed unable to feel a sense of urgency, fear, or even relief at being reunited with her family. It was as if a part of her—the feeling part—had detached itself and floated away in some unreachable place.

She could see the worry etched on her husband's face, could sense the distress in Annie's inflexible posture, and yet she did not pull these emotions inside of herself, as she might normally have done. Her system, it seemed, had suffered a power surge of emotion during the trauma and burnt itself out, like an overloaded circuit. It was not entirely unpleasant, the numbness. It gave her a sense of invincibility.

Her thoughts, as well, were clear, unclouded by the stress of the moment. She could tell that John was heading back in the direction of the harbor and automatically assumed that he'd left the video equipment behind in his headlong flight to rescue Gypsy. Then she remembered the nylon money-bag. Of course they had to retrieve it. Without it, they'd have no real case against Parker Jefferson.

Gypsy knew that returning to the harbor was dangerous, but she felt no fear. She'd conquered death once that night. She could do again, if need be. Hell, she'd faced the dreaded Jigsaw Man . . . and *won.* She caught her husband's eye and gave him a reassuring smile. He tried to smile back, but his thoughts were elsewhere. This did not bother her.

There was absolutely nowhere to park the Blazer where it would not be exposed. Both parking lots were completely barren and there was no one around. Gypsy could see the muscles in John's cheek working in frustration. She said, "You go get the equipment, and I'll circle the car around and come back for you. That way we won't be out in the open here like sitting ducks."

He nodded. Quickly, he pulled up to Mom's Bait Shop and leapt lightly from the car. They could both see the bag, sitting exactly where Jefferson had left it. Such were the benefits of doing anything after midnight in a small town. No witnesses. Not even any thieves to creep up and nab a nylon bag sitting suspiciously out in the open next to a harbor. By the time Gypsy had swung her body over the console and accelerated out of the area, John was sprinting down the pier where he'd left the rowboat docked, bag in hand.

Gypsy drove across the street, cruised around, and headed back toward the harbor. As she prepared to cross back over the street and into the harbor parking lot, she suddenly hit the brakes.

A sheriff's department vehicle was inching along the parking lot, aiming a brilliant spotlight all along the harbor, from Mom's Bait Shop to the shadowy, fog-veiled pier beyond.

TWENTY-SIX

JOHN LAY PROSTRATE IN THE wet, stinking bottom of the rowboat, hardly daring to breathe as he watched the powerful beam of the spotlight cut through the shield of fog and slice over the sides of the little boat. He wondered if they'd be able to see down into the boat from the car. He doubted it, but his heart thudded in his ears like a tribal drum warning, *Dan-ger, dan-ger*.

If they got out of the car and launched a search, he was finished. There was a slim possibility that he could ease his body over the side and swim out of range of the search, but he didn't see how he could do it without making some kind of noise that would carry on this fog like a heartbeat on a stethoscope.

Get out of here, Gypsy, he willed, silently beaming his thoughts to her with all the powers of his mind. *Don't try to save me. Just get away.*

That was all he could do, really. Just lie there like a moth with a pin through its heart, and pray.

Jefferson's stomach lurched. *They'd already come back for the bag.* Shit. How did they do it? He must have been out longer than he realized. Okay. *Think.* What did they have, anyway? A few twenties, wrapped around stacks of paper. There was no $100,000 in that bag—they'd figure that out soon enough. So therefore, there was no real pay-off. He could always claim he was setting them up in a sting.

He allowed a small smile to crease his face. He'd find a way out of this yet. Hell, by the time he was through, he'd come out looking like a goddammed hero.

"You want us to search the dock? I can call for backup. We can enter every boat in port," said the sheriff's deputy. As he spoke, he continued to cruise slowly past the pier, his spotlight searching every crook and crevice. "Damn this fog," he added.

Jefferson hesitated, then shook his head. "Nah. They're long gone." After all, they'd already gotten the money; why hang around? "I'd like to get back to your office and set up a base of operations. Get some agents down here from the Corpus office. We'll find 'em." The implication being, of course, that the FBI would be able to locate the fugitives, whereas the sheriff's department would not.

The deputy stifled a sigh and cut a sideways glance at Jefferson. "There's lots of places to hide in a harbor," he offered.

"Look, if I thought they were here, I'd search myself," said Jefferson, silently cursing this redneck cop who thought he just had to show up the FBI. Huh. He'd show them.

With a shrug that said, *Fine, it's not my responsibility you asshole,* the deputy doused the light and headed the car towards the sheriff's department.

Even after the sheriff's department vehicle had left the harbor, Gypsy waited. It could be some kind of trick.

They could be lying in wait for her behind some building with their lights out, just as she was doing now. But after a couple of minutes, she couldn't stand it anymore and drag-raced for the pier where she knew John would have the little boat docked. Rolling down the window, she called softly to him. Immediately his head poked up, a ghostly shadow in the foggy dim-lit distance, then he clambored out of the boat, his hands full of videotaping paraphernalia and the athletic bag.

"Let me drive," he said, tossing the stuff in the back end. "It might get hairy out there."

"I think I saw Jefferson with that sheriff's deputy, but I couldn't be sure from where I was sitting." She crawled over to the passenger seat. "It could have been another deputy."

"Not likely. They don't cruise with partners. Too small of a town; not enough money in the budget." He got into the car and headed straight out of town.

"But how could he have found a cop so fast? I mean, we were out in the middle of nowhere. I conked the hell out of him and left him in some trees."

John shrugged. "If there were shots fired, and there was a witness, and he didn't shoot the witness, then chances are the guy called the sheriff's department." He gave her a grim grin. "Shots fired in a place like Rockport—even out in the country, if it's not hunting season—is a big deal."

She agreed. "And you should have seen him. He looked crazy, standing there in the middle of the road after midnight in a trench coat, waving a gun around."

John looked sick. "My God," he said. "When I think how close I came to losing you . . ."

She reached over and touched his elbow. "Don't think about it. I'm here with you now, and that's all that matters."

He glanced over at her and his eyes were bleak. "But I was armed, and I let him drag you off—"

She put a warning finger to her lips and gave a significant glance over the seat of the car, in the direction of Annie. "You had a child to think about."

He craned his neck to see over the back seat, where Annie, content once again to have both parents in the car with her, seemed to be dozing. They both knew she could be playing possum, though.

"You should have seen her," he mouthed, not using his voice. "If I hadn't held her back, she'd have jumped right out of that boat, swum for the dock, and attacked Jefferson herself."

They were silent for a moment, both thinking Annie-thoughts, both realizing just how lucky they were. Finally, John mouthed, "So you conked the old fucker, huh?"

The memory might not be so funny, but she had to smile at the way he'd brought it up. Using a voice she hoped was low enough, since he couldn't watch her continually while she signed, Gypsy told him about her first night in Rockport, when she'd been convinced that the Jigsaw Man was watching her through the windows of the house, how she'd taken the shotgun outside and blown a patch of mistletoe to smithereens.

"It gave me an idea. There wasn't much time to think, but that incident was fresh on my mind, so I just threw off my windbreaker and draped it over a bush, then backed off and broke off a rotten tree limb. I knew it would make a noise and draw him out.".

"And when it did . . . *bam!*"

She smiled. "Something like that." Suddenly, she remembered what had happened next, and the memory filled her with shame. Looking out the passenger window, she considered not telling John. After all, she wasn't very proud of it. But on the other hand, she knew he would understand, and she felt an overwhelming need to unburden herself, to confess, as it were.

Touching him to get his attention, she signed, "I almost killed him. I wanted to bash his brains out. I almost did."

He nodded as though he were not surprised. His face took on a grim expression. At first, she thought that maybe he was disappointed in her, but then she realized that he was identifying with her. She wondered if John would have finished the job. After a moment, he merely said, "Why didn't you?"

Gypsy looked down at her hands. This was the crazy part, but she'd gone this far. "I heard my father's voice. He stopped me."

John's eyes widened. He said, "Let me get this straight. You say you *heard* your dad's voice?" He lifted his brows on the word "heard" so she would understand the emphasis.

She nodded.

For a while, he drove in silence. Finally, he said, "There are some things in this world we'll never understand. We just accept them, be thankful for them, and go on."

There was nothing else to be said. Grateful that he understood, she stroked his arm and said nothing.

A highway road sign flashed past. Gypsy said, "Are we going to Corpus? I thought you'd head straight for Dallas."

"Got to ditch this car."

"But it would waste time to go all the way to Corpus Christi, John. Besides, isn't there an FBI office there? Won't they be looking all over for us?"

"It's a chance we've got to take."

Gypsy fought a growing sense of alarm. "But can't we just steal a car around here?"

He shook his head. "Not going to steal one. Then they really *would* be looking." Putting his hand over hers, he said, "It's a risk, I know that. But I've got an idea that might keep the highway patrol from watching for us, anyway."

She gave him a doubtful look.

"Trust me."

She rolled her eyes. "I was taught to look out for guys like you."

"Aww, admit it," he teased, "You really like the dangerous types."

She glanced over at her husband, looking crazily carefree under the circumstances. *I must,* she thought, *I'm risking my life for one.*

Nothing happened fast enough to suit Dash Jefferson. His life was hanging in the balance, and he had to wait around for a bunch of dumbass resident agents to get their lazy asses out of bed and get to Rockport for briefing. In Dallas, he had a whole office at his command; here he was lucky to get a fucking phone.

It was dawn before he'd managed to assemble a sleepy crew in the tiny sheriff's office, brief them on the cop-killer fugitive and his wife and kid, and get them cranked up on the search. Man could be in fucking Mexico by now.

Naturally he'd had to make a courtesy call to the SAC in the Houston field office, which supervised the Corpus resident agency, and get them mobilized for a statewide search which would involve the highway patrol as well as local police departments and the FBI itself.

Frustration scraped at him as he answered one stupid

question after another and then finally made his escape.
The rain had stopped and most of the fog had lifted. The
clouds had lightened considerably, and as he drove past
the harbor, they glowed blood-red over the molten ball
just sneaking above the scarlet-silver water. Some of the
shrimpers were already out in the bay, seeming to float in
low shreds of mist stubbornly clinging to the cool water.
Their masts and booms for raising the giant nets stood out
in black silhouette against the eastern horizon.

There was no sign of the previous night's adventure.

Jefferson sped out of town and hit the open road at seventy. He had to get to the airstrip where his Cessna
waited. The longer John Halden went unapprehended, the
worse were Jefferson's odds that Halden would somehow
take control of the situation and wreck everything.

He couldn't let that happen.

Tomorrow he had to be in Washington, D.C. for the
White House press conference that would announce him
as the president's choice for the new director of the FBI.
Senate confirmation would follow swiftly. This whole
matter had to be resolved by then. He had to get Halden
and his wife in custody, had to find out what they had on
him before they did something insane like release it to the
press. He had no doubt that they would spread rumors and
lies to the media about him, but he had to be sure that they
were completely discredited before that happened.

In spite of the fresh, moist, cool breeze flowing in the
open car window, Jefferson's back was drenched in
sweat. His head pounded from the concussion of the night
before, his eyes were grainy from lack of sleep, and the
stale donuts he'd had for breakfast rested in his stomach
like greasy lard.

He had to get back to Dallas as quickly as possible, get
cleaned up, and get to the office. He had to be there, wait-

ing, when they brought the Haldens in. Had to have first crack at them. Had to see to it that he destroyed them before they destroyed him.

His antsy foot nudged the car up to eighty. No highway patrolman would dare give an FBI agent on the job a speeding ticket.

Especially one about to be appointed director.

TWENTY-SEVEN

CORPUS CHRISTI WAS, QUITE POSSIBLY, the most beautiful city in Texas, but her clean, colorful buildings overlooking the turquoise bay were not visible from the part of town John had to take his family in order to get another car. Nor was it a sleepy fishing village like Rockport, he reminded Gypsy as they reached around the car, making sure all the doors were locked.

As they entered the city from the east, they could see the behemoth, spotlit USS *Lexington*, which had found a permanent home port in Corpus Christi, waiting patiently for her daily onslaught of tourists. John's dad had served proudly aboard the huge ship during the second World War; in happier times, John hoped to bring his family back for a tour. He was thankful that his folks did not live in Dallas, and so were spared most of the public mud through which his name had been dragged since Parker Jefferson had set him up for the murder of the Chief. They did know, however, that he was a suspect in the shooting. He couldn't imagine what they must be going through, and—among other things—he would never forgive Jefferson for that.

They were fighting for so much more than just to bring down Jefferson for the Chief's murder, and perhaps, even at this late date, for the murder of Gypsy's parents; they were also fighting to clear John's name, to restore to him his reputation and the job he loved. Not the least of John's worries was that they would somehow fail in their mission and he would not only spend the rest of his life in prison for a crime he did not commit, but that he would be forever soiled by the dirty allegations that had been brought against him.

He feared that one thing even more than death itself. John would much rather die a hero than live a life of shame, even—and perhaps especially—if it was undeserved.

He sneaked a glance at Gypsy. The slender back of her neck rigid with exhaustion and anxiety, she stared silently out the passenger window. He doubted she'd even noticed the *Lexington*. And why should she? In the past twenty-four hours she had faced her deepest, darkest fears and had overcome them—only to find herself at gunpoint and near death. She'd gathered her wits and fought to free herself—only to wind up on the run from the law.

In this whole miserable affair, his Gypsy was the one true innocent. After all, he'd made his own trouble by snooping around Jefferson to discover the truth about her father's murder—and underestimating the man's cunning. She had done nothing to bring this trouble on herself, not even on that horrible night so many long years ago.

In fact, she didn't even have to be here at all. She had come to find the letters—the infamous, lost letters—in order to save her husband's life. Everything she had done, she had done out of love.

He couldn't say that about himself. God knew Jefferson couldn't. Gypsy, now . . . she was the real hero.

More than anything else in the world, he wanted this to all be over, so that he could start spending the rest of his life making it up to her.

They exited off the high-arcing freeway which circled the city and made their way through the labyrinthine streets of the shady part of town. John was careful to obey every traffic law, even though he saw no police cars cruising the area in these pre-dawn hours. They were out there, though. He thought about that as he gassed up the Blazer, paying cash, and made a quick phone call from the gas station. He was a cop himself. They were out there. Corpus Christi had gotten too big to sleep through the night.

He was following directions he'd scrawled on the back of Gypsy's checkbook and he could hardly see to read them by the dim dashboard lights. He didn't dare turn on an overhead light. Might as well be on stage in the dark, cloud-blanketed night.

After a couple of wrong turns, he finally found the house he was looking for. It was a decrepit duplex, painted flamingo pink. Junk littered the overgrown yard. As he made his way up the driveway past a rusty, sagging Chevy of indeterminate age, a backyard dog set up a furious barking. It sounded though it could eat him in about two chomps. It sounded like it *wanted* to.

The floppy screen door was pushed open on screaming hinges before John even reached it. "Come on in heah in dis house and let me git you da car keys," said the rumbling voice of Fancy Fingers Myers.

It was the sweetest sound John had heard all day.

When the Cessna was well airborne and could handle the automatic pilot, Jefferson switched it on and settled back on the seat, his gaze scanning the instrument panel and the sky all around, as was his habit. He didn't trust *anything* for long, least of all technology.

He was dead tired—too tired to be flying, but he had no choice. Hoisting up the thermos of water he always kept in the cockpit, he took a long drink, then poured a little on his hands and splashed it on his face. Somewhat refreshed, he wiped his wet hands on the legs of his pants. The trench coat was flung over the passenger seat next to him. Reaching over, he groped around in one of the pockets, then another one, until he felt the crackle of paper in his hand. There.

Withdrawing the two notes Gypsy Halden had given him, Jefferson spread them out on his lap and studied them, keeping one eye, as always, on the instruments. It was the first chance he'd had to be completely alone to examine the notes.

Funny. He'd thought those letters would have been burned on his brain after all the trouble they'd brought him. But the truth was that he'd only glanced briefly at them—over thirty years ago—before making that fateful decision to hide the notes from his supervisor and concentrate his investigative efforts on General Walker.

Shit. He'd been so damned cocksure of it. What an idiot he'd been. Two days later, Kennedy was dead, and in the relentless scramble of media and Dallas cops and FBI to close the investigation, he made that second fateful decision—to send them to Mike for safekeeping. He hadn't seen them since.

Judging from the examples of Oswald's handwriting he had seen in the years since that time, they did appear to be accurate. The signature looked legit. Still. There was something bothering him. Something on the periphery of his mind. He just couldn't think of it.

Gazing out the window at the rolling Texan terrain far

below, Jefferson failed to sense that wonderful surge of freedom that flying so often gave him. There'd been nothing free about those terrible days in November of 1963.

The Old Man was shitting a brick to see to it that the FBI proved Oswald was acting alone. He was afraid, considering U.S.-Soviet relations at the time, that irresponsible conspiracy theories would quickly spread like a stain on the innocent American landscape, causing a wildfire panic. As director of America's premier law enforcement agency, he wanted to reassure the American people. He wanted the public to rest assured that the FBI had gotten its man.

Funny. The theories proliferated anyway, more or less *because* the FBI was so insistent on concentrating on Oswald.

If, after Kennedy's murder, Jefferson had turned over Oswald's notes, with their implied threat to assassinate the president—and dated November 20, 1963—to his supervisor, his career would have been over. Even if they wouldn't have fired him, it would have been over all the same. He'd have been stuck in that Butte office, trying to dig his car out of the snow, while somebody else advanced up the ranks.

Oh, the notes would never have been made public, at least not for a full generation, any more than the notes from Oswald threatening to bomb the Dallas field office were not made public for thirty years. After all, nobody would *ever* do anything to embarrass the Bureau (i.e., the Old Man). But nobody would have ever heard of Parker Jefferson again, either.

After scanning the skies for air traffic, Jefferson looked back at the letters. The FBI knew Oswald was working at the School Book Depository. They knew the motorcade, with its convertible limo, would drive right past it. But nobody thought to watch Oswald, least of all Parker Jefferson, who was at that exact moment on that golden Friday afternoon, surveilling General Walker and scanning the streets for any sign of . . . who?

Lee Harvey Oswald.

The moment the news came over the car radio that the president had been shot . . . the very *moment* he heard it, Dash Jefferson knew that Lee Harvey Oswald had done it. In that bullet-splitting second of eternity, Dash had realized the full and complete impact of his mistake.

He should have burned the letters on the spot. To this day, Jefferson had trouble understanding his own motives in not destroying the letters. He was a kid then, really, just a small-town Texas kid, trying not to blow his first assignment in a big city field office. A small-town kid in 1963 who still had the ability to be dazzled by the part—however catastrophic—he had played in history. The truth was that, self-preserving though it may have been, Dash had not destroyed the notes because they were proof that he, a small-town Texas kid, had actually made personal contact with the man who had assassinated the president of the United States—the most infamous figure in American history of the twentieth century.

Somehow he thought that, just like a collector who places priceless works of art in a vault for no one to see but himself, he would put the letters in a safe place and, when he was ready, he could take them out and look at them whenever he wanted. But those intense around-the-clock days in Dallas following the assassination, and later, the assassination of Oswald himself, were paranoia-filled for any investigators involved. Rumors ran rampant and lots of mistakes were made by people who had never in their wildest dreams imagined that the whole world would soon be watching every move they made and every little thing they did.

Jefferson knew, even then, that he dare not risk the letters getting into the wrong hands. So what did he do? He gave them to the only person in the world he truly trusted, his big brother, Mike the Wonder Boy.

Now, looking at it across the years, Jefferson wondered if he hadn't sent the letters to Mike just to impress him.

And look where *that* had gotten him.

The dominoes of life. See where they'd fallen.

The amazing thing of it was, he never really intended to kill Mike that day ten years later, the day Mike threatened to make the letters public. Mike's threat had released some kind of . . . beast . . . that had lain dormant for many years within Dash, a beast of jealousy and envy and hurt and rage. Mike had taken everything Dash ever wanted: his parents' love, the regard of the community, and most importantly, Anna. And he had the audacity, the unmitigated *gall* to threaten to take away Dash's career, too.

He could not stand back and let his brother do it. Would not. Did not.

After all these years, the one thing Dash still wondered was whether Anna really knew about the letters or not. He could still see her face, cowing in terror before him that night, swearing to her death that she did not know what he was talking about, that she didn't have any letters.

He hadn't meant to kill her, either. It was just . . . looking at her beautiful lying face . . . all her lies. They got to him.

Suddenly, the truth fell into place, right in front of Jefferson's eyes. He'd missed it before, but here it was, clear as day.

The letters were not dated.

The one irrefutable fact that Dash Jefferson remembered, over all others, about the notes from Oswald was that they had been dated just two days before Kennedy's assassination.

The beast within stirred.

Maybe Anna had not known about the letters after all, but her bitch daughter sure as hell did.

She'd known enough to get them forged.

In the next instant, Jefferson was reaching for the radio mike. A little thrill—the excitement of the hunt—charged through him. Now he knew how to make everything right again, how to show the Haldens for the fakes they were, and how to save his career with a goddamned grand slam home run.

He'd call Houston, have them patch him through to the field office there, and have those guys relay a message to the boys in Corpus: *Bring in every known forger in the area for questioning.*

John's neck was so stiff he could hardly move it. They'd been driving all night, Annie asleep in the crowded backseat of Fancy's old Chevy. It ran rough, the tires were low, and it belched out black smoke whenever they pulled out from a traffic light, but it ran. The radio didn't work, and the further north they drove toward Dallas, the more an uneasy silence had settled over the car.

Gypsy had been very quiet, and talking to her was too hard when he was driving anyway, so he left her to her thoughts and tried every trick he knew to stay awake. Since the air conditioning didn't work and he couldn't listen to his usual wake-me-up Creedence Clearwater Revival tape, it wasn't easy.

When Annie awoke and begged for food and a bathroom, and not necessarily in that order, he exited I–35 outside Waxahachie and they got out at a McDonald's, parking around the side and using that entrance. While Gypsy took Annie to the restroom, John ordered for them and picked a booth near the side door. He sat facing the restaurant.

Stopping wasn't a bad idea. He was crazy for sleep, but still unwilling to hand over the wheel to Gypsy, since he never knew when they might get into a chase. As if they'd get very far in Fancy's heap.

Annie—ever sensitive to the strain in the atmosphere around her—had awakened cranky. Acting uncharacteristically stubborn, she refused the Big Mac he had bought for her and demanded a Happy Meal instead.

"But you love Big Macs," he coaxed.

She crossed her little arms over her chest. "There's Rooter Racers in Happy Meals this week, and I want one."

Gypsy's face looked like a volcano just before the eruption. In a barely controlled monotone, she said, "Annie, you've got two Rooter Racers at home. Now eat your Big Mac and shut up about it. Here, you can share my fries."

"But there's three in the set!" cried Annie. "If I don't get one this week, I won't have the whole set!"

John took one look at his child's clouded face and his wife's seething one and decided he'd better get the damn Happy Meal in order to avoid making a scene which would attract attention.

Standing at the counter, waiting on his order, John decided that, considering the nightmare his child had lived through over the past few days—and especially in the last twenty-four hours—a Rooter Racer seemed a small price to pay to make her happy.

He had just handed over the Happy Meal to Annie

when the front door swung open and a half dozen local sheriff's deputies sauntered in.

John froze. There had to be a statewide APB out on him—a suspected cop-killer, and here sat six Jim Bobs and one Tammy Jo, sprouting guns and all kinds of redneck good will towards closing this case for their brethren in Big D.

"Let's get out of here," he mouthed at Gypsy. *"Now."* Gypsy glanced over her shoulder, spotted the deputies, and turned back, a sort of controlled alarm in her eyes.

"We've got to stay calm," she signed. "Any sudden moves would only draw attention to us."

His heart a Mexican jumping bean, he nodded.

"They may not have my photograph yet," she signed. "I'm going to check it out—see what I can find out."

And before he could stop her, she'd headed purposefully over to the condiments island in the middle of the restaurant, sorting through salt and pepper and ketchup packages. The cops had all sat down at a large booth near the island with coffee and Egg McMuffins, talking and laughing. Ducking his head behind his burger, he watched as she sorted through the straws for a little while, then returned to her seat.

Calmly, her back to the restaurant, she signed, "I read their lips. I couldn't understand every word, of course, but from what I can tell, there's an APB out for a cop-killer in these parts. And John," she hesitated, fixing him with those soulful blue eyes. "They've got the description and license number of the Chevy."

For a long moment, John just sat there, stunned. He couldn't believe how fast his car had been traced to Fancy. He was now certain that the state was swarming with officers and agents hot on their trail.

While he bent over their food, trying not to hurry too

much, gathering up sacks and drinks to go, Gypsy busied herself with Annie and they quietly left, driving out the back way so as not to pass the window where the cops were sitting.

While Gypsy read the map for him, John took farm-to-market roads through the back country, some of them not even paved. Maize, wheat, and sorghum fields, patch-worked by lines of trees in fall colors, surrounded them, but none of them took notice of the pastoral beauty.

Harvest was over. They drove past several farmers, en-throned in the cosseted air-conditioned cabs of their big green John Deere tractors, listening to Rush Limbaugh on their radios as they plowed under the stubble. Their dusty pickups were left parked on the sides of the roads.

John pulled over behind a pickup. As he had expected in this rural area, the keys were in it. Leaving the Chevy behind and taking only Annie's Barbies, Pooh-Bear, and Rooter Racer, they pulled out in a cloud of dust.

The farmer, half a mile away and concentrating on his task, never noticed.

TWENTY-EIGHT

"SERGEANT HUONG."

"Su Lee?" He took a deep breath. "This is John Halden."

"John! Where the fuck *are* you, man? They got the freakin' *Storm Troopers* out looking for you."

"I know." As he talked, leaning into the outdoor phone booth (though they weren't really booths anymore), John scanned the 7-Eleven's parking lot for any squad cars or unmarked units he recognized. The convenience store was one of hundreds littered along the crowded Stemmons Freeway leading into downtown Dallas. After the isolation of the past few weeks, the shock of wall-to-wall cars and people was almost more than John could handle.

"I'm coming in, Su Lee, and I'm going to need your help." He hesitated. "I know it's asking a lot—"

"Shut up. You need my help, you know you got it. Can do easy GI, fie minutes. Is Gypsy with you?"

"Yeah," he said in relief. He'd been right to call Su Lee. Only the tiny Vietnamese spitfire would offer to help him easy fie minutes. "And we've got Annie."

"You know Fitzgerald got Strickland's job."

"No." John frowned. "I've kinda been out of the loop." Fitzgerald was as prone to chicken-shit as the next bureaucrat. Ironically, John felt himself wishing he could answer to Deputy Chief Strickland about his own murder. One reason the Chief had been so beloved is that he'd been a "cop's cop"—and they all knew they could trust him.

"John, what happened?"

"Would you believe me if I said, 'Hey, man, I didn't do it'?" John smiled. Cops heard those words a dozen times a day.

She laughed. "Remember that guy that broke into his boss's house and hid out in the bedroom closet for two hours with a shotgun waiting for him to come home from his kid's Little League game, and after he blew the guy away, he said, 'I just went over there to talk'?"

"And I don't know how that cocaine got in my purse," John added, his voice rising to a falsetto. "My boyfriend musta put it there."

A sudden and tense silence stretched between the two cops. Laughter was the glue that kept the lid on, that kept them all sane, that made the crazy world they saw each and every day look more like some kind of cosmic joke than the tragedy it really was. But this was too close to home, and they both knew it.

Finally, John said, "All I can say over the phone is that this whole thing was a setup, Su Lee, and Gypsy and I have gathered evidence to prove it."

After a moment, she said, "I believe you."

"I want to show this evidence to Fitzgerald, *and no one else*, you copy?"

"Got it."

"And Gypsy and I want to be allowed to enter the department unmolested. I don't want some damn glory-boy yanking my ass around and clapping cuffs on me in front of my kid, understand?"

"No problem. I'll see to it. Give me an hour to get everything in place."

"Girl, there's nobody else we can trust, and I mean *nobody.*"

"It's an honor, John, and I mean that."

"I owe you."

"You don't owe me a thing. Just be careful. It's really bad out there."

He squinted over towards the dusty pickup he'd stolen, where Gypsy's strained face gazed straight ahead through the buggy windshield. She was cradling a disheveled, sleeping Annie in her lap. He said, "You don't have to tell me."

Gypsy felt as if she were held together by gossamer filaments thin as a spider's web. If one more thing happened to upset the delicate balance, the filaments would break, and she would disintegrate into a hundred little fragments of flesh and bone and mind. The dramatic events of the previous days had piled atop one another with the blinding white efficiency of snowflakes; each one an individual finespun mystery of design, but packed together, a powerful and potentially deadly avalanche. She didn't think she could tolerate the weight of one more flake on her delicate self-control.

Watching her husband as he hunched over the pay phone in front of the convenience store, it occurred to her that, in the span of less than one month's time, he had aged ten years. He'd dropped at least fifteen pounds off his already-lean body, causing his jeans to droop at the butt and the T-shirt to hang like a hand-me-down. Deep creases crisscrossed his forehead and worked their way

down from his nose to the corners of his mouth. Un-
shaven, rumple-headed, stoop-shouldered from fatigue, he
bore little resemblance to the tall, good-looking, confident
intelligence cop she knew.

She found herself wondering if it made him somehow
look guilty.

Bizarre, really. Here they were, in the city they'd called
home their entire married life, living a fugitive's life in a
stolen pickup that smelled faintly of chewing tobacco.
They could be in their house in less than twenty minutes,
luxuriating in a hot shower and falling into bed—but of
course, that was not an option. The FBI was sure to have
the place staked out, and if they fell into the hands of the
feds before they had a chance to talk to the deputy chief,
the case they had so carefully put together against Parker
Jefferson would vanish like morning mist beneath the rising Texas sun.

He would see to that.

John hung up the phone and sloped over to the pickup,
slouching down into the seat like a lazy-eyed high school
kid.

"She needs an hour," he said.

"An *hour?*" It might as well have been a week. "Why
can't we just go over there now?"

"She's got to track down the Chief, brief him, then get
the word out to the uniforms that we are hands-off."

Gypsy's fragile self-control bowed under this added
snowflake, the one more thing she didn't think she could
handle. Working around Annie's slumbering body, she
signed so hard that her hands stung from slapping them
together, *"We don't have that much time! The feds are
everywhere. They'll catch us!"*

Her eyes burned with unwanted tears; tears of powerlessness and fear and exhaustion.

Fixing her in a stern gaze, he also signed forcefully, *"Get yourself together, Gypsy! You've got to do it for Annie, if nothing else."*

She felt heat rising up her neck and flooding into her cheeks. *"I think I've done a damn good job of holding myself together,* thank you very much, *considering the fact that the whole world believed my husband was a lying murderer,"* she responded, exaggerating the sign for "murderer."

John looked as though he'd been slapped.

Gypsy had to look away. With all the predators circling them, here they were, about to self-destruct. She couldn't let stress and exhaustion rob them of what they'd fought so hard to keep. She looked back and signed, *"I'm sorry."*

Reaching out to take one of her hands, he said aloud, "No, I'm sorry. I keep forgetting that you've been through hell, too. We're both just tired and worried."

She nodded and tried to smile, but the effort failed and he did not smile back. Annie stirred in her lap.

"We've got to keep moving," said John. "The longer we sit in one place, the more chance we'll be noticed." He put the truck in gear and headed out of the parking lot.

"Do you think the farmer has reported the pickup stolen?" she asked anxiously.

Concentrating on traffic as he maneuvered back onto the freeway, he shrugged.

Gypsy knew as well as John did that the farmer would not only report the stolen pickup, but the abandoned Chevy which had been substituted for it, which had probably been entered into every police computer in the state. And the mud-crusted old pickup stood out in a city dominated by family-type suburbanite vehicles—mini-vans and compact economy cars and Yuppie-style foreign luxury cars. Even the city boys who drove pickups seldom took them off the pavement; most of them were show-room clean. This was a working farm vehicle, and it was clearly out of place in the tangled urban sprawl that was the Dallas-Fort Worth metroplex.

Suddenly, John's hands tensed on the steering wheel, and his whole body stiffened. The deaf are exquisitely sensitive to body language—it is, after all, the way they communicate—and Gypsy was already on alert before he cried, *"Shit!"*, his gaze riveted to the rearview mirror.

Gypsy twisted around to look, and little needles of panic electrified her body.

A motorcycle cop had swung into the lane right behind them, and was leaning forward, peering closely at the pickup.

Keep cool, John thought. Changing lanes without accelerating, he took the next exit. The motorcycle jockey followed, but didn't hit his lights. *He's curious, but not positive,* John figured, his heart racing. *I've got to lose him before he makes the plate and calls it in.* The problem was not the cop; it was the radio. As soon as the pickup was made and called in, the feds would know about it.

The nylon athletic bag rested on the floorboard between Gypsy's feet. They'd paid little attention to the money, but had stuffed the incriminating videotape and the evidence collected by Gypsy at the house where John had been held captive into the bag. All it took was one little ambitious sycophant—of which the FBI had no lack—to ferret the bag away and hand it over to the SAC with a reverential bow and a genuflection.

If that happened, they'd never see it again.

He took a right and, a couple of blocks later, a left. After the second turn, he checked the prominent side mirrors and a few moments later, as he had feared, the motor jockey popped back into view.

A desperate idea, conceived in fear and born in frustration, crept into his mind. There was no way of knowing if it would work, but fugitives had no guarantees anyway. He headed downtown, taking every opportunity presented to him to put cars between him and his relentless pursuer. At any moment, he expected a police back up unit to show up in front of him and cut him off.

He glanced over at Gypsy, sitting white-knuckled, her unflinching gaze glued to the mirror on her side. She hadn't figured out his plan yet, and he couldn't take the time to explain it to her. Keeping a steady speed, coming to a full stop at signs and only running yellow lights if there was a car between him and the motor jockey, John prayed under his breath that he had the time to make it work.

A cold sweat broke out over his body; he could feel it beaded beneath the stubble on his upper lip. Annie sat up in her mother's lap, looked around her groggily, then stretched out on the seat between them, placing her head on his thigh. John looked down at her. She was staring up at him, her sleepy blue eyes wide and trusting. He was her daddy. He would make everything all right. John cupped the palm of one hand around her soft cheek, fighting back tears of rage and fear-driven exhaustion.

If he failed, they would take her daddy away from her and she'd never see him again except in prison.

It wasn't fair, goddamn it. It wasn't fair.

Then he spotted it up ahead: rusty corrugated tin roofing somehow apart from the other buildings and yet surrounded by them. Gypsy sat up straight; she'd seen it too, she understood. It was a cavernous, open-air space that, in summertime, was usually crowded with pickup trucks and the farmers who drove them.

Anyone could pull up and park, let down a tailgate, and sell their garden produce to supermarket-spawned suburban shoppers hungry for something home-grown.

The Farmer's Market.

But this wasn't summer. This was fall. John's plan was to lose the pickup—pull up and park the rig between other trucks just like it. Then he and Gypsy and Annie could melt into the crowd and catch a bus for the police department down on Main and Harwood. For all he knew though, the place could be closed now.

Turning a corner, he leaned forward to see better, and allowed a nervous smile to flit across his face.

He'd forgotten all about Halloween pumpkins.

They almost made it. Just as the big bus came wheezing up to the bus stop and John, Gypsy, and Annie stepped out of the sheltering downtown store doorway to get on, a DPD unit cruised to a stop just behind the bus. Gypsy and John immediately shielded their faces and crowded into the line in hopes of avoiding notice, but it was too late. They'd been spotted and they knew it as soon as the uniformed officer climbed out from behind the wheel and sprinted over to them, his hand resting lightly on his sidearm.

Annie said, "Uh-oh. We're busted."

Gypsy thought her heart had surely stopped.

Standing directly in front of John and blocking his entry onto the bus steps, the craggy-faced veteran cop said, "John Halden?"

Grim-faced, John gave a slow nod.

"I don't know if you remember me."

"Yes. You're Charlie Speedacker. I remember you from my days on patrol."

"Lots of folks lookin' for you, son."

John met his eyes with a look of quiet desperation. Through clenched teeth, he said, "Please, man. Don't cuff me in front of my little girl."

Speedacker gave the couple a gentle smile, his eyes almost disappearing in the folds of skin around them. "No problem," he said, "The word's already come down. Just don't make a fuss."

John took Gypsy's hand in one of his and Annie's in another. "I won't."

"Raise your arms," Speedacker said apologetically. "I gotta pat you down."

John nodded. "I've got a thirty-eight in the waistband of my jeans." While a gathering crowd stared, he raised his arms at his sides.

"Okay." The officer took the weapon and patted John down. He glanced at Gypsy. "I'm sorry, John. you know I've got to do this."

"It's all right," Gypsy said, raising her arms. He gave her a perfunctory pat-down, but still it made her feel, well, *busted.* She hated the feeling.

Her stomach somersaulting, Gypsy followed the men toward the squad car. John stopped. Speedacker gave him a wary look. "I just have one favor to ask, from one old cop to another. I can't explain why, but I would appreciate it more than you know if you'd keep this off the radio."

Speedacker measured John with one long look. "Halden," he said, "I never thought for one minute that you had anything to do with the Chief's killin'. I won't say a word."

Gypsy said, "Thank you. You don't know . . ."

Brushing away her comment, he held open the car door to the backseat for her as she climbed into the cruiser, followed by Annie and then John.

Now Gypsy knew what it felt like to be a prisoner.

The Dallas Police Department was located in a giant gray brick building that squatted like a dowager chaperone among all the sleek young debs of glass and chrome that towered above it. They met Su Lee down in the basement, just a few steps away from the very spot where Lee Harvey Oswald had been shot dead. There was a rusty dark stain on the cement floor there, and Gypsy never ceased to fancy to herself that it was the mark of Oswald's blood.

They took a back elevator up to the fifth floor. After the initial hugs of greeting, there was very little to say. Annie, however, liked Su Lee and chattered away at the officer about her new Rooter Racer and the stinky pickup they rode in and how badly she had wanted to buy a jack-o'-lantern but that her daddy said no.

"Well, while your mommy and daddy are busy, we'll just have to go and get us a pumpkin then, won't we?" she said, quirking her eyebrows at Gypsy.

Annie jumped up and down, hugging Pooh-Bear, two Barbie dolls, and the Rooter Racer. "Can we cut out the face on it now? Can we?"

Su Lee laughed. "Well, that would be a highly unusual activity for a big bad-ass po-lice department, but I don't see why not, as long as it's okay with your folks."

Gypsy said, "That would be very nice of you, Su Lee. Thank you."

An unexpected lump formed in her throat. Making jack-o'-lanterns was a time-honored Halden family tradition. Their whole life had been turned topsy-turvy and she wondered if it would ever be right again.

Blinking, she glanced away and tightened her grip on the heavy athletic bag. She felt a warm hand over hers. It was John, gently prying her fingers off the handle and taking the bag from her. She leaned her head into his shoulder, and the elevator doors opened.

Su Lee escorted them down the faded hallway to the deputy chief's office. Gypsy limped stiffly, her body pieced together by aches and bruises from the flying leap she'd taken out of Jefferson's car. Even worse, her heart seemed permanently lodged in her throat. She swallowed, but it did no good. Her mouth was too dry to make spit, and it suddenly occurred to her how she must look: her clothes were still muddy from the struggle with Jefferson in the woods, her makeup either rubbed off or smeared off, her face bruised, her hair windblown and wild.

What a pair we make, she thought, giving John a sideways glance.

Fitzgerald spotted them and got to his full, cadaverous height behind his desk, peering down his bony nose like a priest who had just caught the altar boy stealing from the collection plate. Su Lee took Annie and discreetly vanished. Gypsy knew the afternoon was going to be a long one when John extended his hand and the chief ignored it.

Fitzgerald indicated two chairs opposite his desk, and Gypsy and John took their seats uneasily. Gypsy looked at John, studying his lips so she wouldn't miss anything, but to her relief, he signed as he spoke.

"I was framed for the murder of Deputy Chief Strickland," he said. "My wife, who is a qualified crime lab specialist, has assisted me in gathering evidence to prove my innocence."

Fitzgerald frowned. "Where the hell have you been?"

"I was kidnapped, sir, and held hostage. My wife actually tracked me down and helped me to escape."

"Who kidnapped you?"

"We can clear everything up, sir, with the contents of this bag—"

There was a commotion at the door. Gypsy turned to look a fraction of a second after John did.

With his clean-shaven, hawk-eyed, suited self exuding authority, in walked Special Agent Dash Jefferson.

TWENTY-NINE

DASH KEPT HIS EXPRESSION CAREFULLY impassive as John Halden leapt to his feet. "This is an outrage!" he cried, his face stricken. "I specifically stated that I would see no one but you!"

Fitzgerald gave Halden a cold smile. It did not improve on his ugliness. "Sergeant Halden, you should know as well as anyone that when a suspect enters the police department for questioning, he abandons his right to demand *anything,* except his lawyer. It was my decision to involve Special Agent Jefferson in this interview because you are accused of a federal crime in conjunction with the murder of Abe Strickland. Now. Do you want to call your lawyer?"

It was a sweet moment for Dash, one that made all the shit he'd gone through worth it. That bitch who'd tried to kill him the night before looked like she was about to puke. Halden was still sputtering when Dash reached down between the two chairs, grabbed and hoisted the athletic bag. "What's in here?" he asked, a nasty smirk tugging at the corners of his mouth. "More computer fraud money?"

Gypsy burst into tears. It almost made him laugh. "Chief Fitzgerald, *please,* at least *look* at what we've gathered!" Snatching the bag from Dash's hand, she plunged her hand inside and yanked out a clear evidence bag which contained several white cards with transparent overlays. The overlays protected fingerprints.

"We lifted these fingerprints from the house where *this man*"—she paused dramatically, pointing a finger at Dash like a character in some old Perry Mason courtroom drama—"held my husband hostage!"

"What?" cried Fitzgerald. "Have you lost your *mind?"*

He looked at Dash, who raised his hands in the air in a gesture that said, "See how *ridiculous* this whole thing is?" Dash let out a sanctimonious sigh and shook his head for emphasis, saying, "I'm sure you know as well as I do, Chief Fitzgerald, that my prints could be lifted from almost anywhere." He gave Gypsy a withering look.

She was practically frothing at the mouth, which only helped Dash's case. There he stood, cool and calm, the consummate professional, while she blubbered around looking like a bag lady on speed.

"But we've got a videotape!" she cried, grabbing one from out of the bag in such a rush that out popped a stack of money, bound neatly by a rubber band.

A hush fell over the room.

Fitzgerald's voice was funereal. He extended one long, skinny arm and commanded, "Give me that bag."

"But, you have to let us explain—"

Halden looked pained, as though he'd just realized he'd run over his puppy. "Gypsy," he said aloud and in sign language, "Give the chief the bag."

For a long, pregnant moment, she stared at him, doom etched across her face. It was all Dash could do not to give her a wicked little smile.

She handed over the bag.

Fitzgerald dumped out its contents over his desk. "What the fuck *is* all this!" he bellowed.

This was Dash's moment, and he wanted to take full advantage of it. "That, Chief Fitzgerald, is the product of an FBI sting operation to expose an extortionist and a blackmailer. If you'll look," he added, enjoying this whole thing immensely, "you'll find that the money covers stacks of paper." He chuckled. "They thought they were getting one hundred thousand dollars."

"WHAT?" Halden's horrified cry rang off the rafters. "You lying son-of-a-bitch!" He took a step toward Dash.

"Sit down, Halden, before I have you put in cuffs!" yelled Fitzgerald, fixing Halden with a terrible glare. After a few seconds, he plunked down in his seat.

"May I continue?" said Dash, arranging a long-suffering look on his face.

Fitzgerald scowled. "Please."

"Our agents in Corpus Christi have been questioning a known forger by the name of Samuel 'Fancy Fingers' Myers—I believe he has a nephew who has served the DPD as an informant? Man named 'Mooch' Myers?"

Fitzgerald's eyebrows shot up and he glared at Halden. "Go on."

"Anyway. Mr. Fancy Fingers assisted the Haldens in their pathetic blackmailing scheme. I have already turned over the notes he forged to our labs for analysis." The last part was not true. Dash pasted a satisfied smile on his face to cover the lie.

In the silence that followed, Gypsy's voice was small, almost childlike. "At least, just look at the tape," she begged.

Fitzgerald sighed. "Fine." He flipped on a TV on a shelf behind him and picked up the videotape.

Dash stood there, thinking furiously. He wasn't sure what was on the tape, but he had an idea. *But how?* There were no bugs on the dock, and as far as Dash could tell at the time, no one nearby. How good was the quality? What exactly had he said, and what had they gotten on tape? He had to see it first. Had to get rid of it somehow—or at the very least, figure a way to spin-doctor it. He glanced at Fitzgerald as he prepared to shove the tape into the videocassette recorder. It was unfortunate, but evidence got lost all the time. "I'd really prefer if our lab boys got a look at it first, if you don't mind," Dash said. "I'll ship it straight to Washington. They'll have a transcript and a complete report ready in a few days."

Fitzgerald hesitated. "Well, I suppose that might be best . . ."

Halden looked as if he were about to hit someone, only he couldn't figure out who. His wife was clawing at the air toward Fitzgerald, trying in a gesture of almost comical futility to grab the tape out of Fitzgerald's hand, which he held over his head like a basketball player teasing his kid sister. The new deputy chief looked at Dash in total bewilderment.

It was the sweetest moment.

Dash glanced at the scowling Halden. He couldn't *wait* until he got John Halden alone. He pulled a pair of handcuffs out of his pocket.

"John Halden, I am placing you under arrest for computer fraud, a federal crime, as well as extortion and blackmail, and the capital murder of a police officer. You have the right to remain silent—"

"If you don't mind, Chief Fitzgerald, I'd like to take a

look a that tape now," boomed a voice from the open doorway.

Everybody in the room whirled to face the door except for Dash.

He didn't need to.

He recognized the voice.

"Here are my credentials. I'm Special Agent Brook Corruthers, assistant director in charge of the Criminal Investigative Division of the FBI."

Still Dash did not turn around. In that moment, he wondered if maybe he hadn't been right all along—it really *was* a conspiracy of his enemies, designed to bring him down.

"And what is your interest in this case, Agent Corruthers?" demanded Fitzgerald.

Out of the corner of his eye, Dash watched as a clear plastic evidence envelope sailed across Fitzgerald's desk. It appeared to contain a letter.

"This letter only just now made it to my office," said Corruthers. "It was written and addressed to Director Kellerman and put away in a safety deposit box, to be mailed only if . . ."

"Who wrote it?" interrupted Fitzgerald rudely, peering at the signature.

"Your predecessor, sir. Deputy Chief Abe Strickland."

Dash felt every drop of blood drain from his face.

To Gypsy, it appeared as if the man's face had caved in upon itself like a rumpled patchwork quilt, but he stood ramrod straight, scarcely breathing as the chief and Corruthers discussed Strickland's allegations against Dash Jefferson, whose scarred face, blotched crimson and white beneath the merciless fluorescent lights, so resembled the Jigsaw Man who'd stood over her so many years before that Gypsy felt herself holding her breath. Oddly though, she no longer felt the crippling fear such an image usually instilled in her. Just rage. And a sort of scornful pity.

"Due to President Clinton's appointment of Special Agent Jefferson to succeed him and the impending press conference tomorrow, Director Kellerman specifically requested that I give this matter my full attention, especially in light of his recent illness. I've done some checking, sir," added Corruthers, "and this thing goes all the way back the Kennedy assassination."

"*What?*" Fitzgerald's chin drooped in his bewilderment. "What the hell does the Kennedy assassination have to do with John Halden?"

Corruthers turned a kind but steely face toward Gypsy and said, "He's married to Mike Jefferson's daughter, who was deafened at the same time her mother was murdered. Mike Jefferson," he added, "was Special Agent Jefferson's brother. A Dallas cop who was brutally murdered himself back in 1972."

Fitzgerald shook his head. "I still don't get what any of this has to do with anything."

Corruthers pointed to the incriminating letter, lying like a crouching spider on Fitzgerald's desk. "According to Deputy Chief Strickland, Special Agent Jefferson killed his brother when he threatened to expose some letters which would prove that Jefferson bungled an investigation into the pre-assassination activities of Lee Harvey Oswald, back in November of 1963."

"He murdered my mother for the same reason!" cried Gypsy. "And he kidnapped John—all because that bastard wanted those letters, so the whole world wouldn't know what a blithering idiot he really is." She gave Jefferson a defiant glare.

Jefferson's voice, when he finally spoke, sent chills of goose bumps crawling over Gypsy's body. She'd heard it before, the night her mother died.

"This is an outrage, Fitzgerald. I told you, the Haldens hired a professional forger—a convicted felon—to forge those so-called letters in an extortion attempt." He turned and caught Gypsy's eyes in a diabolical gaze. "The letters do not exist."

"Agent . . . what? Corruthers? I gotta say Jefferson's got a point," said Fitzgerald. "This whole thing is ludicrous. I mean, I have a lot of respect for old Abe, but . . ."

"Let's take a look at the tape, shall we?" persisted Corruthers.

Mutely, the Jigsaw Man shrugged and visibly steeled his face.

Fitzgerald plugged in the video, rewound it only partway, and pushed the start button.

Blackness leapt into view, and soon focused to reveal a platform of some kind and two people standing talking under a fuzzy light. It was too dark, and the camera too far away from the subjects to show them very clearly. The camera was not still, either, but jerked up and down in a distracting rhythm.

Gypsy didn't realize it, but the only sounds which could be clearly heard were the lapping of water against the sides of a boat, and the slightly garbled whisper of a little girl saying, "Daddy, are we through yet?"

Dash whirled to face Corruthers, his face contorted with rage. "How dare you butt into my investigation and impugn my character, Corruthers! When I make director, you're out, do you hear me? *Out!*" In a quieter, deadly voice, he added, *"Et tu, Brutus?"*

Then, stabbing the air with a stiff finger, he pointed at the video still playing on the TV screen. "That's *nothing!* This whole thing is a charade cooked up by John Halden and his wife to deflect suspicion from them. And if you don't place them under arrest, Fitzgerald, *I will!*"

John Halden sprang from his chair and took a menacing step toward Jefferson, who made a big show of reaching for his gun.

"Jefferson knows as well as I do that this video can be enhanced with computer graphics to give a reasonably clear picture of the man on that pier," said John, panting as if he'd been running a race. "And if you'll rewind it to the beginning, you'll see footage we shot in that godforsaken hole where he kept me prisoner for two weeks."

"That doesn't prove a goddamned thing, Halden, and you know it," snarled Dash. "You set the whole thing up from start to finish and the sooner you confess, the better it will be for all of us."

"Oh yeah? And did I set up you telling Gypsy that you killed her parents and Chief Strickland because they *got in your way?*" He almost spat the last words.

The two men squared off. The room crackled with the tension between them. A chair scraped as Chief Fitzgerald got to his feet. Neither man blinked.

"You got nothin' on me," snapped Jefferson in a low, rumbling growl, his lip curling at the words. "You saw the tape. You don't have a goddamned thing." Victory glittered in his eyes.

John stared into the despised man's face for an eternal moment, allowing his own glare to communicate all the hatred he felt for him. Finally, slowly quirking up one corner of his mouth in a smug smirk, he said, "Well then, perhaps this will help."

From the breast pocket of his shirt, his movements slow and deliberate in order for him to savor the moment, he pulled out a cassette tape. To Fitzgerald, he said only, "I think you'll find that, when this tape is synchronized with the video, you will have a clear soundtrack."

Dash grabbed for the tape and John tossed it overhand to Corruthers, who deftly caught it one-handed and immediately requested a cassette tape recorder.

Fitzgerald pulled one out of a drawer and placed it on his desk. Corruthers popped in the tape.

Then they all stared, riveted, as the new presidential appointee for director of the FBI admitted that he had murdered and kidnapped people simply because they got in his way, and listened, open-mouthed as he offered a hundred thousand dollars to the people who threatened to expose him.

By the time the tape got to Gypsy's terrifying ordeal on the dock at midnight, and Jefferson's barely recognizable but bone-chilling, *"I'm through fucking with you. Give me the letters or I'll kill you,"* and then his blood-curdling shout: *"I can't let you get away! You know too much,"* and the ensuing nightmarish chase through the woods, every face in the room had gone ghostly pale.

Only Dash Jefferson still stood at attention, staring straight ahead, his scar-patched face immobile, like a man who has just been granted the rare privilege of attending his own funeral.

Fitzgerald punched the off button on the recorder.

The room was dead silent.

Finally, he turned to John and wondered aloud, "How were you able to get that kind of sound? It's perfectly clear. We could hear every word."

Agent Corruthers, with admiration in his voice added,

"Our labs will be able to get a perfect voiceprint match. They're as distinctive as fingerprints."

And John, signing for Gypsy as he spoke, looked at her with love and joy almost overflowing from his eyes and said, "You'd be surprised what kind of transmitter can be rigged from ten bucks worth of stuff from Radio Shack and the components from a hearing aid."

THIRTY

IN THE SHADE OF THE evening, the sun set behind the trees, casting the screened-in porch into cool blue shadow, fanned by Gulf breezes that always picked up at day's end and blew the mosquitoes away. The sky deepened from a high silver-blue to slate to violet velvet as brilliant fuchsia-colored roseate spoonbills cruised in to roost in small squadrons of four or five. The Gulf deepened to midnight blue and the sky to purple until gradually, the two blurred together and the pier lights winked on in an iridescent string. Stars peeked out from under the misty pearl wash cast by the moon. There was a lazy salt taste to the air.

This was Gypsy's favorite time of day. When every ounce of pleasure that could be wrung from the sunset had been, she went to the door and called to supper a reluctant Annie, who had been playing on the newly rebuilt pier with her friends. Still amazingly chock-full of energy after a long, hot, humid summer day, she bounded up the freshly repaired boardwalk and slammed onto the porch, smelling of the sea and salt and sweat and little girlness.

"Don't forget to wash up!" called Gypsy as the child disappeared into the house. How like her father she was getting to be, so tall and rangy. Gypsy turned and smiled at her husband, who had been napping in the shade after a hard day's renovating.

"What's for dinner?" he asked, not bothering to open his eyes.

She gave him a wicked grin. "Bologna sandwiches."

His eyes snapped open, and in a dead calm voice, he drawled, "Lady, I've been known to kill for less."

"Oh. Well. In that case . . . I thought steaks cooked out on the grill would be nice."

He returned her smile. "Happy?"

"Ecstatic. It's over now. Really over."

"Did you really doubt Jefferson would be convicted?"

"Yes, I did—and it all started about the time he hired O. J. Simpson's lawyer to represent him."

He winked at her and said, "Once the judge allowed that cassette tape into evidence, Jefferson's goose was cooked. I don't care if he had God for a lawyer. Anyway," he added, "I expect that the worst punishment Dash Jefferson will have to endure is in knowing that Agent Corruthers got the appointment as FBI director."

Gypsy nodded. "He deserves it. That investigation into Jefferson's doings that he headed was outstanding, and I couldn't believe the way he allowed full disclosure to the press."

"Well, it's a new FBI, they say. And he's in favor of closer press scrutiny of the organization. Says it'll keep 'em on their toes."

"Well, he was on his toes when he traced all those flight plans Jefferson filed each time he flew to Rockport. If he hadn't thought to do that, we'd have no substantial proof that he'd been in Rockport during your captivity, or even that it was he who'd rented the house and built the secret room."

"Plus, Corruthers has been a good friend to us."

"Yes, he has. I think he wants to make it up to us somehow, you know? He doesn't want us to think that all FBI agents are monsters."

"I already knew that. I've worked with a number of good agents. Some not-so-good. But no other monsters."

They lapsed into a companionable silence.

"I got another call from Hollywood," Gypsy said after a while. "They're going to air the TV movie next month, just in time for sweeps."

"Good. Then it really *will* be over," he teased.

"Don't turn up your nose. That movie is paying for all this. " She swept her arm to include the remodeling that had been going on for months while Jefferson's lawyer tried every tactic known to law to keep his client out of prison.

"And I have to admit," said John, "it is helping me get my start down here as a private investigator."

She sat down in a redwood chair next to him and took his hand. "Any regrets?"

"You kidding?"

"I mean about leaving the PD, moving away from the city, starting over."

"How about you? You grew up hating this place."

"I'm different now." It was almost getting too dark for her to be able to follow a conversation. *I've come a long way,* she thought, *and it all started the day I realized that it was not my fault that my mother died that night, any more than would be Annie's fault if she witnessed a car wreck.*

She thought of her mother often these days as she rubbed lemon oil into the old furniture and put up new wallpaper. Her smile, her soft hands.

She realized now why her mother insisted they not sell

the house. From out of the depths of her loneliness and grief and fear, she had recognized it as a place of healing.

Gypsy worried a little about the movie and how everyone in it would be portrayed. The celebrity-actress who was playing the role of Gypsy Halden had gone to the trouble and expense of flying to south Texas to meet Gypsy and get to know her. She seemed in awe of Gypsy, since the script, apparently, had made her quite the hero.

This made Gypsy uncomfortable, and she assured the actress that there was no such thing as a hero; that when a person found himself or herself, or a loved one, in a life-threatening situation, well, they just did what had to be done. That's all.

The actress seemed unconvinced. One night, over wine and fresh south Texas fruit, John and Gypsy and the actress, who was much younger and more glamorous than Gypsy was, talked about it. John said that the country needed heroes; that people needed someone they could look up to as being larger-than-life, someone whose example they could emulate.

"In a way, that's what made John Kennedy such an icon to the American people. In life, he made mistakes and had his political enemies, but in death, he assumed heroic dimensions to us." He savored a sip of wine. "That splendid funeral with the riderless horse and the eternal flame, the heartbreakingly beautiful young widow and the brave children—it all made us somehow feel above ourselves. A real tribute to the human spirit. It was majestic."

"But there's nothing healthy about hero-worship," Gypsy argued. "It creates monsters like Lee Harvey Oswald and Dash Jefferson—people so hungry to appear heroic in their own twisted little minds that they commit unspeakable crimes."

"Are you saying, then, that we should ignore an oppor-

tunity to do something heroic, should it present itself, because we don't want to give the sick minority out there
any bad ideas?"

"But that's just it," insisted Gypsy. "The true hero
doesn't set out to be heroic. If he's a victim of a train
wreck, say, over a Louisiana bayou in the middle of the
night, and he hears people crying for help, he doesn't stop
to think, *'Gee, should I try to look like a hero?'* He just
does what he has to do, what his very humanity *compells*
him to do: He saves lives. He does the right thing."

"I think I understand what you're saying," said the actress. "As members of the human race, we have an obliga-
tion to respect human life, a commitment, almost, to do
what we can to protect it. And yet, when somebody does
something that should be *normal,* should be as natural as
breathing—he helps to save lives when he's got the
chance—then the media jumps on the bandwagon and the
next thing you know, the poor guy finds himself on every
talk show and every news program, interviewed by
swarms and throngs of reporters, telling his story over and
over like it is the most phenomenal thing imaginable."
She smiled her famous flawless smile.

"And they offer him a lot of money to tell his story, to
make it into a movie, and big-time movie stars come calling," added Gypsy with an ironic glint to her eye.

"I see," said the actress, then couldn't resist teasing,
"Of course, the guy then has the option to *turn down* the
money and refuse the offers!"

"At which time," John intoned, "the producers will tell
it anyway, regardless of how accurate it may or may not
be."

Gypsy nodded. "You've just about got to cooperate, if
you want any control whatsoever as to how you are going
to be portrayed on national TV."

"But you can't help but look heroic," said the actress, "and in the long run, we love our heroes."

So there would always be the atmosphere, it seemed that would spawn the little-minded people like Dash Jefferson to do things they hoped would get them some measure of that hero-worship, could, in some way, make them like themselves. That still bothered her.

A schooner moon sailed above the clouds, sending blue-white shafts of light through the tangled boughs of the leaning oaks that surrounded the house like church light through stained-glass windows, and spangled silver off the sea like an angelic halo.

For the most part, things seemed to have settled down in Gypsy's life since her horrible confrontation with the Jigsaw Man. There were still transitions to be made. Gypsy hadn't found another job and was having a little trouble adjusting to that lack in her life, but she was confident that, with time, she would find a new direction.

Maybe they would have another child. Annie had been begging for a little brother or sister.

As Gypsy reluctantly turned away from the glorious view and headed into the kitchen to start supper, the overhead lights blinked on and off. Heading for the guest room—which John had converted into a study, she answered her special phone. "Hello?"

"MAY I PLEASE SPEAK TO MS. GYPSY HALDEN?"

"Speaking."

"PLEASE HOLD FOR DIRECTOR CORRUTHERS."

She waited.

"GYPSY! HOW ARE YOU?"

"I'm fine, Director Corruthers. It's good to hear from you."

"FOR GOD'S SAKE GYPSY, I TOLD YOU, CALL ME BROOK."

"Sorry. I forgot."

"I JUST WANTED TO CHECK AND MAKE SURE YOU'D HEARD THE VERDICT TODAY."

"Yes, we heard it."

"REVENGE IS SWEET, IS IT NOT?"

"Not revenge, Brook. Justice."

"YOU'RE RIGHT. YOU'RE A BETTER MAN THAN I AM, GYPSY. IF SOMEBODY HAD KILLED MY FOLKS, I'D WANT REVENGE."

"I just want the guy put away someplace where he can't hurt anybody else who gets in his way."

"I KNOW WHAT YOU MEAN. LISTEN, I'VE HAD SOME AGENTS CHECKING INTO THE FIRE THAT KILLED YOUR GRANDPARENTS."

For a moment, Gypsy was stumped. What grandparents? What fire? Then, with a small chill, she realized that Brook was referring to the fire from which Jefferson had pulled his brother—her father. Until this moment, it had never occurred to Gypsy to think of the two people who'd died in that fire as her grandparents, but of course, they were.

"YOU STILL THERE?"

"Yeah, I'm still here. You just threw me a little, is all."

"SORRY, I'M USED TO THINKING ON A SINGLE TRACK."

"It's okay. What have you learned?"

"NOTHING CONCLUSIVE. BUT I THOUGHT YOU'D WANT TO KNOW THAT ARSON WAS SUS-PECTED IN THAT FIRE, BUT NEVER PROVED. AND AT LEAST ONE FIREFIGHTER WHO'S STILL AROUND TOLD OUR AGENTS THAT HE'D ALWAYS BEEN A LITTLE SUSPICIOUS OF OUR BIG HERO."

"You mean Jefferson?"

"THE VERY SAME. HE WAS ATTENDING A PARTY

*THAT NIGHT DOWN THE BLOCK. HIS BROTHER
AND PARENTS WERE AT HOME AND THEY ALL
WENT TO BED EARLY. IT WAS SOME TIME LATER
THAT DASH CAME HOME AND SUPPOSEDLY DIS-
COVERED THE FIRE. THING IS, WHAT THIS OLD
CODGER SAYS HE SUSPECTED WAS THAT DASH—
WHO WAS, YOU REMEMBER, A TRACK STAR—HAD
TIME TO DUCK OUT OF THE PARTY, RACE HOME,
START THE FIRE, RUN BACK AND BE SEEN SOCIAL-
IZING WHILE THE FIRE SPREAD. THERE WAS NO
ACCELERANT USED, SEE, AND THAT'S WHY ARSON
COULD NEVER BE PROVED. BUT THERE WAS MORE
THAN ONE SOURCE FOR THE FIRE AND OUR EX-
PERTS TELL US THAT FIRE ALMOST NEVER STARTS
FROM MORE THAN ONE SOURCE. NOT ON ITS OWN,
ANYWAY."*

Gypsy took a few moments to let the impact of what
Brook was telling her to sink in. "Brook, do you realize
what you are saying?"

*"INDEED I DO. IF WHAT THAT OLD FIREMAN
SAID IS TRUE—AND WE'LL NEVER HAVE ANY
PROOF OF IT, YOU KNOW THAT—THEN THE LITTLE
BASTARD HAD EVERY INTENTION OF DELIBER-
ATELY CAUSING THE DEATHS OF HIS ENTIRE FAM-
ILY."*

"But why? Why would he do such a thing?"

*"WELL, HE'S SICK, FOR ONE THING. HE'D HAVE
TO BE. BUT THESE INVESTIGATORS SHOWED ME
AN OLD HIGH SCHOOL YEARBOOK FROM THOSE
DAYS, AND YOUR DADDY WAS SHOWN ON JUST
ABOUT EVERY PAGE. A REAL BMOC. MR. THIS AND
MR. THAT. HERO. MOST LIKELY TO SUCCEED.
MOST HANDSOME. OUR HERO, LITTLE BROTHER
DASH, WAS A NERD OF THE FIRST DEGREE."*

"Well hell, Brook! You don't go killing off your family because your big brother's popular and you're a geek, do you?"

"I DON'T, NO, BUT DASH . . ." There was a pause. *"APPARENTLY IT WAS VERY COMPLEX. THE SITUATION IN THAT HOUSE, I MEAN. OUR GUYS TRACKED DOWN SOME CLASSMATES OF JEFFERSON'S. THEY SAY HIS FOLKS NEVER MISSED ONE OF HIS BROTHER'S FOOTBALL GAMES, BUT THEY NEVER ATTENDED A SINGLE ONE OF THEIR OTHER SON'S TRACK MEETS."*

"If you're trying to make me feel sorry for the guy . . ."

"OF COURSE NOT. BUT IT WAS JUST A COMPLICATED SITUATION, THE WAY MOST DYSFUNCTIONAL FAMILIES ARE. HE WAS FIFTEEN YEARS OLD AT THE TIME, GYPSY. A KID. HIS FOLKS HAVE GOT TO ASSUME SOME SORT OF RESPONSIBILITY FOR THE WAY HE TURNED OUT. EVEN IN DEATH."

"I guess. But let me ask you this. If he really wanted everybody to die, then why would he save my father?"

"NOBODY CAN ANSWER THAT. BUT OUR GUYS FOUND THE NEXT DOOR NEIGHBOR, BELIEVE IT OR NOT, IN A NURSING HOME, STILL SHARP AS A TACK. SHE SAID THAT WHEN SHE CALLED THE FIRE DEPARTMENT, DASH WAS STANDING IN THE YARD, SORT OF STARING AT THE FIRE. SHE FIGURED HE WAS IN SHOCK OR SOMETHING. THEN WHEN THE FIRE TRUCKS CAME SCREAMING OUT, THE FIREFIGHTER WHO SPOKE TO OUR AGENTS SAID DASH WAS STAGGERING OUT OF THE BUILDING, HIS CLOTHES ON FIRE, DRAGGING HIS BROTHER. HE'D WRAPPED A WET TOWEL OVER HIS BROTHER'S HEAD."

"But he didn't take the time to wrap one around his own," she mused.

"GUY SPENT MONTHS IN THE HOSPITAL. HAD SEVEN OR EIGHT DIFFERENT OPERATIONS. EACH ONE SEEMED TO MAKE HIM LOOK WORSE."

"His own living hell. A fitting punishment, I suppose," she said. "Brook, do you think he only saved Daddy's life so he'd look like a hero to the firefighters?"

"I DON'T KNOW. THERE ARE NO SIMPLISTIC AN-SWERS. HE WAS A KID. MAYBE HE REALIZED THE GRAVITY OF WHAT HE'D DONE AND TRIED TO UNDO IT SOMEHOW. WE'LL NEVER KNOW."

"No." Gypsy sighed.

"ANYWAY. I'M FED-EXING THIS YEARBOOK TO YOU. I THOUGHT YOU SHOULD HAVE IT."

"Oh, Brook! Thank you. I appreciate that more than you will ever know."

"IT'S THE LEAST I CAN DO."

"No, you've done so much more than I ever expected, Brook. Please extend my deep appreciation to all the agents who assisted you in the investigation."

"CONSIDER IT DONE. AND IF YOU EVER NEED ANYTHING, ALWAYS REMEMBER YOU'VE GOT A FRIEND IN WASHINGTON."

"Well, I could use a job!" she cracked.

"WHAT?"

"I was just kidding—"

"YOU NEED A JOB? SERIOUSLY?"

"Well . . ."

"YOU KNOW EACH OF OUR BUREAUS AND SATELLITE OFFICES DEPEND ON SUPPORT PER-SONNEL WHO AREN'T NECESSARILY AGENTS. I'LL SPEAK TO MY GUYS IN CORPUS. SEE IF THEY CAN

*USE ANYBODY WITH YOUR BACKGROUND AND EX-
PERIENCE."*

Gypsy felt a little thrill of excitement. It would be a
long commute, but maybe she could work something out
on a part-time basis, or arrange something at home.
Maybe. Maybe not.

"Brook, you don't have to . . . but I won't stop you!"

*"I JUST WANT YOU TO KNOW THAT THE FBI AP-
PRECIATES THE SACRIFICES YOU HAD TO MAKE
BECAUSE OF THE MISTAKES AND CRIMES OF ONE
BAD AGENT. I CAN'T HELP IT. I FEEL RESPONSI-
BLE. LET ME HELP YOU SO I DON'T HAVE TO FEEL
GUILTY ANYMORE."*

She laughed. "Whatever I can do for my country."

*"JUST IN CASE YOUR PHONE DOESN'T TRANS-
LATE THIS: I'M LAUGHING. HANG IN THERE, AND
WE'LL TALK TO YOU LATER."*

She hung up with that pleasant afterglow that talks with
Brook Corruthers always left. As long as there were more
FBI agents like him and less like Dash, she figured the
country was in good hands.

Roaming through the house turning on lights, Gypsy
paused to appreciate the hominess of the old place that
she and John and Annie had brought. With their books
and things around, fresh flowers on the table, candles and
seashells Annie had collected on the windowsills, the
house was taking on the personality of home.

Even so, there was one thing of which Gypsy was certain: home wasn't something that could be found in a
place or things. Home could only be found where there
was love. As she went around lighting some of the candles, Gypsy reflected on something she'd read recently.
While cleaning out the old house, she'd found a timeworn
bible, high on a shelf in a closet. Flipping through the

bible's delicate gilt-edged pages, she'd come across the ancient story of the two brothers, Cain and Abel.

While Gypsy reread the story, she came across something she hadn't remembered from her childhood Sunday School days when they'd been told about the man who "slew" his brother because he was jealous of the favor the brother had found in God's eyes.

It said that God's punishment for Cain for the murder of his brother Abel was that he would be doomed to wander the earth for the rest of his life. In a way, Gypsy could see that happening to Dash Jefferson, too. After his ignoble and public dismissal from the FBI, and now his conviction for the types of crimes he once investigated with almost demonic fervor . . . he would spend the rest of his life in search of an identity.

For her, Gypsy knew, the wandering days were over.

AUTHOR S NOTE

IN THE WEEK BEFORE PRESIDENT John F. Kennedy's visit to Dallas, an allegedly unsigned note was left at the FBI offices in Dallas from a man threatening to "take action" if the agents did not "quit bothering my wife."

The note was hand-delivered to the office for Special Agent James Hosty. Hosty claimed "the note could have been left by anyone" and that the Dallas office was too busy worrying about the upcoming visit of President Kennedy to pay much attention to it.

In April of 1994, the FBI released another 80,000 pages of documents pertaining to the Kennedy assassination. Tucked in amongst the thousands of papers was a note which said, "If you don't stop bothering my wife, I will bomb the Dallas Police Department and the FBI." It was signed by Lee Harvey Oswald.

The note Agent Hosty claimed to have received was not unsigned, after all, and did not offer a veiled threat. It was very specific in its threats and was signed by a man the FBI had been keeping an eye on for some time.

In a memo written after the assassination, Hosty instructed his secretary to "bury the note" so as to "not embarrass the Bureau." Like all loyal FBI employees, she did as she was told. The note from Oswald was carefully hidden away for more than thirty years.

This is very typical of the reactions of the Bureau during the infamous Hoover years toward any kind of development which would portray them in any way as incompetent, inept, or just plain careless. An organized effort was made in those days to perpetuate the "FBI myth" that Hoover made famous: the clean-cut, jut-jawed agent, wearing a dark suit and conservative tie, who always got his man.

As far as we know, there were no other notes delivered by Oswald to the Dallas office making threats in the days before President Kennedy was killed. That is . . . as far as we know.

ACKNOWLEDGMENTS

THIS BOOK COULD NOT HAVE been written without the assistance of several fine special agents of the Federal Bureau of Investigation, who gave me as much help as they could without revealing any national secrets. They were tolerant of my eagerness to learn, appreciative of my desire for accuracy, and patient with all my questions.

I would especially like to thank Special Agent Marjorie Poche, media representative for the Dallas office, who gave generously of her time, offered a tour of the facilities, and gave me a small peek into the hectic, demanding, and satisfying life of special agents who happen to be married to one another.

I am so very grateful to Special Agent Ralph Harp of the Houston field office, who did not seem to mind in the least when I hijacked him for a cup of coffee one day, and who never seemed to regard my relentless probing or phone calls as an intrusion. He gave me a rare glimpse into the private world of a field agent who loves nothing more than simply to do his job.

I would also like to thank Special Agent in Charge of the Houston office, Michael Wilson, who somehow managed to embody in his appearance and character the FBI agent who commands respect and gets it, the one we've all got in the back of our minds as the quintessential agent, for offering this author the same respect when asked for an interview.

I have got to thank a very fine friend of mine, Rick Cassells, United States Secret Service, retired, for guiding me through the back doors of the White House, and for being just an all-around great guy.

And I would be terribly remiss if I neglected to thank the indomitable Susan Dunn for making the world of the hearing-impaired come to life for me.

The FBI has a reputation for carefully guarding its secrets; library research tends to produce the Hoover type books that offer up the myth and the image, but I could not have written my own book without a few works I considered essential. The most important would have to be Ronald Kessler's defining missive: *The FBI.* Thanks to Kessler's impeccable research and unprecedented access, I was able to ascertain many of the basics of the organization, from bureaucratic structure to the floor plans of the headquarters building in Washington, D.C.

Two other books provided a refreshing irreverence toward the Bureau, which can be more important, in its way, than organizational charts: *No Left Turns,* by Joseph L. Schott, who gave a hysterically funny look at the craziness of the Hoover years, and the fine bestselling novel, *Witness to the Truth,* by Paul Lindsay, which reassured us that, bureaucratic and frustrating though it may be, the FBI is still the finest law enforcement agency in the world.

I would also like to offer praise for the very excellent and completely dignified museum about the assassination of President Kennedy, which is located on the sixth floor of the School Book Depository in Dallas. You won't find a better compilation of facts and photographs which completely reconstructs, not just that terrible day, but that entire innocent era in American history. Most touching are the messages left by people of all ages and cultures and from all over the world, which express the simple but powerful feelings they have toward a man who was truly a hero for our time.

Author of the #1
New York Times Bestseller
MR. MURDER

Dean Koontz

__THE EYES OF DARKNESS	0-425-15397-5/$6.99
__THE KEY TO MIDNIGHT	0-425-14751-7/$6.99
__MR. MURDER	0-425-14442-9/$7.50
__THE FUNHOUSE	0-425-14248-5/$7.50
__DRAGON TEARS	0-425-14003-2/$7.50
__SHADOWFIRES	0-425-13698-1/$7.50
__HIDEAWAY	0-425-13525-X/$6.99
__THE HOUSE OF THUNDER	0-425-13295-1/$7.50
__COLD FIRE	0-425-13071-1/$7.50
__WATCHERS	0-425-10746-9/$7.50
__WHISPERS	0-425-09760-9/$7.50
__NIGHT CHILLS	0-425-09864-8/$7.50
__PHANTOMS	0-425-10145-2/$7.50
__SHATTERED	0-425-09933-4/$7.50
__DARKFALL	0-425-10434-6/$7.50
__THE FACE OF FEAR	0-425-11984-X/$7.50
__THE VISION	0-425-09860-5/$7.50
__TWILIGHT EYES	0-425-10065-0/$7.50
__STRANGERS	0-425-11992-0/$7.50
__THE MASK	0-425-12758-3/$7.50
__LIGHTNING	0-425-11580-1/$7.50
__MIDNIGHT	0-425-11870-3/$7.50
__THE SERVANTS OF TWILIGHT	0-425-12125-9/$7.50
__THE BAD PLACE	0-425-12434-7/$7.50
__THE VOICE OF THE NIGHT	0-425-12816-4/$7.50

Payable in U.S. funds. No cash accepted. Postage & handling: $1.75 for one book, 75¢ for each additional. Maximum postage $5.50. Prices, postage and handling charges may change without notice. Visa, Amex, MasterCard call 1-800-788-6262, ext. 1, or fax 1-201-933-2316; refer to ad # 227g

Or, check above books and send this order form to: The Berkley Publishing Group P.O. Box 12289, Dept. B Newark, NJ 07101-5289 Please allow 4-6 weeks for delivery.	Bill my: □ Visa □ MasterCard □ Amex ____ (expires) Card#_____ Daytime Phone #_____ ($10 minimum) Signature_____ Or enclosed is my: □ check □ money order

Name_____	Book Total $_____
Address_____	Applicable Sales Tax $_____ (NY, NJ, PA, CA, GST Can.)
City_____	Postage & Handling $_____
State/ZIP_____	Total Amount Due $_____